Ann Oakley is Professor of Sociology and Social Policy and Director of the Social Science Research Unit at London University's Institute of Education. In addition to her many well-known feminist and academic writings, she is the author of six previous novels, an autobiography and a biography of her father, the sociologist Richard Titmuss. She lives in London and enjoys cycling and grandmotherhood.

Overheads

ANN OAKLEY

Flamingo
An Imprint of HarperCollins*Publishers*

Flamingo
An imprint of HarperCollins*Publishers*
77–85 Fulham Palace Road,
Hammersmith, London W6 8JB

Flamingo is a trademark of
HarperCollins Publishers Ltd

www.**fire**and**water**.com

Published by Flamingo 2000
1 3 5 7 9 8 6 4 2

First published in Great Britain by Flamingo 1999

Copyright © Ann Oakley 1999

The Author asserts the moral right to
be identified as the author of this work

ISBN 0 00 651218 6

Set in Meridien

Printed and bound in Great Britain by
Clays Ltd, St Ives plc

Contents

Acknowledgements

All the characters in this book are fictional; no resemblances to actual people, places, events or circumstances are intended. Apologies to Alice Kessler-Harris for creating yet another somewhat unsympathetic American individual; I promise to try harder next time. Thanks to the Swedish Collegium for Advanced Study in the Social Sciences in Uppsala, Sweden, for providing the kind of peace necessary to ruminate on the themes in this novel; to Catherine Cullen for her insightful comments (as always); to my family and other friends for technical help and moral support; to my agent, Rachel Calder, for her support and valuable criticism; and to my publishers, Michael Fishwick and Rebecca Lloyd, for steering the book in the direction of what we all hope will be a marketable product.

CHAPTER 1

One PHOD Among Many

There was a single tree outside the window of the purple meeting room. Justin studied this obsessively. Its craggy branches made little movement today; the wind which had chased over the ironstone hills to the east of the campus all weekend had sighed itself to rest early in the morning, just as Jim Sanders, the Security Officer, swallowed his last cup of tea of the night, and wrote a vengeful note to his opposite number in Domestic Services about the state of the walkway between Environmental Sciences and the so-called Student Health Centre.

The tree on which Justin Leopard's eyes were fixed, although motionless, was nonetheless faithful to a certain aesthetic ideal, which was more than could be said for the faces of most of his colleagues at the University of the East Midlands ('EMU', for short) in and outside meetings. Justin wasn't a great meeting man, and he regarded these PHOD meetings as especially irksome. The designation 'PHOD' – Professors *and* Heads of Department – had been chosen after a tiresome discussion at the University Council in which three or four ageing professors had reacted to the new ruling that Heads of Departments didn't have to be professors by insisting that their own title should continue to appear in the name of the committee. It wasn't because the purpose of the PHOD meetings was vague that Justin disliked them, because this could be said of most university business, or because the meetings dragged on past their appointed hour, because they didn't – the chairman, Professor Callum Wormleighton, saw to that. If there was one thing Wormleighton was good at, it was chairing meetings.

He had taken them at a breakneck speed through the first part of the agenda – the long-running saga of security in the Students' Union, by which was meant the open access the building offered to itinerant drug-dealers; how to introduce the new no-smoking policy (with difficulty); and the rationalizing of sixty-four committees into about half that number, which was claimed to represent a twenty-eight-per-cent saving in efficiency (Callum had paused for a moment on the arithmetics of this). The meeting was thinly attended; several key figures were absent, including the two other Heads of Department within the School of Social and Cultural Studies (SSACS) – Professors Lydia Mallinder and Elliot Blankthorn. Wormleighton had given their apologies. Lydia – Professor of Gender Studies, and a distinctly rising star in the dusky firmament of EMU – was on her way back from Rotterdam, where she'd had an exalting few days with a group of (other) European researchers interested in Gender and the Distribution of Time. No one knew where Elliot Blankthorn was.

They'd now reached item four: Implications of the current financial situation of EMU for the role of PHODs. Wormleighton read it out like a news item and then allowed his large frame to sag comfortably backwards into his purple chair. The word 'financial' was always an emotive one these days. Dr Stephanie Kershaw from Environmental Sciences and Professor Roscoe Proudfoot from Business Studies tried speaking together. Proudfoot won because he had the louder voice. 'With due respect, Chair, we ought to be apprised of the details of the financial situation before we

2

can sensibly discuss this item.' Stephanie had been going to say the same thing but more conversationally. There was a lot of nodding from round the table and general affirmative noises, like those of the sheep which baa-ed on the hills beyond the tree outside the window. Of course they all knew that EMU had money troubles, but so did most universities these days. Who wanted to know the details? So the world had at some point been made, so the budget was in deficit, so what?

'I agree. I suggest we defer this item until the next meeting of Council which is, when is it, Phyllis?'

Phyllis from SAR (Secretarial and Administrative Resources) looked in her green EMU desk diary. '19 March. Two weeks' time.'

'That'll do. The point being that Council will debate this item fully then. The V-C is expected to make a detailed report. Good. Very sensible.' Wormleighton beamed at them. One way to get through meetings quickly was to defer everything.

'May I make a suggestion?' This was John Mapstone from Modern Languages. 'I think we should arrange a special meeting of PHODs to discuss this item after the Council meeting. And we should invite a representative from the AUT to come along.' He waited expectantly like a naughty schoolboy who's just kicked a ball through a window.

'Come, come,' objected Wormleighton. 'I think we can handle this ourselves, without the AUT, can't we?'

'An overstatement,' agreed Proudfoot. 'We shouldn't anticipate a litigious climate.' He hunched his shoulders, and made his characteristic odd ha-haaing noise, a cross between a laugh and the warning sign of an epileptic fit.

'Well, I'm not sure.' Like many at EMU, Stephanie Kershaw had begun to smell trouble, and Proudfoot's defence simply confirmed her suspicion. But the tentative, feminine

tone of her utterance allowed Wormleighton to drown it
easily in a display of arm-waving and overbearing committee phrases such as 'now, now, comrades', and, 'thank you
for that', and, 'it's time we moved on'. He wanted to get
on to the new system for room bookings and the remodu-
larization of the Cultures of Science degree. The first was
an obvious failure, and the second not yet so, partly because
no-one except Roscoe Proudfoot understood the concept of
TRUs (Teaching and Research Units), which had recently
been introduced as part of the technical vocabulary of the
new Inter-Departmental Structure (IDS). Proudfoot understood it because he'd invented it, on a train coming back
from a German conference on the rise and fall of welfare
economies in Charlottenburg. He always had his best ideas
on the way back from conferences. As the sun set over the
Rhine it had come to him that what EMU needed was a
new conceptual and economic framework that would make
everyone think things were getting better when they were,
in fact, getting demonstrably worse. As he stepped off the
train at the railway station in Berlin, he'd noticed a rat
scampering under a hamburger stall. But it was the appearance of things that mattered; all the underneath scurrying
should be covered up. He went straight to the V-C with his
new scheme when he got back, knowing full well that one
of the things the scheme would mean was a discretionary
element added to certain professorial salaries.

'It's very simple, Leopard,' Proudfoot had explained to
Justin only the other day. 'The nomenclature of Teaching
and Research Units represents an attempt to recognize and
bridge the binary divide in higher education between those
who teach and those who do research and those of us who
do both.' Here he'd paused for a smirk, because he himself
did do a little – although only a little – of both. 'A Teaching
Unit is counted as two undergraduate lectures or four

4

undergraduate seminars or one postgraduate seminar per term, and a Research Unit is £5k of research income over a commensurate period. Of course, one can play around with the figures, and an advantage of the system is that it's flexible enough to be adjusted to reflect the changes in the four-year cycle of the HE funding system, that is the different weightings attached to the quantity and quality of teaching and research.'

Proudfoot went through it all again now in front of all the other PHODs. Mapstone, still wearing his AUT hat, pointed out the contractual implications of the TRU formula for research staff, and Jeremy Krest from Biological Sciences complained about the failure of the TRU model to recognize the lack of parity between different fields of research (his and theirs); Justin used the time for a surreptitious sort through his mail. The pile today included some for Jim Leonard, one of Jeremy Krest's biological colleagues, whose name, being only slightly different from Justin's own, gave insufficient clues for successful delivery to the disaffected postroom staff. In Leonard's mail was a glossy catalogue of research apparatus – the Argos brochure for bioscience – featuring some truly frightful looking gadgets for animal experiments, including a new system for ventilating mice, rodent sampling cages with counter-balanced lever arms, and items called rabbit jackets made of nylon mesh with zipper closures.

Alan Livingstone from History spearheaded a wearing discussion under AOB about why chairs which belonged in one room kept turning up in another. A certain amount of remodelling had been inflicted on the buildings of EMU when it first became a university, and the architect who did it had arrived fresh from colour-coding a Danish hospital. The floors of EMU's main buildings had consequently all been painted different colours, and broad bands of bilious gloss stretched from the floor to half way up the walls, just below the comfortingly consistent green fire exit signs. Noticeboards on the ground floors provided clues to the meaning of the colours – navy blue for the History Department, yellow for Modern Languages, grey for Administration and so forth – but these were only clues, as the expansion of some departments and the contraction of others had interfered with the original colour-coded system. (Bits of Administration, for example, now turned up everywhere.) Since his attention had been drawn to it, Justin could see that there were three orange chairs in the purple meeting room, and also one black chair, twinned in its stick-like economy with the one tree outside the window.

At the punctual conclusion of the meeting, Justin walked out of the building behind Stephanie Kershaw. Her legs gleamed the sleek synthetic suntan of tights beneath a skirt made of a curious red material with a raised pattern on it – like an acreage of birthmarks. She wore lots of silver chains everywhere, and had a habit of painting a thin dark line round the outside of her lips, as though colour-coding them, like the building.

A faint pre-spring light fell from the sky as Justin and Stephanie came out of the building. It illuminated the weariness on Justin's face, and the outline on Stephanie's lips, beneath the lunar stretches of her cheekbones, high under prune-dark eyes. 'I think we'll all lose our jobs,' confided Justin mournfully. He bent to pick up the wrapper from an ice-cream Mars Bar which lay on the ground in front of them. He screwed it up and put it in his pocket. 'Why can't people pick up their own damned rubbish?' His family called him the litter dictator, and his daughter, Carey, who was in a Difficult Phase, made a point of dropping as many provoking items in as many places as she could.

'Is it really as bad as that?'

'I've no idea. You heard what Callum said. They're discussing it in Council next week. For what it's worth. It's probably all been decided anyway. Did you see the *THES* last week? ''Three thousand jobs to go''. You haven't got tenure, have you? Neither have I. Perhaps you should think about a career move. It's too late for me, I'm stuck with it.'

Stephanie looked at him intensely for a moment. Once you knew Justin's name was Leopard, you couldn't help seeing it in his face. The cheeks resembled jowls, but that made him sound ugly, which he wasn't – he was too nice for that. Niceness was written all over him. The combination of jowls and the thin light brown hair streaked over his balding head might have been animal-like, but his eyes had the light of human kindness in them. He stopped in front of the heavily used coffee machine by the SAR office and fumbled in his pocket for the right change. 'I can never make these bloody things work!' He pushed and pulled the buttons with an aimless venom, so Stephanie had to help him.

'Thanks. Thanks very much.' Unreasonably grateful, he stood there for a moment sipping his polystyrene coffee. Jobs and money. Sometimes he couldn't understand how he'd got into this university business at all. It was difficult to retrace his steps from a South Manchester comprehensive to a chair at EMU. Justin's had been one of those 'new blood' chairs. As a colleague of his in Cultural Studies had pointed out, there was nothing accidental about applying the metaphor of eugenics to academic expansion. It was all about the survival of the fittest. Justin, like all boys, had wanted to be something magnificently manual in his youth, like a steel welder or a weight trainer, and then something terribly authoritarian, like a policeman. The football bit had passed him by, because he was so hopeless at it. He'd been a lecturer in social policy at Cardiff when he'd seen the advertisement for the Chair in Public Policy at EMU, and he'd rung up and asked what Public Policy meant in this context. The Dean's secretary, a nice woman who'd been forced to take a job when her husband gassed himself because of some city council scandal, had said she thought it covered a multitude of sins, or words to that effect. He'd applied and been interviewed and got the job, and then been faced with transplanting the family from Cardiff, and trying to work out what public policy really was. The opposite of private policy? The rhetorical truth behind public practice? From the university's point of view, it seemed that the unhappy secretary had been right, and it didn't matter a fish's tit what the subject was as long as the fees and the research income flowed nicely in.

One of EMU's major troubles was its unfortunate location just off a roundabout outside Motley, a medium-sized Midlands town known these days for its high juvenile crime rate and impressive incidence of teenage pregnancy, the second highest in the whole of the country. But it also had the first experimental lighting scheme for reducing urban violence, and in the 1950s a novel housing estate modelled on some of the first garden suburbs had sprung up and had been moderately successful, as a place where aspiring garage owners and Tory-voting teachers wanted to live, though latterly it had fallen from favour with the expansion of the motorway to eight lanes, and the building of a huge Morrison's supermarket and an Elf petrol station on the edge of town. To reach EMU, you went north and then east off the roundabout, following the signs to the A43. This road actually bisected the campus, causing students to drop books on the asphalt, as they tried to cross and worse. But in the days when EMU had been Motley Poly, no-one had planned anything, and the sprawl of buildings had just sprawled, and when Jenson's Farms had refused to give up any more of their land on one side of the A43, the only option had been to obtain some on the other. The line of traffic crossed and recrossed Justin's office window – he was often mesmerized by it during seminars, when for the Nth year the Nth student repeated the Nth version of Teitel and Mandon's text on *The Development of Public Welfare and the Twentieth Century State*. The thick hum of the traffic on the A43 made EMU more metropolitan than rural, and the question of just what kind of university this was remained a source of puzzlement to many. However, this wasn't revealed in the university's prospectus, which referred to Motley as an 'up-and-coming vibrant city', well-served by take-aways and pubs, 'and all the other essentials of student life'. Black and white pictures taken by Nathan Horrell in the Arts Department showed a gang of his friends (only one of whom was actually a student) posing outside a heavily retouched union building.

The blurb on the jacket of the book that had got Justin his chair, snappily entitled *Public Administration and Citizenship Rights*, described him as dedicated to developing a theoretical understanding of the ad-hoc nature of social and fiscal policies in what he preferred to call market economy societies, though in this he'd been taken to task by Elliot Blankthorn, who thought the distinguishing feature of such societies lay more in the relationship of professionals to authority. But then he would, being a sociologist. The thing that puzzled Justin was why some policies developed and not others. This puzzlement ought to have produced a plethora of research projects, but Justin had only managed to acquire one research grant in recent years, or, rather, a share in one – an extremely complicated European affair with eight countries, twenty-four investigators and a budget of Monopoly money – ECUs – very little of which could be spent in the country that was actually doing the research. It was consequently difficult to get the work done. The French were taking advantage of this, and were enthusiastically misappropriating most of the funds. Justin himself had employed two part-time research officers, Beverley and Candida, and put them in a poorly lit room at the end of the corridor, where he visited them from time to time.

When Justin got back from the PHODs meeting, there was a student waiting for him. She wore a long skirt reminiscent of the sixties, and dark green Doc Marten boots, and she had a clipboard perched ominously on her knees. Through thick, rimless glasses she bore down on him interrogatively. 'Professor Leopard, what I really want to do is study the operation of equal opportunities policy and practice in higher education over the period from the mid 1970s. Now is this part of public policy or isn't it? That's the question!'

It was her question, but was it his? The question for Justin was whether he wanted to be her supervisor or not. Then he remembered Proudfoot's soliloquy on TRUs. The headline in the THES about jobs disappearing flashed through the hindpart of his brain. He moved the papers around on his desk and found Judy Sammons' letter. She had a first in legal and social studies from Sussex. Why on earth would she want to come to EMU? 'Well, Judy,' he said, beginning as he meant to go on, 'what brings you to this part of the world? After the purer climes of Brighton?'

'It wasn't Brighton,' she replied, 'it was Lewes. I lived in Lewes. I had a motorbike. And the answer to your question is love.'

'What?'

'My partner lives in Motley.'

'Ah.' He wondered briefly what 'partner' meant in this context.

She moved swiftly on. 'Of course I would aim to do a comparative study of several universities.'

'Of course you would.'

'Of course, you're not the most obvious person here to be my supervisor, Professor Leopard. Professor Mallinder has the background in gender studies and equal opportunities which you lack.'

Justin wouldn't have put it quite like that himself; he might have been more inclined to mention his positive qualities; the fact that his book, *Public Administration*, did, for instance, contain a useful section on the expansion of higher education, with some thin, but nonetheless present, references to other European countries. But Judy Sammons was right; Lydia Mallinder, and not he, was the appropriate supervisor. Lydia was known to be a tough supervisor, a good teacher, an unrelenting worker, a person with uncompromising views. Men tended to be afraid of her, sensing the probability of sharp personal encounters, but they were also discomfited because she represented something they might have been too.

But Justin needed to boost his TRUs more than Lydia did, which was unfair, as she'd only been at EMU for four years. 'Joint supervision,' suggested Justin, for want of two better words. Such an arrangement might turn out to be rather like the European research grant, considerably more of an administrative nightmare than it was worth. But there was something in Judy Sammons' demeanour, in the way she presented herself to him. He'd seen hundreds of keen young would-be doctoral students over the years, and many more who were not so keen; this one was unusual in the strength of her determination, her disconcerting ability not to mince words, and the fact that she had a concrete, studyable subject, whereas most of them wanted to study the world. You spent the first year convincing them that they couldn't, and then they lost interest, and so did you.

About Judy Sammons, there was also something else: an aura of – of – Justin couldn't put his finger on it. He stared

11

through his window at the Nissan Micras and the articulated food lorries and the Volvos and the occasional stuttering farm vehicle on the A43, and then he looked back at Judy's cropped hair, and intelligent grey eyes, magnified by those glasses, and at the conjunction of the shiny green leather of the DMs and the didactic slope of the clipboard on what he imagined would be white, cleanly angled and above all, young, knees. It brought to mind a dreadful film he'd seen as a teenager – he thought it'd been called *Claire's Knee*. But, anyway, the film had been full of pubescent limbs and unrequited love, though this bit of his memory might just have been a function of the stage Justin himself had been at, lusting in a quietly acne-d way after Sandrine, a young woman in the class below his at the South Manchester comprehensive, with earlobes like unripe pears, hung with silver paste earrings from Woolworth's, which she kept in her blazer pocket and clipped on defiantly just outside the school gates.

'It could work,' Justin observed, referring to the joint supervision, as an enormous frozen food lorry passed. 'But why do you want me to be involved at all? Professor Mallinder has quite sufficient expertise on her own, doesn't she?'

It started to rain. The rain hit the window diagonally, imposing a new geometry on the A43 rush-hour traffic. For some reason, Justin caught himself wondering whether Judy's green boots were waterproof. Between the SSACS building and the campus exit there were some nasty potholes which would be filling up with water now like nobody's business.

'As a subject, equal opportunities doesn't only belong in gender studies, conceptually and ideologically speaking,' reprimanded Judy Sammons, in case Justin thought it did.

Justin pasted a stray bit of hair back on the top of his

head. 'Doesn't it?' Like most academic men, he regarded equal opportunities and gender as something of a turn-off. But one wasn't supposed to say so. Gone were the days when one could happily ridicule women for being interested in themselves, confident of not getting the rejoinder that in a patriarchal world that's only what men have been for aeons. No, now you had to pretend to be on their side. Of course, on another level there was a considerable incentive to do this, because you wanted women to like you. The psychology of it was odd, because if you liked them and they liked you, then you couldn't help but see they had a point in going on about gender.

'If equal opportunities is to work in practice as opposed to principle, then it must be integrated with public policy,' declared Judy.

'I suppose you're right.'

'That's why I want you.'

Justin knew Judy Sammons didn't want him in the *Claire's Knee* sense, but nonetheless her phrase, 'I want you' had a certain impact on his brain. Before he left, he looked up the University Council document entitled, 'A new model for assessing academic performance.' He wanted to find out what happened to your TRUs in cases of joint supervision. After scanning the dense paragraphs for twenty minutes, he gave up and decided it was easier to let Judy Sammons decide his fate.

Stephanie Kershaw, on the other hand, wanted to decide her own. She sat in her streamlined office and swivelled round a few times on her black anti-static computer chair, lightly touching the surface of her pentagonal link desk as she did so. She'd had to wrestle the smart office furniture out of Building Services, but appearances *were* important, especially when it came to attracting bright students and consultancy income of the sort they all needed these days.

The PHODs meeting had been irritating; Stephanie disliked most of her colleagues. She'd hoped to see Lydia Mallinder at the meeting, as she and Lydia were taking on a new module in gender and development, and Lydia had sent over a draft earlier in the week. Stephanie was the country's first Reader in AgroEconomy. Her specialism was agricultural markets and sustainable development, but you wouldn't think it to look at her. The draft had enraged Stephanie, who didn't share Lydia's enthusiasm for seeing gender everywhere. Personally, Stephanie wouldn't have touched gender with a bargepole, but the pressure was on to get the student numbers up. EMU's projected student numbers for 1999 were twenty-five per cent down on the 1992 figures, and the overseas numbers were derisory. Although Stephanie couldn't understand why anyone would want to take a course in gender and development, she was a sharp enough businesswoman herself to seize any opportunity for generating profit.

She stopped swivelling, and started writing, in red, all over Lydia's draft. After a while, composure returned. She spread the red-marked sheets out in front of her across the pale oak surface of her desk and looked at them with equanimity as a job well done.

In a corner of the library, Judy Sammons sucked the top of her biro and looked thoughtfully out of the window. A non-picturesque array of bird droppings met her gaze, but as she didn't really work here, the reduction in window-cleaning from four times yearly to only once was of no concern to her. It was raining slightly. She moved the biro from her mouth to the lined paper on her clipboard. 'Send e-mail,' she wrote, 'to let them know the first bit was easy. What next??'

CHAPTER 2

Citizens of Motley

The orange cat squinted at Lydia Mallinder from the patio. Unlike other people's patios, this one was naked – there wasn't a tub of daffodils or a distressed miniature rose or an overwintered bay tree in sight.

Lydia abhorred nature. She couldn't stand the country – swathes of vacant green, the dross of sheep, flowers stupidly reappearing year after year in the vain hope of what? In her experience, it didn't get better, but worse. Nature stood for culture, and culture itself was marching backwards. Everything died at the end of its season.

That Lydia was a professor of Gender Studies was a sign of the times. She would have preferred to be a professor of Women's Studies, but because the world was going backwards you couldn't any longer study women without always taking men's interests into account. That was why one used this apparently innocuous, masculine-ego-pleasing word *gender*. But for Lydia Mallinder – and this was what most people didn't understand about her – neither gender nor women were the thing, really: the thing was the apocalyptic decay of modern culture, the escalating march towards a chaos of self-seeking hooliganism; from football matches to nuclear armaments, the world was fast disappearing into a sucking bog of competitive, muddy materialism. What was happening to gender, and to women, was merely part of the whole crumbling super-structure of decay. As various (masculine) giants of social theory had proclaimed, you could tell the state of a civiliz-ation by the condition of its women, but what mattered was the civilization and not the women. In the end, women were only markers, symbols, metaphors.

The house attached to Lydia's patio was close to the centre of Motley. Because the landscape of Motley was more town than country, Lydia found it a perfectly accept-able place in which to live. Her little modern house suited her; she lived in it alone with Huneyball, the orange cat, and both of them took solace in its clean, white, right-angled lines – the absence of dust-containing crevices, the lack of cracked tiles on the roof and of the kind of cement between bricks which drew gangs of masonry bees to other Northamptonshire houses and set their owners in a panic of worrying and consulting bee-keepers (who only wanted to keep bees, not to get rid of them). Huneyball had the disability of only one eye, so a small, tidy house prevented him from banging into things; he'd got into some kind of scrape when Lydia was away giving the plenary address at the World Conference on Gender Studies (COGS) in Barcelona in 1991. Antibiotics prescribed by the vet had been too late to save his eye, which ever since had been a different and much duller green from the other one, giving out the clouded funereal gaze of a cod on a fishmonger's slab.

Lydia tapped on the glass of the patio window. 'Come here, Huneyball!' She sat at her desk, a simple black table pushed up against the wall with a black anglepoise lamp on it, and her Prolinea slimline Pentium computer with two sound boxes like ear muffs arranged on the sides, out of which came various jingles as she closed down one pro-gramme and opened another with the slight, practised click of a regular mouse-user. Huneyball, who was used to sleeping between the keyboard and the monitor of Lydia's computer, occasionally reaching up with a lazy paw to bat the flashing fly of the cursor on the screen, had at first taken exception to the jingles, and had fled to the wastepaper basket, where he had rested his mound of orange fluff on the screwed-up minutes of the Degrees Board, the Student Affairs Committee, the University Council, the Teaching Quality Committee, and more prosaically worded memos from Domestic Services announcing a further decline in the extent to which they were able to live up to the promise of their name.

Lydia was replying to one of these at this very moment: 'Memorandum from Professor Lydia Mallinder, Head, Department of Cultural Studies, School of Social and Cultural Studies,' declared the by-line conveniently retrieved from the computer's memory, together with a copy of the icon for SSACS, which had cost £5k from a London consultancy firm run by a friend of the V-C. The letters S-S-A-C-S were arranged in a V-shape, with the representation of a three-riveted bronze dagger in the middle. This was copied from an original which had been found in 1862 when part of Motley was dug up to build the railway, and was thought to be an artefact of the late Neolithic period when warrior-traders from the Rhine, known as the 'beaker people', had first set foot in that part of the country. 'To: Professor Callum Wormleighton, Dean, SSACS. I am writing to protest about the latest memorandum from Domestic Services,' Lydia clattered out, absolutely to the point as was her wont. 'Deliveries only every two months of furniture and equipment from stores represents a quite unacceptable level of service which compromises the efficient functioning of both our teaching and research functions.' She dragged the icon backwards and put a full stop after 'services'. Short sentences were better than long ones. She deleted 'functions' and substituted 'activities'.

Huneyball clunked through the cat flap with a leisurely heave and strolled towards her over the bare wooden floor. 'Oh how boring all this is!' declared Lydia, scooping up the cat and burying her face in his fur, being rewarded by a purr of enjoyment far more satisfying than anything she would ever get from dispatching or receiving a university memo. 'I'm not sure I can be bothered, Huneyball. There are so many more interesting things to do.' She leaned over the purring mass and sifted through the pile on her desk, which had grown during her brief absence at the research meeting in Rotterdam: an embryonic research proposal for the ESRC on gender, unemployment and mental health; a paper on feminist post-structuralism to review for a new Californian women's studies journal; her own draft chapter provisionally entitled, 'When We Speak of Gender, We Mean Women: A Comment on the Mnemonics of Postmodernism'. At the bottom of the pile were a clutch of students' essays on the family for a module she taught jointly with Elliot Blankthorn in the sociology department. Elliot, who was much less conscientious than she was, took the view that, as they now had to teach twice as many students as they used to, they should spend half as much time marking each essay. But Lydia took essay-marking as seriously as she took everything else.

It was a Sunday evening at the end of March; cold, but without that dampness that sometimes creeps in from the Fens, wrapping everything in a shroud of mist, bringing a kind of sad, dull ache to the bones and sending the inhabitants of Motley in their droves to their local pharmacies for packets of Panadol, Hedex Extra and Aspro Clear. Lydia often found it difficult to get back to work when she came back from conferences and meetings, especially abroad. Her trips to Rotterdam always left her with a sense of frustration, because her colleagues there in gender and cultural studies seemed to have a so-much-more comfortable time at their university than she did at hers.

She decided to take a walk. Her little house opened onto a walkway which led directly to the city's main shopping centre. The decor there was bright blue and bright yellow, a clamour of colour intended to cheer, but serving only as a garish reminder of the general syntheticism of modern life, of that very aesthetic and moral hideousness associated with cultural decay. Lydia walked between the plate-glass shopfronts: Granada TV – 'no deposit slot TV available here'; The Baker's Oven (with its lingering smell of meat pies); a shop called The Wearhouse boasting clusters of gold and silver accoutrements and cropped tops for impossibly small-chested women; the usual bland incitements to consumerism such as Kwik Save and Foto Processing. A fast food stall called The Snack Shack, in the middle of the pedestrianized area, tried unsuccessfully to look like a Hawaiian grass hut. Next to it a keycutting and shoe-mending shop promised 'superior services with experience while U wait'. Lydia wondered whether this might do as a statement of the University's Mission, a topic that was at the moment much debated in the corridors and offices of EMU. Indeed, a special subcommittee (the EMU Mission Subcommittee – EMUMS) of the University Council had been set up with a budget that would mostly be paid to the V-C's friend's London consultancy, which apparently produced Mission statements just like that. Lydia did often wonder what the Mission of the University really *was*. To produce students who could write half-decent essays and would remember a thing or two from textbooks that might or might not be useful in their subsequent lives? To find out things, such as how not having a job might affect the health of men and women differently? Or where the current malaise affecting higher education had come from, and how its symptoms might best be treated? To become repositories of cobwebs of formulae and acronyms which would layer human understanding with just as thick a mist as wandered in from time to time from the Fens? Why did the University have to have a Mission anyway?

Try as she could (and she did try) Lydia couldn't banish such dreary thoughts from her Sunday-evening brain. She came out on the other side of the shopping centre opposite the police station which had two hanging baskets of plastic ivy in front of it. Here the road twisted away from the town and into yet another new housing estate. Under an unidentifiable flag a sign ordered, 'MOVE IN FOR UNDER £49'. Nobody seemed to have done, for under £49 or any other amount. A couple of metres further on there was another sign: 'WARNING: SITE CLEARANCE TRAFFIC'. Beyond this, and the Monopoly-board red mock tudor, loomed the late-winter countryside: the grey-brown earth of the ironstone hills with patches of Upper Jurassic clay. Pylons marched above it, saving the landscape from that monstrous rurality Lydia so detested, and drawing the eye comfortably back to the irrepressible urban impulse.

There was a church beyond the housing estate, left over from some Norman village or other, and its bell chimed eight as she stood with her back to Motley in the fading light. Last summer, she'd taken a brief holiday with her lover in the Auvergne area of France. This is the volcanic region; on the plateau running across the middle, the blue hills, which shimmer in the August heat, carry snow on their tops for eight months of the year. Lydia and her man had rented a house, a converted barn with a sloping garden. In the evenings they had sat after dinner drinking cold sweet white wine, watching the pale orange light on the hills, and arguing – arguing about love and commitment and treason and faith, and what it means to fuck so hard in the middle of the night before the cock-crowing dawn, or so gently in the long afternoons that they seemed to be part of the soft covering of sun over the landscape.

Why Lydia thought about this now, she didn't know, but so strong was the feeling of being back there with Jeremy Krest, looking at the countryside with the last of the sun on it, that she forgot for a moment where she was and what she was doing there.

The sky was streaked with pink in the trail of the sun which had slipped over the edge of the world. As Lydia stood and stared at the landscape poised on the edge of winter, wondering if it might dare to take the step into spring, whether it was worth defying the insalubrious frosts, the grey cloudbursts, the law of putrefaction which rules all living things, she felt a moment of sympathy with the natural world that was rare for her. For an instant, fixed between the pustular grime and litter of the town, and the cold clear gaze of the countryside, and remembering the volcanic summer landscape of that loving-and-hating time, she felt jealous of the inner regulation which caused the countryside to move imperceptibly but surely into the next season. She herself and the town were more chaotic. Who knew what might come next for either of them?

Elliot Blankthorn, coming out of Motley on his motorbike, spotted Lydia walking down the hill from the roundabout. He roared up beside her, but he had to remove his helmet before she'd stop, because a gesticulating man on a motor-bike is any man to most women. 'Rum lot, aren't they?' he said, then, when she recognized him.

'What?'

'The essays on the family.'

'Oh, I haven't read them yet.'

'If I read another reference to that damn Bethnal Green study I think I'll throw up.' He had an odd accent – a combination of a boyhood in Brooklyn, an adolescence in Delft, a first degree in Montpellier and a second in Glasgow, according to his CV. 'Want a drink?' he inquired, grinning, he hoped, boyishly. There were rumours that Lydia was a lesbian, but Elliot Blankthorn was sophisticated enough to understand this probably wasn't true.

'Bugger me,' he swore as he slopped beer all over the table in an effort to deliver her Campari and soda and two packets of McCoy Crisps in pristine condition. 'I've been looking for a chance to socialize, but you English have barriers like steel. How long have you been at EMU, Lydia?'

Elliot was a new arrival. The question everyone at EMU asked everyone else was why they had ended up there. Sometimes the answer was obvious, for example, in the case of John Mapstone from Languages who had the disability of all sorts of phobias (enclosed spaces, open spaces, cats, dogs, fish, tomatoes, Clingfilm, telephones, envelopes, etc.), or Roscoe Proudfoot, eighty per cent of whose sick mother's nursing-home costs were defrayed by an unusually charitable local authority, or Fern Meredith in Justin Leopard's department, who'd married a local artist, and had another life as the mother of four small boys. While it was clear why these people had come to EMU or why they stayed there, there was some puzzlement about the likes of Lydia Mallinder and Elliot Blankthorn. 'I was desperate,' Elliot told Lydia, over his beer and crisps. 'What I really want to do is write up my research on the precursors of ethical thought in Glaswegian schoolchildren. I was heading for a nice Oxford or Cambridge college, but I guess I'm not their sort of person.' He looked like a version of Woody Allen with blacker hair and a strange pair of reddish-brown glasses. 'I had to get out of the States,' he went on invitingly. 'Relationship problems.'

'Oh yes?' Lydia didn't really want to know.

It came out like a flood then, like the Thrapston bitter all over the table. 'Child support, you see. If I'm in the States, she can get me for it, but if I'm here she can't. It's not that I'm not willing to support them, you understand, though I don't see why Millie needs any alimony, she's an able-bodied woman with a teacher-training certificate and a degree in newspaper journalism. But the twins, well, yes. If I could afford it, but I can't.'

He reached for Lydia's crisps. 'I've been a bad boy, you see. I'm guilty of what you feminists,' he paused to give her a chance to repudiate this label, 'what you feminists would call very reprehensible behaviour. There was wife number one, she was Scottish. Came from one of those monosyllabic islands – Rum or Egg or something. I was doing my PhD, it was winter, I was very miserable, you know with all that grey stone they have up there. Malvin was born soon after. It's Gaelic, means smooth brow, which he had, but then I suppose all kids do. Malvin's twenty now, he's a trainee chef in Colorado. When I finished my PhD Malvin's mother didn't want to come with me back to the States and I didn't much want to take her. So we agreed to split. My attentions were engaged elsewhere by then. I guess she knew that, which didn't help. She was called Medwenna. That's spelt M-E-D-W-E-N-N-A. Lovely name, don't you think? It's Welsh for good mannered. Medwenna and I had a great time. I bought a boat and we sailed to Miami and then there was Rhidian, also Welsh for "he who dwells by the ford". Not immediately, but when we got back to Southampton. Excuse me, am I boring you?'

Lydia thought about Huneyball's dinner, and about Jeremy and the blue-misted hills of the Auvergne. But

Jeremy was in London, and the Auvergne was in the past. In her disconsolate mood, perhaps some entertainment was better than none. 'I think you'd better finish the story.'

'They all begin with M – my wives' names. Moira . . .'

'Who begat Malvin,' said Lydia helpfully.

'You've got it! And Medwenna, who began Rhidian. And then there was Millie.'

'Who begat?'

'Twins – two boys, Joel and Jethro. They're ten now, they're great kids, I miss them like hell.'

'If you miss them, why didn't you stay with them?' Lydia didn't mean it altogether nastily.

'What is this, some kind of inquisition?' Elliot sat back on the wooden bench in the dark smoky interior of the pub with his hands on his knees – a masterful pose. 'I expect you've got – what's the English phrase – some skeletons in your own cupboard, haven't you? But I guess it'll take me more than one Campari and soda to get the cat out of the bag, won't it? Maybe my tale's a bit sordid for middle England. You all seem such settled types here at EMU. Naturally I don't plan to stay – this chair's only a route to somewhere else.' He laughed, a hollow, uninteresting, self-amused sound.

'That's what they all say.' Lydia reflected that there was something singularly uninviting about talking to a man whose idea of a conversation was a narrative about himself. Most people divulge their identities in small pieces of reciprocated information: you tell me this and I'll tell you that. Conversation is an act of taking as well as giving. But Elliot Blankthorn only gave of himself, in gestures of such magnanimous charity that nobody really wanted them.

Back in her little house, Lydia made herself an omelette and gave Huneyball a tin of pilchards. He was asleep in the laundry basket when she came in, on top of her dirty purple

IKEA sheets and a week's worth of knickers. He ate one pilchard and then came to sit on her, purring like a steam engine, his chin glistening with pilchard oil. His fishy tongue grazed her hand like sandpaper. There was nothing like the love of a bad cat. With the aid of several cups of strong tea, Lydia marked the essays on the family, correcting the mistakes in red as she always did – not 'cereal monagomy' but 'serial monogamy', not 'Tallcock' but 'Talcott' Parsons, etc., etc. Elliot had been right about Bethnal Green. She fetched the book to compare these comic sophistries with the original account. It was a long time since she'd scanned it for her own undergraduate degree, cooped up in a cheap bedsit in suburban Bristol. Michael Young and Peter Willmott's nostalgic *Family and Kinship in East London* read now like a defence of the New Man – gone were the days when a man would rip a woman's contraceptive cap out of her (gone were the days of contraceptive caps, anyway) and throw it on the fire to keep her pregnant. Twenty-nine out of forty-five husbands had washed up for their wives in the previous week. It was, as the students caricatured, really rather an over-cosy picture of three-generation families living in unproblematic proximity and woven tightly into a cultural web of the local markets, pubs and so forth: the very blueprint of the television soap opera, *EastEnders*. But the sense of belonging, of which the authors wrote, held some attraction for Lydia, despite herself.

Huneyball had fallen asleep at a dangerous angle on top of her computer monitor. She pushed him off gently and switched on the machine and finished her memo to the Dean about the decline in Domestic Services which meant that the new chairs for the Department office would stay in the storeroom indefinitely. Then she dialled into the University electronic mail system. 'Mentor login,' flashed the message. 'Immdcs', she typed back. 'Password? Dialup password?', 'emu1996,' she entered. It had seemed a bit obvious, hardly much of a protection against illicit users. 'You have new mail,' it informed her.

Five messages had gathered since she'd last checked in. One was from Callum Wormleighton: 'Dear Colleagues,' it read, 'There will be a special meeting of the SSACS Policy Committee on 12 March at 2 PM in the orange meeting room. Phyllis will circulate an agenda beforehand. Because of the sensitive nature of the agenda, this will be sent to members by e-mail only.'

The second message was from Stephanie Kershaw: 'Dear Lydia,' (this term, thought Lydia immediately, was a lie) 'Thanks for the draft of the Gender and Development module. I've made some changes to this, which you may want to discuss. Next time, perhaps you could send it via e-mail as an attached document? It always saves time if one has the document to work on directly.'

Yes, thought Lydia, but then I wouldn't be able to see what you've done to it. Working with Stephanie hadn't been her idea. It was all part of this new interdisciplinary collaborative way of working which was supposed to be so good, though it led to so many interdisciplinary, not to say interpersonal, fights that it simply wasn't worth it.

The third and fourth messages were from Disa Loring, a senior lecturer in Lydia's department. One was from Disa to Shepley Harrod of room bookings and had merely been copied to Lydia. Room 604, which Disa had thought she'd booked for her course on 'Women: Fragmentation and Resistance in Urban Lives' had been found to be occupied by Dennis Rudgewick's 'Health of the Older Population' option. Shepley had replied tersely to Disa's complaint: 'Don't blame it on me. The software EMUCS wrote for us has got a lot of bugs in it' (EMUCS stood for EMU's Computing Sciences department, which mostly meant a couple of men with a bag of screwdrivers and a dubious level of expertise picked up on the job).

Disa's second message was of a different nature. 'Did you know that the V-C's PA was seen coming down the road from St Nicholas's church with the V-C's new boyfriend last weekend? What do you think is going on here, Lydia?'

Disa came originally from Helsingör in Denmark, which is not to be confused with Helsingborg, which is in Sweden (though the two towns are only four kilometres apart). Her English was excellent, with the slightly staccato musical tone of Danish. She was writing a book on metaphors of friendship in urban communities. This had nothing to do with Bethnal Green, but reflected a concern in cultural studies with social relations of the non-family kind. Disa was a cheerful, open person, with a white moon-shaped face and straight light brown hair in a pudding-basin cut. Lydia always felt she had a sort of eternal stability about her, a calmness which could be relied on. Disa lived with a long-distance lorry driver. Danny and she made a remarkable pair: he was short and stubby, and she looked like a giraffe next to him. The physical disparity was paralleled by a whole host of others. People wondered what they saw in each other, but Disa said they only wondered this because of the modern myth about heterosexuality – that men and women had to *be* like one another, whereas the opposite was, in her experience, true.

'I expect they're just having a fun time,' typed Lydia. What did she care about the antics of the local gay community, even if this did include EMU's very own Vice-Chancellor?

Lydia's last message was from Jeremy. He wanted to know how she was, and was she coming to the School of Business Studies' annual professorial lecture on Managing Change in Chaotic Organisations?

She exited from the system without replying, turned the machine off and stepped onto the patio to call Huneyball in to bed. The clear evening had lapsed into a cold navy night. The streetlights of Motley, and particularly the bright lamps that burnt over the shopping centre, reflected their meretricious gleam into the sky. The stars were consequently a good deal less bright than they might have been. The effect was rather like the office uplighters Phyllis from SAR had just ordered to illuminate her corner of the office and foul up the mid-year budgets.

The last time Lydia had seen Jeremy, he'd told her about the first eyewitness description of a nuclear explosion, at Alamogordo in New Mexico in July 1945. Suddenly the hills had been bathed in a brilliant light, as though somebody had turned the sun on with a switch. The scientist who wrote the account had his back to the explosion to protect his eyes, but when he turned round he saw a perfect red ball, as big as the sun, joined to the ground by a short grey stem. Then a second mushroom grew out of the first one, and the red glow faded. The cloud layers above wore the appearance of spilt milk, and the spreading pool of milk marked the impact of the blast waves on the earth's atmosphere.

'You see,' Jeremy had said, 'how the scientist marvels not only at science but at art! The two kinds of imagination are connected, and there's really no difference between the two.'

Jeremy was always trying to prove there was no difference between things when there really was. He was the main reason why Lydia had come to EMU. The Affair, or The Relationship, or whatever it was they had, had been kept a secret for many years. Ages ago they'd passed the point where either of them knew whether it being a secret was one of the things that made them go on believing they loved each other. Jeremy lived in London with his wife and their child, a daughter, who'd been born with cerebral palsy, and was in some complex conditioning programme which involved an army of helpers and 150 per cent dedication. So Jeremy felt he had no choice but to be dedicated. This was what he told himself and also Lydia. Erica, Jeremy's wife, being very occupied with the child, was mostly too busy to speculate on the finer details of Jeremy's own motives. For mothers it's always simpler: motherhood stares them in the face and they have to get on with it. The child, Claudine, needed the network of neighbourhood helpers Erica had been clever enough to build up. Who in Motley would have exhibited such altruism? Time is money and money is time. The unemployment rate in Motley was 20.5 per cent and one in three families with children lived below the poverty line. Things configured differently in Hampstead.

So Lydia and Jeremy's week in the Auvergne was only one of many make-believe episodes of domesticity. The Affair had had its ups and downs – more ups than downs; but seven years was a long time.

Jeremy was a bear of a man, bearded, rose-cheeked, replete with body hair (recently discovered to be linked to high testosterone and high IQ). He liked to wear colourful plaid shirts and sixties' corduroy trousers with pale suede shoes and heavy-knit cotton waistcoats with pockets. In this garb he resembled an East-Coast American intellectual who'd migrated to a self-sufficiency homestead in Maine with a long-haired breastfeeding wife and a brood of children. In reality he was half-Jewish, and, on his non-Jewish paternal side, the upper class English family connection could be traced back and sideways to Charles Darwin. Jeremy himself as a child had been most impressed by the serendipitous nature of scientific discovery when he'd read about how Charles Darwin nearly didn't make it on to the *Beagle*, the ship which carried him on his voyage to discovering evolution. Furthermore, had it not been for the party of Tierra del Fuegans who were on board the *Beagle*, Darwin probably would never have understood the symbiotic relationship between biology and culture: the interplay between them, which means that neither is truly in the ascendant.

Jeremy was no ordinary biologist. His original work on the role of the chemical messenger acetylcholine in brain disorders had earned him international recognition, but he'd always had his sights set on something much more important – communicating ideas about science to the world in general. He wanted to demystify it, so that people were no longer in awe of its concepts and complexities, but could use its principles in their everyday lives. He wanted them to understand that scientific theories and imagination were no different from any other kind; they were just as beautiful and just as useful. So he'd become something of a media guru. Whenever any new scientific discovery burst on the scene, which they did all the time – the so-called breast-cancer gene, giving children leukaemia via vitamin injections at birth, fiddling with the DNA of parsnips – there was Professor Jeremy Krest up there on your TV screen, even on the news itself sometimes, or in the newspaper headlines, and although the solidity of his announcements seemed at first a little challenged by the mention of 'East Midlands University' in conjunction with his professorial name, over time this began to work the other way round, and the School of Biological Sciences, East Midlands University, started to resonate with a more authoritative ring.

So Jeremy Krest was an interesting man; and this helped to explain Lydia Mallinder's desire to have a relationship with him, even in unpropitious circumstances. It was the light in Jeremy's eyes, the bounce in his words. Throughout the relationship, Lydia had never regarded herself as a tragic figure. It was her decision not to have a man at the centre of her life. She was the centre of her own life. She didn't envy her friends whose existences were like puddles of soup settling themselves in the bowl of a man's attention.

Take, for example, Helena Sutton, with whom Lydia had been at university; Helena lived like that. Every now and then Lydia went to see her, so as to re-remember this alternative fate. Helena lived on a farm in Cornwall with her husband, Bruno, and everywhere she went the children and the ducks and the chickens and the bottle-fed lambs and the smelly goats and the dogs came too. Bruno was off circling the globe making money. He called in now and then to check that Helena had remembered to get the roof mended and pay the electricity bill and buy his mother a birthday present. When he came home, he would stand in the big Cornish kitchen and inquire as to the whereabouts of his clean shirts and his supper, and the children would cry 'Dadd-*ie!*' as though he were some long-lost treasure.

Jeremy had a tiny cottage five minutes off campus where he stayed three or four nights a week. It had a garden of wild flowers about which he tried vainly to educate Lydia – *Arum maculatum*, otherwise called cuckoo-pint for unmentionable reasons; purple loose-strife, with its reputation for quietening an argument; lords and ladies, so called because the black dots look just like the beauty spots aristocrats wore to disguise their pimples.

Like most men, Jeremy patronised Lydia from time to time. He would berate her for not checking the oil and the water and the tyre pressure on her car; and also for her housekeeping habits – her kitchen cupboards were unhygienically full of little black things that moved (Huneyball had given up on them a long time ago); and Jeremy sometimes thought Lydia didn't know what was best for her. On these occasions, he would begin his sentences with, '*Lyd*ia,' said very loudly, and she would take this as a warning sign of what was coming, and turn her head away from it.

'I don't want to own you,' Lydia had protested to Jeremy so many times, standing in his disgusting wild-flowered garden, sipping wine in the interval of a concert in London, or on a canal boat in Bruges (a conference on Cultural Understandings of Science). 'It's not about ownership, and it's certainly not about the amount of time you spend with me. What I have to be sure about is the nature of our communication.'

But latterly Lydia had found herself in a newly disconsolate mode about Jeremy. She felt she deserved better than half a man. This was no kind of life. She wasn't just a bit on any man's side. Her head was full of clichés, common texts about relationships she'd got from other people, from the culture, floating like fluffy clouds low in the atmosphere. They imbued her thought, but she also resisted them, being both in the culture and outside it. She wanted and she didn't want; she felt and she didn't feel. She liked to think of herself as free from all the normal silly conventional restraints, but it was hard. Like most things in her life, the challenge of carving out new ways of relating to men was much more easily accomplished in theory than in practice.

Lydia, who could explain most things, couldn't explain her current mood of discontent. It wasn't age, because Lydia wasn't that old. But time passes nevertheless, constantly, and as Darwin would have said (or people would have thought he'd said), where's the evolution, then? You're not supposed to go through life in the same way all the time. There's meant to be movement, transition, transformation, the self-developing shock of change. The monotonous persistence of Lydia's relationship with Jeremy was at odds with her vitality. What had started out as an adventure, as well as a passion, time had turned into a routine. They knew where they were with one another. But was that where Lydia wanted to be?

The greatest truth about Lydia's life was the plague of self-questioning and self-doubt that besieged her all the time. This was rarely obvious to others; even those who shared some intimacy with her found the core of her, a soft, melting, lugubrious core, impossible to believe once they discovered it. And sometimes the fight simply seemed too much for Lydia; the reward no match for the effort it cost her. She was aiming for something, but all the aiming was itself only an escape. To get there meant she had to drive herself all the time; a voice inside her egged her on, kept her restlessly occupied with meetings, with memos, with papers, with chapters, with students, with examinations, with tidying her office or her house, with scouring Huneyball's orange fluff for underlying sores and fleas to be treated with trips to the vet and expensive potions and lotions. Routines, rituals, procedures: you must never let go, because if you let go, the black hole awaits you, and into it you'll fall, like any other set of loosely connected atoms hurtling round this sad universe of ours.

She felt the relationship with Jeremy wasn't enough for her, but she also felt she didn't want any more, at least not in *theory*. She liked living by herself in her neat little house with her unneat cat. It was a controlled environment. She could invite people in, or not, as she chose; it was *her* space. But life is also about being wild, about allowing the tide of the unanticipated moment to carry you along with it, right out to sea where the blue silk rippling surface of the ocean lets you sit bobbing in your little white-sailed ship, deliciously half-conscious of the risks beneath: the whales, the rusty skeletons of shipwrecks, the momentous watery shifting of the whole earth's crust. Caught between these two opposing sentiments, Lydia was finding that she dwelt more and more on what she *didn't* and *couldn't* have with Jeremy – the open embrace, the adventure round the world, the spontaneous combustion of heart, mind, body and soul. What was regulated could not be free.

The divergence in their views about freedom and fidelity was a fundamental problem. For him it was freedom *to*, while for her it was freedom *from*. While Lydia was pleased to be rid of the tyranny of the sexual chase and ready to see Jeremy's body as the only one for her, Jeremy deemed sexual liaisons the very stuff of life, and women's bodies as a limitless succession of combinations in the DNA sequence. She was never sure what he was up to when he wasn't with her, especially at conferences, which for him tended to be the medical sort held in plush hotels covered in bougainvillaea with multiple opportunities for meeting new and exciting combinations of DNA. While she was well aware that Jeremy's availability to other women kept her on her toes, she would never admit that it increased her addiction to him. The problem was that Jeremy didn't see any of this. He, who was much practised in the smooth articulation of complex facts, was either unwilling or unable to share Lydia's understanding about the quandary they were in. This characteristic he had, of being able to cut through and put aside other people's perceptions, helped to make him a good scientist and it gave him that no-nonsense abrasiveness that television science and news producers so loved. So, for Jeremy, things were just fine. He loved Lydia, he loved fucking her, he loved being able to see her when he wanted, he loved knowing that she would always be waiting for him, and their times together, and he loved to think that what he did the rest of the time, either with his wife, Erica, in Hampstead, or with anyone anywhere else, didn't detract from the essential gratification of their union.

Lydia was tired of it all. She was restless, and she wanted resolution, but resolution couldn't be summoned as simply as Huneyball from her neighbour's patio. Lydia sat down at her black desk and pulled her manuscript on post-modernism towards her. After reading for a while, she switched the computer on and typed: 'Women's double vision within the master discourse produces an alternative and more troubling version of those canonical texts about the nature of the "real" world. As Luce Irigaray said, years of looking in straight mirrors mean that the rule of patri-archy is reflected back at us, we ourselves are perfected as receivers of these images. But we also know that in the mirror everything is "really" reversed.'

The only way to avoid absorbing the false logic of mirror images was to stop looking at them. Lydia laughed at this midnight thought; for mirrors were, after all, such an omni-present feature of women's world. Every day one looked into them to check the arrangement of one's hair, the absence of removable blots from one's complexion, to observe again how others might see one, to ensure that the cartography of one's face and body was the same today as it had been yesterday. It wasn't, of course, but time's inroads happened slowly, and one never knew what cancers might be growing underneath. As Lydia had just said, in theory mirrors lie, because in them reality is reversed. But in prac-tice we often speak instead of the ineffable, sometimes unpalatable, truths mirrors tell.

Theory and reality; seeing and not seeing. Sometimes Lydia suspected her relationship with Jeremy Krest and university life these days were all of a piece. They shared the same rhetoric of openness, of integrity, of authenticity; on the surface it was all on the surface, and what you saw was what you got. But that was by no means all there was to it. University scholarship and successful heterosexual relationships shared the same essential deception, that passion and perseverance would make it alright in the end. Neither took account of what, in the old days, before the obscurantisms of post-modernism and other apparently liberal philosophies, had been called power.

Power inheres in people, in men like Jeremy Krest and Callum Wormleighton, but also in women who ape them, like Stephanie Kershaw, and who are willing accomplices in this major cultural myth of our time, that if you want something enough you can have it – there's the hill, just climb it; there aren't any real rocks and gulleys on the way, and if your heart and lungs aren't up to it, you only have yourself to blame.

CHAPTER 3

A Definite Deficit

Professor Callum Wormleighton and his wife Sidony lived in a delightful village about half an hour's drive from the EMU campus. The Wormleightons' back garden sloped down towards the valley of the river Soke, which was extremely polluted by the illegal effluent of the rubber tyre factory upstream, but as you couldn't actually see the pollution unless you looked for it, the appearance of an old English house smiling its historic secrets at the landscape, with perfumed floribunda and climbing coral roses and honey still for tea, was preserved more or less intact. Many of those whom the Wormleightons invited to Haddon House felt they were being invited in order to be impressed, and so it was, they were.

This morning Worms, as he was called by most of his colleagues at EMU, took the car out of the drive with a heavy heart. Sidony called after him to remind him to fetch a case of claret for the weekend, but he revved the engine and pretended not to hear her. He had more important things on his mind – the meeting of the special SSACS committee to discuss the implications of the Council's paper on the budget deficit.

There was really no way of breaking the news gently. 'Colleagues,' he said formally, as he usually did, when they were all assembled in the orange meeting room (with two purple chairs), 'we have a serious position to contend with here, or with which to contend,' he added thoughtfully, mindful of John Mapstone's admonitions about the declining quality of the English language. 'It goes like this. Because of the cut in the HEFCE grant, which is due, erhmm, to, erhum, government policy, we haven't got as much money to play with as we usually have. Or even to work with.' He tried a laugh but nobody stirred: the room was more silent than the graves in Motley cemetery. 'The University's HEFCE grant has been cut by four point seven per cent. Some of you may have read the figure in the *THES* which was incorrectly quoted at two point eight per cent. Nonetheless, we haven't fared as badly as some.' Worms paused in a minute's silence for those less fortunate than they. 'The final figure represents an overall cash reduction of four hundred and seventy k,' he went on briskly. 'Split between the six schools of the University, this means that, to put it baldly, we in SSACS must reduce our liabilities by approximately seventy-eight k this year. The exact figures have yet to be finalized, but they will be of this order.' He paused again, but not for too long, understanding that what he had to do next was to give them a plan of action that would fill the void of uncertainty.

'So what I propose to do is to set up a Resource Implementation Planning Sub-committee – RIPS for short.' This had seemed like a good idea last night over the cognac in the silk-papered sitting room of Haddon House. But nobody laughed. 'We will nominate six people to serve on the committee – two representatives from among the PHODs, one from Student Affairs, one member of the Research Sub-board, and one ANOTHER.'

'That makes five,' noted Lydia.

'Does it? Well, how about a representative from among

38

our Senior Lecturers? For my sins, I shall chair the committee,' (nobody laughed again) 'and Phyllis,' he turned round to look for her as he was wont to look for his wife when something practical needed doing, 'Phyllis will serve the committee with her usual high standard of efficiency.'

Phyllis's light gaze flickered round the room. She knew who would get nominated – Lydia Mallinder to represent the PHODs, because Lydia always wanted to be where the action was, and probably that American professor whom Phyllis disliked on instinct without having been exposed to any of his self-centred narratives, but then, when you'd been on the job as long as she had, you learned to trust your instincts. She turned over her agenda and scribbled on the back. £78k. Now one professorial redundancy plus something like cutting the Dean's entertainment budget and modularizing a few more degrees would achieve that nicely. She giggled.

'I'm sorry, Phyllis?'

She bit her lip and did the sum another way. Disposing of three part-time secretaries and not having any new computers equals £70k. Not redecorating the purple meeting room and not plugging the hole in the roof of the examination hall (the students complained that the noise of water dropping into the bucket disturbed their concentration) and not cleaning the statue of Sir Robert Sharpe-Palmer, the great Midlands industrialist, that had got itself painted a strange bright blue during the England–Germany football game last week, would undoubtedly be seen as cost-effective ways of what Worms had called 'reducing our liabilities'. She made a note to backdate an order for two new laser printers and some nice navy blue filing cabinets for the SAR room. Last year's reorganization, in which all the secretaries and administrative assistants and so forth who'd hitherto had their own nice little rooms in the departments had been centralized in the old gym, had been bad enough without this as well.

'We need to think,' continued Worms gravely to her left, 'of creative ways of reversing the straitened circumstances in which we find ourselves. The vacant chair in economics in the Department of Public Policy will not be filled. You'll just have to make the best of Professor Proudfoot, Justin. But you will be pleased to hear that the axe shall not be allowed to fall unequally. Lydia won't get her computing support post, and there will be changes in the arrangements for dealing with research overheads which will affect research-intensive departments particularly heavily. I'll come to those in a minute. So far as Sociology is concerned, Elliot, I'm afraid you won't get the extra teaching post you asked for, and the special grant to buy twenty years' worth of *Theoretical Perspectives in European Sociology* and five years' of *Ethics and Meta-Ethics: A journal for Transformative Social Praxis* will go out of the window. I do hope this shortfall won't adversely affect the quality of teaching in your department, as we need all the TQVs, not to mention all the TRUs, we can get!'

Elliot frowned and started to say something.

'You mentioned the change in the allocation of grant money, Callum,' commented Lydia menacingly.

'I did, and as I said, Lydia, I'll get to that in a minute. But I'd like first, if I may, to make a couple of points. The first is that none of these changes is being made without a great deal of heart-searching on my part, and on the part of the other deans, and, of course, the V-C himself.' He lowered his head and peered over his glasses at them so they could see how serious he was. Actually, he'd gone through it all with Sidony last night, who did the sums on the calculator she kept in the kitchen drawer for working out the budget of the village committee, which she chaired with an aptitude which was even more impressive than Callum's. He'd had to check with Phyllis the precise payroll costs, as he could never remember how much it actually cost to employ people. He only knew it wasn't the same as what they were *paid*, because you had to add on all kinds of extras like pension contributions and national insurance and so forth. But Sidony had phoned Phyllis for him while he had a whisky and watched the news.

'The second point,' he said, in exactly the tone he used for the few lectures he still gave every year when forced to justify his existence as something other than a chairman, 'is that the strategy being imposed on SSACS was, of course, fully discussed in the Council meeting last week. This means that your colleagues in the other Schools of the University will be subject to similar deprivations. Of course,' he added, 'we shouldn't regard them as deprivations. They're more in the nature of *challenges*, aren't they Phyllis? That's right, *challenges*.' He beamed happily at the sound of the word. 'Now, are there any questions?'

'Perhaps you could tell us about other strategies Council is using to cut spending, Callum?'

'Not *cut spending*, Elliot, extend limited resources in a challenging way. Have you got the Council minutes, Phyllis? I need to refresh my memory before answering Elliot's question.'

Justin stared out of the window, but this view was treeless and he looked out on to the brick wall of the building which housed the University's emergency electricity generator. A tired ivy spread a few crinkly brown and dusty green leaves up the wall, and someone had left part of a bicycle there. Its amputated appearance, without a back wheel, saddened Justin further. Was nothing safe these days? Not the back wheel of a student's bicycle, nor the future of the University? Last in, first out. He glanced pityingly at Elliot Blankthorn. The only people at EMU who had tenure were those who suffered from some personal incapacity, like Jon Pitton in Environmental Sciences, who had narcolepsy. 'What do you think, Dennis?' he scribbled at the top of Judy Sammons' PhD outline: *Women to the Top? The Problem of Patriarchy in the University Sector*.

Dennis Rudgewick was a senior lecturer in Justin's department. 'SSRs up,' he wrote. 'Top-up fees next?' He put his pen down and started cleaning the nails of one hand with those of the other. Dennis's hobby was vegetable-growing, and some of the earth from an energetic digging session last night had come to the meeting with him.

'More research?' scribbled Justin. Dennis raised his heavy eyebrows at him. Those two ROs down the corridor on Justin's European project hadn't a clue what they were doing, and Justin wasn't about to tell them.

Callum looked at them sternly. 'I ordered coffee, didn't I, Phyllis?' Phyllis sighed. He did and she had, but catering was usually late these days. She got up and peeled a phone off the wall. 'Hallo, Khadeeja. This is Phyllis, in the orange meeting room. Professor Wormleighton asked for coffee at eleven. Yes. Oh, did he? Well, alright then.'

Dennis Rudgewick didn't need to worry, he'd just got £75k out of the ESRC for a project on trends in old-age morbidity. He'd decided to specialize in old age a long time ago. It wasn't a sexy subject, but it did have a future, as everyone had it to look forward to and there was a lot more of it around these days.

Callum had found the Council paper. 'Ah, here we are. Yes, of course, the ARQ. Assessment of Research Quality. This is a purely internal exercise designed to give us some grasp of the nature of schol – uhm, research, in which we are all, as professional academics, engaged. Or ought to be.' He looked over the top of his glasses at no-one in particular, although several people thought he was looking at them.

'Forgive me for being obtuse,' said Elliot, 'but I fail to see how assessing research quality will cut – will reduce liabilities. Perhaps you could enlighten us, Callum?'

Callum thumbed through the Council minutes.

'The short answer is that it won't, will it?'

'Certain forms of research activity are unproductive,' remarked Callum, for want of anything more productive to say.

'Are they?'

'Yes. Unfunded research, for example.'

'Ah. You're using "productive" in rather a narrow sense, there, aren't you, Callum?'

'Anyway,' boomed Callum, raising his voice against what he regarded as petulant banter from Elliot, and waving the Council minutes in his defence, 'there are a few other ideas here. More consultancy income, I remember that one. I'm sure we can all make a contribution here. Elliot's quite a TV star these days, isn't he?' This was a reference to a brief appearance Elliot had made a few months ago on *Newsnight*, when he had been asked to comment on a new code of ethics introduced by a health authority in Devon to prevent paediatricians from experimenting on newborn babies. The problem was (and Elliot had stated this most authoritatively) that cleaning up your act always meant revealing what a dreadful mess it had been in. It simply wouldn't have occurred to most parents to think that doctors were using their babies to experiment on. 'Council has set up a working party to consider the matter. How best to retrieve consultancy income, you know, fairly. The Consultancy Income Sub-Committee – CISC for short. You're on it, aren't you, Justin?'

Justin sighed. The phone on the wall rang – something about a fire practice. 'New degrees, that was another,' recalled Callum from the minutes. 'We ought to consider whether we're really maximizing the potential for inter-disciplinary work. We are the School of Social *and* Cultural Studies, after all. It's not healthy to work in pockets. Now, Lydia, I was wondering about your MA, Critical Pedagogy and Liberal Education. Whether there might be some room there for a creative partnership with, say, Post-modern Discourses on Power, or even, dare I say it, with Social Work Today?'

Lydia frowned, remembering the interdisciplinary collaboration with Stephanie Kershaw, and thinking that real post-modern discourses on power were actually a good deal more interesting than what Rhena Malik in Sociology taught, with which Callum wanted her to collaborate.

'Hmm.' Callum looked down for renewed inspiration at the Council paper. 'Ah yes, this one came from the V-C himself. There's a proposal, well not a proposal, because it will happen, in our efforts towards cut—, towards liability reduction. It is proposed that we enlist the help of a team of management consultants. A name was suggested, I think, but I'm not sure . . .'

'Is that the same firm that we paid all that money to to design our notepaper?' asked someone.

'Maybe, maybe. Anyway, what do we think of the idea?' Callum looked round the table with the air of an adult at a children's birthday party suggesting a new game of musical chairs.

'A waste of money,' declared Lydia.

'A waste of time?' suggested Justin.

'Sometimes,' said Elliot, 'it can be a good idea to gain an external perspective. Helps to see the wood from the trees. There's a lot of it in the States right now.'

'Will whoever it is from whoever they are consult with the students?' This was from the Student Affairs Committee representative, a worried-looking young woman who carried lots of canvas bags, the daughter of a Norfolk opthalmologist.

'Oh I expect so,' said Callum airily. 'That's our usual practice, isn't it?'

'What about equal opportunities, Callum? What steps will be taken to ensure that the effects of the cuts won't discriminate on grounds of race, gender, age and so forth?'

Callum thought they probably would discriminate – that was the whole point of them, and it was probably why Lydia had asked the question. He and the V-C and others from the inner circle had already had what you might call informal discussions about Gaynor Scudamore who ran the library, who was a nice enough woman (the students liked her, she ran a one-woman counselling service from her room behind the Accessions desk), but she'd definitely passed her sell-by date. Others in the firing line were Fern Meredith in Justin's department – she'd cost EMU a fortune in maternity leave, and still looked threateningly fertile – a woman in Environmental Sciences Callum couldn't remember the name of, and Martin Pippard in EMUCS who'd got rather unfortunately addicted to what Callum understood was called Surfing the Web. Apparently this was now a recognized form of addiction, akin to drugs or alcohol. That reminded him: 'Are we on the Internet?' he asked.

'How would we know if we were?' asked Peter Handyside, an administrator from SAR.

'Check it out, Phyllis, will you? And liaise with someone from EMUCS. Perhaps we need an Internet working party. Yes, that's a good idea. Any volunteers?'

Eventually they got round to the subject Lydia wanted to hear about – the new proposals for handling research income.

'Heretofore,' began Callum pompously, 'the University Finance Committee allowed you' (he then changed this hurriedly to 'us', though it hardly applied to him as he wasn't what was called 'research active') 'all to retain a portion of the overhead element on research grants. This was in order to increase incentives to attach an appropriate overhead element when preparing the budgets. That is, when Peter prepares the budgets for you – us.' He threw a sympathetic glance in Peter Handyside's direction, as he knew it was no mean feat to sit down with these people and reduce their airy-fairy ideas to figures: number of travel trips needed to the British Library, or to collect data from Glasgow, how many questionnaires, how many pages long, how many second-class stamps with how many reminders, and so forth. 'However, the mechanism doesn't seem to have worked particularly well . . . where's the paper for the research sub-board, Phyllis? Ah, yes, that's right. Our overhead recovery rate in 1994 to 5 was thirty per cent; last year it was twenty-one per cent. Dismal, really. Come on, chaps, we're going to have to do better than that.'

'The formula doesn't offer much of an incentive,' murmured Lydia. Various people round the table were looking quite puzzled.

'What do you mean? What formula?'

Phyllis had long ago ceased to be surprised at how little these people could remember about the rules they themselves had invented. 'The first twenty-five per cent of overheads goes to central funds,' she spelled out wearily. 'After that it's split sixty per cent to the School and forty per cent centrally. Schools vary in the internal carve-up – SSACS' ruling is half of the sixty per cent to the department. Then departments vary in what they give back to the grant-holder.'

'How complicated,' commented Callum.

'It means,' explained Phyllis impatiently, 'that on an average small grant of, say one hundred k, with forty-five per cent overheads on salaries, the person who wrote the research proposal and who has to do the work would be lucky to get more than a thousand quid back in overheads.'

'Oh.'

'A large proportion of our research income comes from charities, Professor Wormleighton,' explained Peter. 'Charities don't pay overheads.'

'Well, they ought to. I must talk to the V-C about that.'

'I've got a class at twelve,' said Lydia. 'Can we please get on and finish this meeting?'

Callum looked at her sharply. Too bloody efficient, that woman. But maybe you had to be when you had a non-subject like gender studies to look after. Like many very clever women, Lydia was attractive: long brown hair arranged in a knot on top of her head, grey-green eyes, a compact body, hands (Callum always noticed people's hands) of unusual delicacy.

'Yes, yes. We will finish the meeting. I myself . . . what have I got next, Phyllis?'

'Lunch with a group of government officials from Mauritius,' intoned Phyllis. This was one of Callum's three stock excuses for not being able to be engaged in university business. Actually, he was bound for the 1.15 to London and an afternoon at the Cézanne exhibition before joining his sister, a Baroness, at the opera in the evening. They were going to Monteverdi's *The Coronation of Poppea*, a particular favourite of his. It was the first opera ever written on a historical subject (if one discounts Aeschylus's *The Persians*, that is), and he was looking forward to watching a good Roman orgy.

'The new system,' pronounced Callum, drawing himself abruptly back to the present, 'will be different.'

'Fancy that!' exclaimed Dennis. An enormous £9.1k of his £75k ESRC grant was overheads, so he had a personal interest in what happened to them. Dennis was a very parsimonious researcher, unlike some of them. He had the same attitude to research as he did to gardening. A few reliable seeds, a few reliable ideas, enough good soil, a decent dose of hard work, a bit of luck with the weather.

'The whole of the overhead element will now be retained centrally,' Callum informed them. 'In addition, there will be penalties for obtaining grants carrying no overheads, and for those on which the overhead element falls below the threshold figure of forty-five per cent.'

'What penalties?' snapped Lydia.

'A pro-rata reduction in the size of the relevant departmental grant has been suggested.'

'What do you mean, "suggested"?'

'The finer points of the new improved system of research grant administration have still to be finalized,' deferred Callum. They'd known this particular bit of the liabilities reduction exercise wouldn't go down well with staff. Overheads were a funny thing. Research Councils and so forth were supposed to pay this money to institutions to support the basic costs of the research – the labour needed to direct it, the researchers' rooms, their wastepaper baskets, and their anglepoises, a share of Domestic Services, the illiterate postroom staff, and so forth, even the office and the salaries of the deans and the V-C himself. Of course, the grants also paid the salaries of the contract researchers who did the work, and the direct costs of the research – the tape recorders, the questionnaires, the envelopes – and this encouraged one to believe that each research project was a law unto itself, a closed system, a micro-climate separate from everything else that was going on. But it wasn't true. Research was an expensive business for universities. So Callum Wormleighton and Sir Stanley Oxborrow, EMU's V-C, had learnt recently, as a result of their exposure to the self-interested revelations of the management consultancy firm, Winkett and Bacon, who had designed the EMU note-paper, who would soon determine EMU's Mission, and whom Sir Stanley had decided it would serve everyone's interest for EMU to use as much as possible in future.

But it was unhappily the case that universities also *needed* research. This was because a proportion of the grant they got each year from the government was for research; the more research you had, the more government money you got. The weakness in the whole system wasn't hard to spot. It was that it all depended on the calibre of the staff them-selves. Intellectual capital, that was the nub of it. That and the ability to get off your backside and turn it into some-thing. It was a pity that nobody had worked out a foolproof way of hiring staff who would do this successfully. Callum knew that of the three departments in SSACS – Public Policy, Cultural Studies and Sociology – only one was doing much in the way of research, and that was entirely due to the efforts of Lydia Mallinder. Oh, Dennis Rudgewick did his bit, but it was pedestrian stuff. Dennis's problem was that he'd never finished his PhD and the title 'Mr' didn't look good on a research application. Callum kept meaning to have a word with Justin about Dennis's PhD.

Callum's dislike of Lydia followed from the fact that her performance gave her power over him. But he couldn't do anything about it – when she kept raking all that money in. He'd been terribly dubious when Stanley Oxborrow had said to him five or so years ago after a Council meeting, 'You know, Callum, I can't help thinking we ought to be doing something about this women thing'. Afterwards he'd learnt that the V-C had a feisty granddaughter who was something of a feminist, and Stanley listened to her. When

Callum first told Sidony they were going to have a chair in gender studies, she'd laughed like a horse and said something about pollination and courgettes.

He'd vetoed a chair in *women's* studies. 'Don't we want whomever it is to study men as well?' he'd argued.

'Gender – women – same thing,' retorted Sir Stanley. 'But have it your way, you're the one who'll have to manage her or him, most probably her.'

Lydia had come to them from the LSE. She'd applied for a readership there, which was half-way to being a professor, but they'd refused to give her one, and so out of pique she'd looked for somewhere else to move to. This was the official story of Lydia's migration to Northamptonshire. The unofficial one was, of course, the story of Jeremy Krest.

In those days, not so long ago, the first principle of capitalism – invest – had been understood by most universities. Paying Lydia Mallinder's salary had produced a huge profit in terms of research overheads for EMU. With luck, this would now get huger as the new procedures for holding onto overheads came into effect. When EMU had become a university, and there was money around, the V-C, who, whatever else he was, was a man of some foresight, had looked around him for figures of intellectual stature who might be lured away from wherever they were to establish what in the jargon were called new 'centres of excellence' at EMU. Thus Jeremy had come, fresh from some Cambridge college or other, to head the School of Biological Sciences, and to develop his own research laboratory. In this laboratory he and a stream of acolytes continued the research that inspired him, and led to a succession of scientific papers and lucrative research grants. It all went on slowly and steadily the way in the popular imagination scientific work is supposed to do, while its leader, Professor Jeremy Krest, fronted all the latest scientific frauds and scandals and elements of half-truth, wearing his latest soft flannel tartan shirt which made the TV sets of the nation dazzle.

Naturally the V-C would have liked to get his hands on all the money Jeremy earned from these appearances, but Jeremy, like the rest of them, either maintained he didn't earn any or stashed it away in a secret account from where it could be siphoned off to pay for the unbelievable technical devices featured in the catalogues that mistakenly found their way into Justin Leopard's pigeonhole, or to keep some poor part-time researcher in work for a few more weeks, or for the annual School festivity in June, an event famous for its experimental fireworks and for the calibre of the food provided, which quite made Khadeeja in Catering's eyes pop out.

When Lydia had applied for the chair in gender studies at EMU she'd undoubtedly been the strongest candidate for the job. This didn't stop Callum from trying to give it to the only male applicant, an ex-psychiatric nurse with eyes that reminded him of Sidony's spaniel and a matching fawning attitude, but little in the way of relevant teaching or research experience. The man did have good references, and his performance in the interview was much crisper than Lydia's, who rather took the attitude that if EMU didn't snap her up there'd be plenty of others who would.

The persona was important, the sociology of the body, because of course these days you couldn't tell much about people's private lives from their CVs, except in the case of some women, where a gap of several years lay, poorly accounted for, in the story of their past: '1970–2 Caversham Girls' School, 4 A-levels (3As, 1C); the University of Nottingham 1972–5, BA Hons in Politics and Sociology; 1975–82 various part-time research assistantships, etc.' That was the gap where children had happened, where, in the old politically incorrect days, women would have been able to write with some pride the dates of birth of their children and before that the appellation 'Married', all of which enabled other people to place them, to know what kind of people they were, what could be expected of them. If only Fern Meredith, for instance, had put 'Married' on her CV, and also warned of her intention to have multiple progeny, for whom she would continually have to rush home for one thing or another, they'd never have hired her. Nowadays the most that CVs gave away were absurdities such as 'fellwalker' or 'marathon runner' or 'clean driving licence', as if anyone would ever admit to having a dirty one.

So they knew nothing about Fern when they hired her, not much about Lydia, nor about Elliot Blankthorn, but then Callum thought there was always less to find out about men. Men were more transparent. Simpler, somehow.

This business of overheads was undoubtedly tricky. Sir Stanley had told Callum in confidence that when he'd talked to Richard Winkett, the senior partner in Winkett and Bacon, the management consultants, Richard had told him that if he played the game right, a healthy balance of research overhead income could wipe out the entire deficit in a couple of years. 'Work'em to death, Callum,' had advised Sir Stanley, 'that's what we've got to do.'

It wasn't the same with teaching. The pressure was on there, too; but teaching couldn't earn directly the way research could. You packed the students in, increasing the staff-student ratio (SSR) in leaps and bounds, and you lowered admission standards to almost below the point where literacy was a criterion for university admission at all. You taught them what they wanted to know rather than what they didn't want to know, and their local authorities and their daddies and mummies paid and they managed or mostly didn't manage on the student grant, and with the student loan, and on the crumbs or the credit cards their parents gave them. Richard Winkett had told Sir Stanley he should organize some public relations exercises abroad. There must be at least a few courses that could be flogged to third-world countries. Winkett had flipped through the catalogue. 'What about Equine Studies, or Band Musicianship? Maybe Prosthetics and Orthotics – what the hell are they? Certainly Applied Consumer Studies and Computerized Accountancy – now *there* are a couple of things the rest of the world *must* need to know about!' It occurred to Sir Stanley that PR abroad would be a good use of some dead wood, by which he meant chaps who got by with four hours' teaching a week, and spent the rest of their time in The Squirrel Inn, the other side of the roundabout. 'They'll soon get tired of it, Callum. After the first dozen or so, one hotel's much like another. Like universities. Or women, dare I say, but don't tell that Mallinder woman, she'll have us hung, drawn and quartered if we're not careful.'

CHAPTER 4

Theories of Risk

'I know it's going to be difficult to get the statistics,' admitted Judy Sammons in the faintly sunlit atmosphere of Lydia's room on the green floor of the SSACS building.

It was the day after the special SSACS meeting. Lydia was looking for something in her filing cabinet. 'Ah, here they are. The minutes of the last Equality Committee. They aren't exactly scintillating, these meetings. The committee was only set up because the V-C thought EMU should be being seen to be doing something to clean up its act.'

'You're on it, aren't you?'

'One representative from each department. But most of them don't turn up. We had some very good anti-sexist training sessions a couple of years ago, but I said I couldn't see the point unless the men at the top were trained as well. Ah, this is what I was looking for.' Lydia pulled a sheaf of papers from the filing cabinet. She sat down, moved a loose strand of hair from in front of her eyes and leafed through the papers, extracting a series of bright lemon pages.

'Staff recruitment monitoring information. This is the sort of thing. School of Business Studies, Economics Department, clerical posts: twenty-seven applicants, sixteen white and one a woman. A white man was appointed. And here's the 1990 statement from the CVCP on Equal Opportunities in Employment in Universities. It says there's a statistical appendix on the position of women in universities, but I don't think there is. No, that's right,' her finger jabbed at a lemon sheet, ' "the statistical survey of the position of women nationally in universities has yet to be completed". I wonder why! We used to have a part-time equal-opportunities officer. She had a terrible time. They kept forgetting to pay her, and in the end she resigned over the installation of braille buttons in the lifts.'

Judy Sammons listened attentively and held her hand out to take the papers Lydia was reading. 'I'm sorry, I can't give you these, they *are* confidential.'

Judy looked at her quizzically. But of course: Lydia Mallinder was part of the establishment. That, after all, was one of the subjects she wanted to explore in her thesis: the transpositions of loyalty and affiliation that could be the making and the scourge of successful academic women. She decided to be matter-of-fact about it. If she was allowed to take EMU as a case study, then Lydia Mallinder's own political identifications would be part of the story. The notion of including her supervisor as data amused her. Nell, Judy's partner, had been reading a book about women scientists and had told her a story about one who in the early 1900s was interested in theories about sex differences in intelligence which related these to head size. So she measured lots of skulls, including her supervisor's. He turned out to have a particularly small one.

Lydia defended herself: 'I'm sure that what happens here is typical of other British universities.'

'That's why it'd make a good case study.'

'You'll need to write formally to the V-C for permission to observe the workings of the Equality Committee, and carry out any staff and student interviews you might want to do.'

'I've already done that.'

Lydia smiled.

'There's nothing wrong with being keen.'

'Indeed not.'

The girl beamed and pulled a sheet from her clipboard. 'I've sketched out a rough timetable for the first year. I'd be glad if you could comment on it. I've given a copy to Professor Leopard as well.'

Lydia had lunch with Disa Loring in the staff canteen. She had a pallid vegetable curry. Disa spent some time inspecting the label on her wholemeal salad bap, because coleslaw or mayonnaise had started to appear everywhere ever since the sandwich side of EMU's catering had been contracted out.

They sat by the window, from where they could see directly into the library building. Students peered glumly at piles of books or ploughed hopefully down the stacks with crumpled reading lists in their hands. All but the very keen were disappointed, because the library budget had been one of the first areas to suffer cuts, and at the same time most of the undergraduate courses had expanded hugely, which meant there were even fewer textbooks to go round. Dedicated teachers photocopied chunks of books illegally and then photocopied photocopies as though this excused them from the photocopying law.

Behind the library rose the chimney of Biological Sciences, piling its normal nasty effluent into the air. No-one knew what Biological Sciences did to produce this discharge, but most of them had lived with it for so long that they no longer found it remarkable. Lydia would ask Jeremy Krest, but Jeremy always distracted her by laughing and saying that the beauty of science lay partly in its violence and the fact that there were always mysteries to be unravelled. Secrets, if you like. Lydia didn't; the trouble with secrets was that they could also be lies.

'Here's a lie for you, then,' Jeremy Krest had said. 'Or maybe not? If you took a glass of water and you somehow tagged the molecules in it, and you emptied it into the sea, perhaps at Trenarvon Bay where you and I might find an excuse for a few days away in the summer, and then the sea with the glass of water in it flowed through all the oceans, and then you filled the glass again, what do you think would be the chance of collecting some of the original molecules in it?' Of course Lydia had said none, which was what he'd expected her to say. 'Not true!' said he gleefully. 'There are more molecules in a glass of water than there are glasses of water in the sea, so you'd almost certainly find some of the original molecules in the glass.'

'If you believe that, you'll believe anything.'

'That's what I said to begin with,' said Jeremy.

Behind the chimney of Building Services the vast countryside unrolled, slightly green with advancing spring and dotted with early daffodils, always for some reason a uniform pale yellow in this area, without those healthy orange middles that remind one of the yolks of really free-range eggs. Perhaps the air was polluted, and that's why all the daffodils were anaemic.

'What are we going to do, Disa?'

'About what?'

'About all these awful cuts and threats, and the fact that we're going to have to fight so much harder to get any decent work done.'

'It is the same everywhere,' noted Disa dispiritedly. 'It is even the same in Denmark.'

'It's alright at the top.'

'Naturally. Perhaps we should form a committee – women against the cuts?'

'I think not.' Lydia played around with the square of rehydrated carrot and parsnip and pea on her plate, arranging them around the edges in an alternating pattern: white and orange, green, orange and white. 'The days have passed when anything can be called a conspiracy against women. "Woman" isn't even a category any more. Dual systems theory has gone out of the window. We're so busy investigating the discourse that we've quite forgotten about sites of male hegemonic power.' Judy Sammons would love this. 'Try telling that to the likes of Stephanie Kershaw, though.'

Lydia had shown Disa Stephanie's red markings on the draft of the Gender and Development module. They'd drunk one and a half bottles of wine over them, and had composed a reply which referred Stephanie to a recent ESRC report on female entrepreneurs and sex discrimination, according to which 82 per cent of male business owners wanted to get rich, but 76 per cent of the women merely wanted a good reputation; 40 per cent of the women (none of the men) had had to give up for domestic reasons, and 63 per cent felt their sex got in the way of something called 'market credibility'. 'If these aren't reasons for encouraging students to explore gender differences,' wrote Lydia to Stephanie, 'then *I'd like to know what are!*'

'This is all extremely unpleasant to live through,' concluded Lydia. 'Especially the business about overheads.'

'Of course, yes.'

'It's extremely powerful as a metaphor,' she observed. 'It's not only what they're trying to do to us *but what it all means*. How can they really think they can treat us like this? Like machines to be bled for money.'

'We are machines,' murmured Disa, 'full of blood.'

Lydia stared at her curiously.

'Don't pay any attention to me. I'm only an alien!'

'But the other part of me,' continued Lydia, 'says there must be some mistake. Reason must be made to prevail. We have to convince them that the model isn't a rational one. I want a research centre of my own, Disa, and I'd rather have one which is part of a university than one which isn't.'

'I want a good selection of sandwiches which do not have mayonnaise in them, no coleslaw anywhere, cycling tracks across the country, absolutely no smoking, meat-eating to be illegal, organic farming, an end to pornography on the Internet, a baby without being pregnant, and then also I would like the toilets at Motley station to re-open. But I don't think these things will happen.'

'Why did they close them?'

'Men weeing on the floor. And worse than that.'

'We've got to resist, Disa. We can't let them do this to us.'

'Perhaps I should tell you something that will make you even more cross,' offered Disa. 'Or maybe I won't. Don't you have a class this afternoon?'

'Psychoanalytic Theories of Gender Development.'

'I expect you can do that on your head.'

'Tell me, then.'

'Our friend old Oxymoron. He's slipping his boyfriend in as a professor. Without going through any of the proper channels – the UPC, the Council. And in EMU's present – what is the phrase? – straitened circumstances. Now, don't you think that is a little difficult to swallow?'

Nothing would surprise Lydia, but this didn't mean she didn't want to know the latest EMU gossip.

'The boyfriend is called Trent Lovett. He is a cyclist like me. We are both on the Central Cycling Campaign. He has a very nice mountain marathon bike.'

'Spare me the technical details, please. So here we are in

the middle of all this cost-cutting, and the V-C suddenly finds the money to pay a friend of his a full professorial salary.' Lydia sighed. Sir Stanley Oxborrow's gayness was widely known. There was no need to hide it now in the 1990s as there had been in the 1960s. Homosexuality in men had a masonic character to it; it was common, easily recognized by insiders, and afforded a glue-like solidarity to its members. 'He won't get away with it.'

'He will. Remember we are all vulnerable now. I do not think you should step out of line, Lydia. Maybe he is not such a bad guy, this Trent Lovett, although probably if he wasn't Sir Stanley's boyfriend he would not be worth more than a senior lectureship. He hasn't done very much. I looked him up on the library database – there are five papers in peer review journals, two edited books. His field is risk. Theories of risk, you know. He has come from the University of North-west London. In Acton.'

'I don't,' said Lydia. 'Know about risk theory, I mean. Where is this man going to go? He's not coming to Cultural Studies, is he?' She went pale at the thought.

'I told you you'd have done better with a sandwich. You must look after yourself, Lydia, no-one else is going to.'

Particularly not Jeremy Krest. Like the rest of EMU, Disa didn't officially know about Jeremy. It sometimes seemed unfair to Lydia that other people could brandish their unrespectable personal relationships when she couldn't. She wanted to talk to Jeremy, to hold him; but most of all to be held by him. But Jeremy was at home with Erica and Claudine, playing the good family man. It was time for Claudine's three-monthly check up at the hospital. Then he was off to Los Angeles to another one of his conferences.

'Would you like some coffee, Lydia? They sell decaffeinated now.'

'I need a few pints of caffeine after what you've just told me.'

But it was Justin who got Trent Lovett and this, on reflection, was the real reason why he wasn't going to get the post in economics he'd asked for. Callum Wormleighton had known about the V-C's plot all along. Justin retired to bed with a sore throat and glands – stress, he called it, but his wife Rosemary decided it was a virus.

Callum phoned Justin at home to tell him that Trent would be moving into the room next to his fairly promptly, i.e. the following Monday. 'But what will he do?' inquired Justin, much more politely than Lydia would have done, though less politely than if he hadn't had a temperature of 103 degrees at the time.

'He'll boost your TRUs for you, that's what he'll do,' shouted Callum. Building Services were drilling next door, reinstating a partition they'd taken away the year before. 'He'll be an asset. He can teach on one of your health and welfare courses, I should think. I've told him to contact Dennis Rudgewick to discuss it. Or perhaps the joint course with sociology. And then of course there'll be the research grants. Enormous sums of money. Don't worry, Justin, you'll still be Head of Department, Lovett'll just labour alongside you. He's a good worker, and then there'll be that fruitful exchange of ideas, the very essence of scholarship, don't you know?'

Rosemary had given Justin a double dose of Night Nurse, so after this he fell into a deep coma. He woke to a tremendous amount of shouting from downstairs – Rosemary and Carey, their teenage daughter, having one of their arguments. Carey burst in on him all fiery from the fray: 'Daddy, what's wrong with The Moon and Sixpence? Why does Mummy think it's full of drug pushers and heroin addicts and underage sex?'

'Because it probably is,' reasoned Justin from the depths of his sickbed. He was just beginning to realize what Callum had done to him. He felt like a defrocked priest or a king whose kingdom had suddenly been whipped away from under his feet.

'Daddy!'

'Alright, alright.' He held out a sweaty hand and pulled Carey towards him. Rosemary couldn't stand it that he especially loved Carey when she was angry. It was for that display of spirit he so lacked himself. Try as he might, he could never whip up a frenzy about anything. He never felt terribly angry or terribly excited or terribly anything. Sometimes he thought his brain had been wired differently from other people's – theirs responded much more than his did to the same level of stimulus. This didn't mean he didn't feel things, because he did, but there was an inordinate sameness about the feelings which bored him no end, and the boredom was also the same day after day, year in, year out.

'Alright, I'll talk to your mother, but you have to promise me that you know how to take care of yourself, and you won't take any risks. Because if you do, and there's trouble, I don't want her shouting at me, I've got a lot of problems at work at the moment, and I'm going to need all my energies to deal with them.'

The Leopards lived in Suckley Green, a delightful village far enough away from EMU's Biological Sciences chimney and all the other contaminations of Motley to provide that microclimate of false reassurance so loved by the middle classes. Theirs was a thatched cottage even – fondly known as 'The Thatch Palace'; Justin had had to do a consultancy at a dreadful university in the States the previous year to pay for the repair of the thatch. He'd muttered and moaned about it, but Rosemary had made him go, and she'd arranged for him to stay in a plastic Howard Johnson Inn while he was there so he could save as much money as possible. Under the new arrangements for consultancy that money would now belong to EMU, instead of the Leopards' house account. Try telling Rosemary that!

He heard the back door bang and the whirr of bicycle wheels going through the front gate as Carey disappeared for her evening's entertainment.

'Has she done her homework?' he asked when Rosemary brought him a cup of tea.

'Of course she's done her homework, what kind of mother do you think I am?'

'A good one. Oh Rosie,' he rarely called her that these days, although he was fond of her, and she did sometimes endear herself to him, 'Rosie, d'you think we could go away for a few days, just the two of us?'

'What about Amos?'

Amos was four, and not the easiest child, either. It was the same spirit that Carey had, only it showed itself differently with him, in bursts of inattention that could be called naughtiness, and a habit of waking several times in the night. Justin usually found Amos in bed with them, and if he wasn't there he was in with his sister, who complained bitterly about the indignity of sharing a bed with a four-year-old.

'Rosemary,' tried Justin more seriously, 'when was the last time we had any time together?'

She pushed a strand of hair off her face, and he noticed how she'd recently spread a bit around the middle, so when she sat down her blouse or sweater bulged slightly all the way round. Today it was a red sweater, and it had a hole in the arm. Her elbow poked through it like a dried mushroom. He felt strangely touched by this symbol of her vulnerability. Rosemary was a capable woman, the anchor of his life. In this cottage, sequestered safely away from the pollutions of town and gown, down the lane in Suckley Green where the horse chestnut trees were even now preparing to hold out their magnificent pink candles to the spring, demonstrating anew that exact angle of erection that must be every man's dream, he knew that his life was made, even if he was usually incapable of feeling it.

Warm in bed, with domestic fevers raging below and the languorous perfume of the magnolia grandiflora drifting through the window, Justin struggled with Judy Sammons' research proposal on the position of women in higher education. 'Patriarchal discourses are reflected in the institutional-attitudinal climate of higher education,' he read. 'The aim of this thesis is to examine the operation of patriarchy in the Academy using the self-reflexive analytic techniques of feminist post-structuralism. Feminist post-structuralism is crucially underpinned with a reconstruction of language and discourse as constituting subjectivity.' Justin had a feeling he'd bitten off more than he could chew. Did he want the hassle? Was it worth it to get a couple of extra TRUs? The white image of Judy's knee flashed before him like a stork, or a heron.

As April advanced and the hedgerows under the horse chestnut trees in Suckley Green grew milky with meadowsweet, some of it crept as far as the shopping centre and car parks in Motley and poked its creamy waving lace through cracks in the asphalt. Jeremy Krest telephoned Lydia Mallinder at all hours of the day and night from Los Angeles, and from an ensuing much-publicized conference on Science and the Media in Seattle, and Lydia was no nearer finishing either with her book or with Jeremy Krest. It was all, thought Lydia resentfully, so much simpler for other people.

Rosemary and Justin Leopard went to the Costa Brava, to a three-star hotel with pots of pink geraniums and two swimming pools, and Rosemary lay by one of them alternately reading a P.D. James novel about brutal murders in Norfolk and worrying about Carey and Amos, who had gone to stay with their grandparents in Somerset.

Justin kept coming to sit beside her and sighing deeply, 'This is the life, isn't it, Rosie, this is the life!' He'd brought two books with him, a textbook of women's studies which he thought might help him with the problem of Judy Sammons, and a new book by a whizzkid American called Victor Malvesen about the crisis in government welfare policy, but both of them stayed in his suitcase. Instead he and Rosemary ploughed their way through the Spanish spring flowers to take a look at Salvador Dali's wild fisherman's house by the deep blue bay out of which all manner of weird and dreadful things came, courtesy of Dali's imagination. There, on a little hill, they picnicked off olives and bread and warm white wine, and Justin found himself launched on a speech about overheads. 'It's unacceptable, Rosemary,' he complained.

'When did you last have a proper research grant, Justin? You can't count this messy little European thing,' she added. Periodically either Beverley or Candida, the two women employed part-time on the project, would ring Justin up at home because they couldn't find him at work to ask him what they ought to be doing. Justin always promised to tell them. The 'professor of promises', Rosemary called him.

Justin screwed his eyes up and focused on the white balls on the opposite hill which represented Dali and his wife, Galia. 'I can't remember. 1976 or 1977, I think. That was the project on crowd behaviour. I did it with Malcolm Watson. It was a good project. Unfortunately we never published anything because we had that disagreement about the data. Malcolm took it with him to Cuba,' he remembered gloomily.

'You should have insisted on getting it back.'

'I did,' insisted Justin. 'I wrote and I phoned, but the Cuban phone system doesn't work very well.' Rosemary pulled her skirt up to her knees and lay back in the sun. 'I know what Worms is going to do next,' said Justin desperately. 'I bet he's plotting with the V-C at this very moment. Departmental targets for research income. The whole caboodle.'

'No bad thing, if you ask me.' Rosemary spat an olive stone into the sea. 'You've had a cushy life, Justin.' She thought of the uncushy life she had as a freelance copy-editor and the mother of Justin's children, especially in Suckley Green in the winter, when the mists overflowed from the fens and everyone stayed inside their houses, and even the ducks retreated to their little wooden box in the middle of the duckpond.

'Perhaps I should leave EMU. What d'you think, Rosie?'

'Where else would take you?'

'There's no need to be so horrible.' He lay back in the scratchy grass with his arms behind his head squinting at the sun. Perhaps he should have an affair. An image of Judy Sammons floated into view. There was a definite ethical problem about that. Momentarily, he glimpsed Stephanie Kershaw's pencil-like skirts and her polished legs, and that strange dark line round the outside of her lips, exactly like the contour lines on a map. Stephanie kept herself to herself, or else gave herself to others when no-one was looking. Justin fancied Lydia, but they were friends, so that wouldn't do. In any case, he'd known about Jeremy ever since he'd driven past Jeremy's cottage one evening, dispatched by Rosemary to pick Carey up from somewhere or other, and he'd seen Lydia tripping gaily up the garden path which had been lined at the time with miniature golden sun-flowers Jeremy had proudly bred from seed. 'I wish you luck, Lydia,' Justin had said to her afterwards. 'My lips are sealed.' And so they had been. Justin was a man of honour.

Back at EMU the sun was also out and Lydia, following the path of reason, but also of risk, went to see the V-C about this overhead business. She wore a sparkling white blouse, a pearl necklace, and a tight black skirt and knew that Sir Stanley would admire her efficiency, even if he didn't fully appreciate her femininity.

He sat behind an enormous antique desk in his office. Unlike Lydia, he no longer needed to pretend he was some-thing he wasn't. He'd come out as gay just after he'd got his knighthood for services to industry ten years ago, leav-ing the usual wife and two grown-up children. His wife had intimated to the *News of the World*, for a large sum that enabled her to buy herself a pension, that Sir Stanley had been carrying out his clandestine sexual activities for many years before he became a Sir. He was now a pert, bright-eyed sixty-five-year-old with a penchant for young Aryan types whom he entertained to ribald feasts in his four-teenth-century manor house, which was several steps up and a few miles away from the Wormleightons, which in turn was in a different social echelon from the Leopards' Thatch Palace in Suckley Green. Sir Stanley's manor dated back to 1375, when the original owner, one Simon de Keynes, had been granted a licence to crenellate it. It had been an Elizabethan hall with octagonal piers and cham-fered ribs. Sir Stanley was especially fond of showing his young friends the Jacobean Powder Closet, which these days boasted a heart-shaped, high-technology, high-speed jacuzzi, with the usual accompaniment of odiferous milky lotions.

It took Lydia a while to cross the new Wilton carpet in Sir Stanley's office. On her journey she noticed new prints on the freshly painted ivory walls. They were shadowy etchings in tones of grey and dark red and brown; groups of figures, ambiguously joined with far too many limbs and apertures of light in unexpected places. Doubtless they were by someone famous, but Lydia knew nothing about art. Ivory wall-lights were dotted between the etchings, illuminating golden-globed curtain rods, and painting a silk sheen on a vase of apricot lilies standing in the corner.

Lydia placed herself in a chair to the side of Sir Stanley's desk, and sat a little forward on it, like a piece of strung elastic.

'I wanted to see you, Sir Stanley, because I'm concerned about these Council decisions which relate to the future of scholarship,' she stressed the word so it sounded as sparkling as champagne, 'here at EMU. To be frank, I believe that on several key points they are likely to prove counterproductive. I believe that what they will do is decrease our research and teaching standing and therefore lead to a fall in our share of the overall HEFCE cake.'

She wasn't visibly nervous, but she was doing something that everyone had advised her not to. What reason do you have to believe that he'll listen to reason? they cried. But there lay in Lydia Mallinder a lingering childlike faith in justice. It might be against reason, but she simply believed that anyone presented with a rational argument would eventually give way to it.

'Now "believe" is an interesting word,' ruminated Sir Stanley by way of reply. 'Interesting and possibly dangerous. You see, what you believe about the future of this university, Professor Mallinder, is quite different from what I believe. Which of us is right? That's the question. I shan't pull rank over you, because it's not my style, but as you know I do have considerable experience of strategic management, not only in universities but in industry and international public relations. I served my years in the electronics industry. I was associated with the British Council office in Hong Kong. That's why I *believe*,' he paused, in order for the word to carry the right element of force, 'that introducing a more rational system of planning and accountability to our schools and departments will be like a breath of fresh air that will sweep EMU successfully into the twenty-first century.' Sir Stanley was the kind of man who knew what he thought before he said it, but he still liked hearing the words in his own voice. 'Yes,' he said, answering himself like a boomerang, 'that's the key principle here. We must have a New System for a New Age.'

'I was thinking specially of the new procedures for centralizing research overheads, Sir Stanley,' observed Lydia doggedly. 'My concern is that the effect of these will be to reduce rather than increase incentives for staff to be productive in pursuing funding opportunities.'

He looked at her with his blue laser eyes, periwinkles in the tanned earth of his face. 'We'll have to see, won't we? As your colleague in Sociology, Professor Blankthorn, would no doubt say, the proof of the pudding is in the eating.'

'My father was a businessman,' stated Lydia.

'I dare say; so was mine, but is it relevant?'

'Please let me finish, Sir Stanley. What I was about to say was that he was a very successful man, financially that is. As no doubt your father was also,' she added quickly. 'And one of the precepts he taught me when I was young was that even in times of financial stringency, one must invest. Money must be spent on some things while it isn't spent on others, so that income may accrue in the future.'

A young man stepped out of a door at the end of the room bearing a tray with a gold cafetière and two white bone-china cups on it. 'Ah, Jevon, what excellent timing. This is my new PA, Mr Jevon Tricker. Jevon, this is Professor Lydia Mallinder, whose speciality is cultural studies, and within that this interesting thing called gender.' An amused look shot from Sir Stanley's periwinkle eyes towards Jevon Tricker's muddy ones.

'Pleased to meet you, Professor Mallinder.' Jevon shook Lydia's hand and minced away across the Wilton – she was simply unable to think of any other word for it.

While Sir Stanley poured the coffee, Lydia went on: 'I don't know how familiar you are with the current details of the EMU research portfolio, Sir Stanley.'

'You yourself have three grants currently and another two in the pipeline. Total overhead income last year of £74.7k of which you have had £16.8k. You spent just over £8k of that on consultancy fees for Dr Dagmar Folsen at the University of Rotterdam, who is, I understand, a particular friend of yours, four point eight k on additional fieldwork in the Electrolux factory in Luton, and then you bought yourself a very nice laptop with a CD-ROM drive. How is the screen, by the way? I always find the screen on laptops difficult, but then that's probably my eyes. I've been lucky, vision is the only one of my capacities age seems so far to have affected.' He smiled at her.

'Very impressive.'

'I didn't get to where I am because of nothing, my dear.'

'These grants,' she said, 'are very attractive and potentially mobile resources.'

'We are all attractive and potentially mobile, my dear, well – some of us more so than others.' He thought, looking at her Persil-white blouse, with the collar sticking up towards her petite ears and the hair contained so nicely on top of her head, that if he'd been at all that way inclined, he might have been tempted to buy off Lydia Mallinder's suspicions and utterly righteous anger about his self-serving manoeuvring and plotting with a healthy spot of screwing in the best hotel in Northamptonshire. But as it happened he wasn't, and anyway he'd just booked the premier suite in it for himself and Trent Lovett that weekend.

'I could move my grants, Sir Stanley.'

'Yes, I have gathered that you consider this to be a theoretical possibility.'

'But I won't do that because I expect two sets of circumstances to become more propitious.' Lydia took a deep breath. 'One relates to the new overheads policy. I'm confident that we can expect this to be reversed, or at least some compromise reached between the old policy and the new one. Secondly, there is the position of Dr Disa Loring in my department. As you are so well informed, I'm sure you'll know that Dr Loring has been with us for three years. During that time she has managed, almost single-handedly, our one-year MA in Modernity and Cultural Studies and has published three books, one of which got very warm reviews in the *THES*.'

'Whereas the other two were only edited collections,' remonstrated Sir Stanley acidly, 'and as you know, Professor Mallinder, edited collections do not count as publications in the ARQ exercise.'

'They ought to,' she commented lamely.

'I agree. But the rules have been made and we must abide by them. Nonetheless, I do realize you want a readership for Dr Loring.'

Lydia finished her coffee and put the cup down on the dark green tray, just inside the two gold lines that ran around the rim. 'Dr Loring deserves it.'

'My dear,' began Sir Stanley, 'you as a social scientist – I take it you would agree with that designation – must surely realize that deserving has very little to do with it.

Deserve, want, need, promise, get – the rhetoric and the practice are like Rudyard Kipling's proverbial East and West. In the days when those were politically correct, of course,' he added. He put his fingers together in the shape of a church. 'There are a number of applications for chairs and for readerships this year. In view of our financial position, only a few will be successful. Your colleague, Dr Kershaw, has a deserving case – female AgroEconomists, let alone those of Dr Kershaw's calibre, are hard to find, as I'm sure you, of all people, will be prepared to recognize. And then I understand that Professor Krest, a fine biologist – I much admired the lecture he gave last year on the scientific imagination – has a very deserving young colleague whose work on the Human Genome Project has apparently been quite brilliant. Did you know, Professor Mallinder, that the alphabet of DNA has just four letters? A, G, C and T: adenine, guanine, cytosine and thymine. No, I didn't either, until I read young Neal Burnell's work. But I expect you've discussed all this with Krest. That must be a true meeting of minds: biology and culture. But in the path of all true meetings there are usually a few impediments, aren't there?'

Lydia stared at Sir Stanley's unbelievably blue eyes, at the centre of which burned a cruel flicker of light.

'You see, Professor Mallinder, questions can be asked about all sorts of things. About academic links and about non-academic ones. About research expenditure as well as income. We've got to run an honest show here, but more than that, we've got to be *seen* to run one. As to the overheads question, yours is only one of a number of representations that have been made to me about it. I've also had Professors Blankthorn, Carter, Cunningham, and Tudor. Proudfoot's in favour. So is Carter in Accountancy. I shall review the position in a year's time. EMU values your work,

Professor Mallinder, and I hope you will decide to stay with us. But the greatest mistake any human being can make is to believe, against the evidence, that he or she is indispensable.'

Having delivered his speech, Sir Stanley took the decision, there and then, to let Winkett and Bacon loose on Lydia Mallinder and her department. He'd already discussed with Richard Winkett a programme of management-consultancy exercises. There needed to be some general rooting around and measuring of different characterizations of the truth, and a little imaginative book-keeping, with sums being done this way and that, and then they'd see how dispensable Lydia Mallinder really was.

CHAPTER 5

Men at the Top

When Justin had come back from the Costa Brava, Lydia had phoned him to talk about her unsatisfactory meeting with the V-C, but he wasn't in his room because he'd gone to look for Beverley, one of the researchers on his European project who'd missed one of the team meetings he'd instituted after his Spanish holiday in an attempt to get a handle on what the thing was about. Phyllis told him the time had clashed with Beverley's aerobics class, so she couldn't make it. When he got angry, Phyllis reminded him for the Nth time that Beverley only had a point six FTE contract, so what she did in the remaining point four was her business.

'Okay, okay,' Justin had said petulantly. 'But how do I know which percentage of her time she's going to her aerobics class in?' He went back to his room and sighed. He was sighing a lot these days. In Spain, Rosemary had told him he needed to lose weight. He didn't really need to be told: his back hurt, and his knees hurt, and his trousers did up below his hips rather than above them. Two and a half stone he had to lose, according to Rosemary's calculations. She'd bought him a book about calories. It was pocket size, like the manual witch hunters had used in the Middle Ages. He immediately looked up beer and crumpets, his two favourite foods. Rosemary had also bought him a little green notebook in which he had to write down his daily calorie intake. So far today he'd had one Weetabix (seventy calories with diluted virtually-fat-free milk) and he was ravenous. He pulled his stomach in: yes, it'd definitely made a difference. But he wasn't doing it for himself, that was the problem.

Lydia sat in her room now going over and over her interview with Sir Stanley. It had been unpleasant, but she'd expected that. She flinched when she remembered the atmosphere of complacent opulence, the way Jevon Tricker had held his hand out to her and smirked as she moved off the Wilton cushion onto the bare boards of the corridor, smarting from Sir Stanley's remark about people being ultimately dispensable. Jevon's look said, you're not one of us, so don't pretend to be.

To take her mind off it, she started to correct the proofs of a paper which would shortly appear in the journal *Gender and Culture*. Elliot Blankthorn put his thinning head round the door. 'Hi. I've got some notions about how to pull more students in for our joint Theorising Culture module. Maybe we could talk about them sometime? I guess now's not the time, though?'

Lydia's red Pentel was poised over a student's 'hermeneutics', which had lost its 'r'. 'No, not now if you don't mind, Elliot.' In this morass of obligations and encounters, she wanted to get at least one task finished. She also didn't think she wanted to hear any more tales about wives whose names began with M, so she forestalled his suggestion that they might meet over another drink or worse, and proposed instead a meeting in her room the following afternoon.

Elliot went away a disappointed man; but he was a man with a strategy, even if this wasn't entirely clear from his saga about wives.

The proofs finished, Lydia put them aside. Thin lines of spring sunlight lit the grey dust on the desk. She took a tin of lavender polish out of her top desk drawer and sprayed it on to the surface of the desk. She used a tissue to wipe it off. She polished the computer screen as well. Then she switched it on and started to send Jeremy Krest an e-mail message, and then thought better of it, and turned it off again.

Justin was fantasizing about food when Lydia knocked on his door. He'd only had an apple for lunch and could have killed for a bacon sandwich and a glass of beer. He could almost smell the scent of frying.

'We've got to do something,' insisted Lydia. 'We can't just let it happen.'

That was how Justin felt about his diet. 'Come with me to the canteen, and we'll talk about it.' On the way he told Lydia about the trials of being on the CISC committee. 'The meeting went on for three and a half hours, we spent the first two hours trying to define consultancy. Certain people,' he paused here, remembering the absolutely vitriolic nature of the discussion, 'were determined to make sure it excluded all their favourite activities. You know, giving lectures for fat fees, and so forth. Especially Alan Livingstone. And Stephanie, that surprised me. And, er-hum, Jeremy Krest.'

'So he *is* back,' she murmured.

'Anyway, it was decided that all consultancy activity from now on would be declared and recorded centrally. Though who will actually *do* the recording wasn't decided,' he reflected. 'Anyway, half of it will go to central funds, forty per cent to the department, and ten per cent to the person who earned it in the first place.'

'Predictable,' reflected Lydia.

'Of course, all consultancy activities will now cease. At least visibly.'

'Of course.'

Yula behind the counter, who liked Justin, gave him a plate of chips with his bacon sandwich.

'About 1,500 calories,' he noted, not needing to look in his little book. 'Oh well.' Fortunately, he'd forgotten the green notebook.

He tucked in while Lydia told him about her and Sir Stanley's exchanges on the matter of overheads. 'We need the money, Justin. Especially now. I don't know what happens in your department, but in mine we pay one of the secretaries out of it, and we've been able to upgrade all our computers, and have a staff fund for conferences as well. Bridging money for researchers between contracts – that's something else we do. Why should we go on doing research, that's what I want to know!'

He was beginning to feel much better now. 'I meant to ask you, Lydia,' he said, 'what do you do with part-time researchers?'

'How do you mean?'

'Well, how do you work out which part of the time they're supposed to be working in?'

'You have to set them targets. Agree timetables,' she said, impatiently.

'Yes, but how . . . ?'

She interrupted him. 'The question is, Justin, why should we be part of a university at all?'

'Well, they pay us.'

'Yes, but for how long?'

'I know. PRP.'

'PRP?'

'Performance-related pay. Though I expect they'll set up some working party to find a fancy acronym for that. You know, like PAYE – Pay As You Earn. It'll be the other way round, Earn As You Pay. Mind you, I don't think you should get so worked up about it, Lydia.' Justin's normal complacency had returned now his stomach was full.

'I want you to talk to Worms for me. And I'd also like to know what's happening to Disa Loring's readership application.'

'I think we considered it in November. As I recall, there was a problem about the external reviewers. But I can't remember what it was. Anyway, Lydia,' he said cheerfully, 'I'm not supposed to tell you – the workings of the committee are confidential.'

'Yes, I know,' she said, impatiently again. 'But I've rung Personnel and Marcia what's-she-called has been off with a mouth abscess for six weeks. I wouldn't ask if it wasn't important, Justin. Can't you remember what the problem with the reviewers was?'

'I'll have a look,' he offered.

'Of course, if you're really feeling brave,' Lydia went on relentlessly, 'you might be able to get at the V-C through your new professor. About the other business, I suppose that depends partly on how well you're getting on with him. How well are you getting on with him? The other thing is, you're on the Promotions Committee, aren't you?'

'Oh my God,' said Justin, feeling suddenly overwhelmed by the calories and Lydia's barrage of demands, 'I've got my own problems, you know.' Trent Lovett was being a bit of a pain, throwing his weight around really rather unpleasantly. On his first day, Trent had looked round his office and phoned up Phyllis and demanded she come and sort it out for him. Phyllis had taken her time, having a currant bun in the Students' Union on the way. When she'd got to his office, Trent had read out of a copy of *Personal Computer World* at her: 'An Olivetti Pentium, a one-twenty megahertz processor, sixteen megabytes of memory, a graphics card with two megabytes of memory and a one gigabyte hard disc; a six-speed CD-ROM drive and a sixteen-bit Sound-Blaster-compatible sound card. And a fifteen-inch colour monitor, or preferably a seventeen-inch one.'

'Oh yes?' Phyllis had stared at Trent. His hair was cropped like a wheatfield and she suspected peroxide. His skin was pink like a pig's and freckled, so he looked like a piece of pastel-coloured candy. One ear bore two thin gold rings. His trousers, of bright green cord, were extremely tight.

'They've got some good offers at the moment.' He'd handed her the magazine which weighed about a gigabyte and had the corners of a number of its pages turned down. 'You can order it, can't you?'

'I'll need a budget code first,' Phyllis had said firmly. 'And of course there are the new purchasing procedures to be gone through.' She thought with unusual joy of the large red looseleaf book Jasbir in Domestic Services had taken a year to assemble. Most of the information was out of date, the prices were far from reasonable, and Jasbir's grammar and punctuation were up the creek, but at least it stopped silly orders like this one from going through.

'And I want an ergonomic mouse, and one of those special chairs for my back. I've got a bad back, you know.'

At his age? It was probably because of some of the things he got up to in his leisure time. Phyllis was unrepentantly of the view that God created men and women for each other and that sexual congress between men implied the kind of hyperbolic risk that Trent Lovett was rumoured to study for profit in his professional life.

The newly created Professor Trent Lovett thus got himself impaled on the matter of a budget codes; he didn't know what it was or where to get it. The first Justin had known about this was when he came back from a searching encounter with his Welfare-Society-in-the-Twentieth-Century class, normally thirty-two strong (or weak) but now usefully depleted by a stomach virus that was decimating the campus (there were rumours of a connection with Catering Services' new cheap source of mayonnaise). Justin had explained that it wasn't only the budget code that was the problem but the budget. Money. Or, lack of money, to be blunt. Trent was of the opinion that he would be unable to do his work at all without the fancy equipment whose specifications he'd read out at Phyllis. This Justin found hard to understand, as he'd only just about got to grips with the old Toshiba and WordPerfect 3.1 he'd inherited from a retired geographer. Mostly Justin worked with a biro and that awful cheap yellow lined paper that kept appearing in the stationery cupboard. 'Risk theory,' Trent had pronounced, 'is a sophisticated science. There are some extremely important innovations in the software field. For example, we now have software permitting algebraic calculations of cumulative different systems risk.'

'You must tell me about them sometime,' Justin had suggested untruthfully. 'But I'm sorry – there just isn't any money. I used up the departmental grant by December. We're skint till the start of the next academic year. We can't even go to any conferences.' He did actually have a few hundred put away in the book-purchasing account as there was a conference on social theory and welfare policy he wanted to go to in Sicily in June.

'What about e-mail? I don't even have an e-mail connection.'

Justin admitted that Trent was right about this, but it was hardly unusual. EMU wasn't an e-mailer's paradise. Some people like Lydia were assiduous users, there was in theory a system for allocating usernames to staff, and Martin Pippard in EMUCS had designed an EMU home page for the Web – indeed, this was what had got him started on his distracting career of web-surfing. But, as Callum had suspected at the meeting the other day, the EMU Home Page said very little. It led onto a series of other Home Pages, all of which were entertainingly blank. Justin made a mental note to get started on e-mail himself sometime soon.

The colour in Trent Lovett's cheeks had now turned magenta. 'How can,' he expostulated, 'this place consider itself to be a *properly functioning* and *competitive* university when we don't even have an adequate infrastructure in place!' He had stormed off and slammed his door. Justin had been about to observe that he didn't think anyone *did* claim that EMU was either competitive or properly functioning, but a strange commotion from Trent's room put him off. The slammed door had dislodged a noticeboard on the wall which had been hanging on for dear life with one screw and the noticeboard fell into the small pot plant which Marcia in Personnel had instituted as a welcoming present for all new staff (they also got two sharpened pencils, a rubber and a selection of notepaper). Dried up potting compose from the Plants 4all Garden Centre had scattered all over Trent's floor. He'd ground it viciously into the threadbare grey carpet with his designer trainers as he tried to reach Sir Stanley on the phone, but Sir Stanley was entertaining a representative from Winkett and Bacon in the bar of The Country Pie Hotel, with his mobile phone safely locked away in the glove compartment of his sapphire BMW.

Round the back of the hotel on the left of the car park was a tired-looking wine-bar-cum-pub-cum-disco called The Black Cat. The Black Cat, of which there were various representations in plastic appended to the walls, didn't have a tail, and thereby hung several, but the place was under new management, so these were getting harder to recollect.

Judy Sammons, Marcia from Personnel, Charlie, the secretary from Sociology, Veronica and Ola from the

Women and Leisure project, and Beverley and Candida from Justin's ill-fated European one, were all gathered round a shaky brown table, nursing glasses of lager and rum and Coke. There were three others from History, all lowly researchers, and one from Biological Sciences, a young woman who worked for Neal Burnell, the colleague of Jeremy Krest's who was in line for a readership. It was a slightly witch-like gathering, reminiscent of the women's-liberation consciousness-raising sessions of the 1970s, though without the same verve, and of course the context in which it was happening was entirely different, because history had moved on, as Lydia Mallinder was fond of saying: women had been deconstructed, which meant that feminism itself had been reconstructed as some kind of transient aberration.

This lot weren't what feminists then would have called feminists, anyway. But they did share a common nose for some of what Lydia and Disa called the de-liberatory pedagogy of the patriarchy. In other words, they were having a good old moan.

Judy was trying to persuade Marcia to commit some dastardly deeds for her, involving the minutes of Equality Committee meetings and so forth, but Marcia was resisting on the grounds that the unemployment rate in Motley was already too high. Charlie, whose first job this was, was tickled pink to be sitting here with the rest of them, although she did feel a bit sorry for Lydia, who had been very nice to her, and who seemed to be coming in for considerable attack from Judy. Judy was using a lot of long words. The researchers, Veronica and Ola and Candida and Beverley, and the woman from Biology, who was extremely short-sighted, were much easier to understand. Charlie had every sympathy with them, especially on the question of the lack of light in their rooms.

'Of course it's in the interests of the university,' said Judy with predictable pomposity, 'for contract researchers *not to see*. They won't give you lights because they want you to remain blind to your structural position.'

'I thought there wasn't enough money,' objected Charlie sharply. 'I thought that was why we couldn't have any new anglepoises. And what about the what-did-you-call-it position of secretaries, anyway?'

'As Adrienne Rich said – the American writer, you know –' added Judy, seeing a tablefull of blank expressions around her, 'as Rich said, universities keep going largely on the backs of the exploited, low-paid or unpaid labour of women. As contract researchers, as wives, as mistresses, as cleaners, and so on.'

'The cleaning's not much to write home about these days,' reflected Charlie.

Judy scowled at her. 'Neither is the management. The point is, this is *institutional* discrimination on a massive scale. Until we realize this, nothing's going to change.'

'But even if we do realize it, how are we going to change anything?' enquired Beverley.

'You'd be lost without your aerobics classes,' pointed out Candida.

'Professor Leopard gets very cross sometimes,' said Beverley thoughtfully.

'You should think of yourselves as having *careers* not just *jobs*,' insisted Judy despairingly.

'I want to get married and have a baby,' confessed Charlie.

'Oh, for God's sake!'

'What careers?' asked Veronica and Candida, both at the same time.

This essential problem, of different people having different perspectives on the same set of facts, was also afflicting

Lydia Mallinder and Jeremy Krest. When Jeremy admitted he'd come back from Seattle and not contacted her, Lydia put all the various things of his that lay around her little house – a pile of colourful shirts, some Calvin Klein under-wear, the soap he liked to use, his nasty fennel toothpaste, a large gardening dictionary, some back copies of *The Scientific American*, a box of chewy unsweetened muesli, etc – into four plastic bags and drove them round to his cottage one evening, intending just to drop them outside the front door and be done with it. But Jeremy heard her coming, and opened the door and drew her inside, like a grizzly bear pulling a child into his cage at the zoo. She looked round at her bars – at the small, disordered square room, full of books and growing plants, and the kind of sticky silvery-white dust that afflicts the possessions of men for whom housework is itself a dirty word – and tried not to remember the happy times she'd spent there, being entertained by Jeremy's body and his mind, such entertainments success-fully banishing most thoughts of Erica and Claudine in Hampstead, and the whole tiresome cost-cutting and squab-bling world of EMU.

'Sit down,' ordered the bear.

'Thank you, I'd rather stand. I only brought your things round for you.'

'That was kind of you. Though it's perhaps not so kind that you're apparently trying to remove all traces of me from your life.' He practically glowed with indignation. In the falling darkness, he definitely seemed fluorescent to her – larger than life, a reservoir of power and energy.

'I meant what I said. I've got to go.'

'Lydia, stay, please. Please stay!'

It didn't suit him to plead. As she turned to go, he got hold of her and moved her easily, like a Barbie doll, round to face him, so that when he pressed her to him, the odours of his body, its doings and being, not only flowed into hers, but made her confront again the whole seductive biology of opposition in which he specialized – a man's body and a woman's body, united in their humanity but in practically nothing else. More specifically, Jeremy wanted to remind Lydia not only that he desired her but that she desired him.

She got the message. But she'd decided to be a woman of resolve tonight. 'I'm going, Jeremy.'

As he watched her walk, trembling, past the curled brown remains of spring flowers down the garden path back to her car, he called from the doorway, like the zookeeper he was, 'This isn't the end of it, Lydia!' He turned on the light outside the door, so that when she looked back at him from the deceptive safety of her car, he would still appear to her to glow with a bright, magical light.

CHAPTER 6

Oxborrow's List

Fern Meredith's journey from Lower Byfield to the EMU campus was mostly flat, which was just as well, as the three gears on her rusty Raleigh had given up the ghost long ago. As she climbed the slight incline before the roundabout, another cyclist whizzed past – Trent Lovett on his flashy orange mountain machine in full cycling gear: a Duofold Coolmax T-shirt in electric blue, a pair of black Celange Hot Bots streamlining his bum on the saddle, Kevlar gripsters on his hands and Shimano boots on his feet. His Giro Air Blast helmet was the same blue as his T-shirt, and his Moah glasses featured ergonomically designed polycarbonate frames. It was hard to see in this high-tech persona any representation of what Lydia Mallinder called scholarship, though its configuration with Trent Lovett's own interest in risk was clearer.

On this sunny day at the beginning of June, the North-amptonshire countryside had moved itself decisively into the next season. Sharp yellow fields of rape seed were edged with vermilion poppies; the hedgerows were rife with umbrellas of cow parsley. As she rode, Fern breathed in the scents of the countryside. These meadowy scents gave her far more pleasure than any number of testers of expensive perfumes in an airport duty-free shop. She pitied Trent Lovett, for at his speed (twenty-five point eight miles per hour measured on his Sigma BC 1100 cycle computer), he would smell only the air zinging past his face.

Trent cycled out of choice, but for Fern it was a necessity. She and her artist husband, Jake, had only one car, a rattly old Peugeot. On the days when she had to be in early to teach or would have to stay beyond the end of the school day, Jake had the car so he could ferry the boys to and from school. The baby, Karl, who was two, went to a child-minder in the village. Thank God the other three – Eiran, five, Magnus, seven, and Zadoc, ten – were now for a brief time all at the same school. Fern had given birth at intervals of two and a half years plus or minus a few days, not because they'd planned it like that, but by the time she'd finished with her maternity leave (six months, the EMU provision was quite generous), plus some extra sick leave (three months, she was always dogged with mastitis and bad veins, and after Karl she'd had a bad case of shingles which had meant an extra two months off), and then got the childcare and the transition back to work organized, not to mention the expressing and freezing and unfreezing of the breastmilk – after all that, it seemed to take a while for her body to get back to normal, and then, as soon as it did, whoosh, they were off again.

The history of motherhood was marked on her body, but regular cycling and the constant on-the-go nature of her life combated its legendary drooping. Her status as a mother of four amazed many who met her. She had the face of a schoolgirl, totally ungrazed by time; and the way she looked at one was so open and straightforward that it was easy to discount the experience which must loiter behind those pellucid eyes. Innocent she looked, and innocent she was – guileless, loving, loyal, virtually a pre-twentieth-century woman.

Fern and Jake had wanted to have a good-sized family,

so she had no objections to the way it had panned out, and many were the times she'd thanked her lucky stars for the fact that she'd got a secure job with a reasonable salary at EMU, an institution proclaiming ungrammatically on its notepaper that 'equal opportunities is university policy'. Fern knew her colleagues complained about the extra work she caused them. It wasn't only the maternity leave, but the numerous occasions on which Zadoc or Magnus or Eiran or Karl had a tummyache or an earache or a pattern of spots on his little body that called for a diagnosis by the long-suffering Dr Macadam in Oakingham, or when there was an infection of lice or threadworms or parents' events at school. Jake did his best, but he was an artist, not a mother. He created art and she created children, and that was the nature of the agreed partnership between them. Jake had a studio overlooking a bird sanctuary, where he put together vivid, thickly textured representations of man and nature in which wild birds swooped like gigantic items of prehistory across the sedentary terrain.

The other downside was that when she was at work, Fern could really only manage the teaching. She did sixteen hours a week on four courses: Fundamentals of Social Policy; Modern British Society; The Origins of the Welfare State; and Policy and Values. All the basic stuff nobody else wanted to do. It was a much heavier load than most of her colleagues. But Fern liked the students; she did, after all, have a teaching job, and so long as her teaching hours were of this order she could always point to them to justify the fact that she hadn't published anything except a few book reviews since Zadoc was born. And every time she contemplated the possibility of doing some research, one of the children got ill, or Jake had to take a trip to sell his paintings or collect some inspiration for a new batch from somewhere a bit wilder than the East Midlands.

Fern knew that her contribution to the ARQ would be zero. Justin had called her to his room one day last year for one of those serious talks which he did so appallingly, with so little understanding of how best to encourage people to do the kind of best you want them to do. He'd tried to explain to Fern her dismal record of TRUs, and her negative contribution to the new IDS, but as he himself didn't understand either, they'd both ended up even more confused.

While everybody knew that EMU's new Mission had something to do with making money and not much to do with education, the exact form of words for saying this without causing offence had not been found. The Mission Statement Working Party – a committee for which, unusually and perhaps ominously, no suitable acronym could be dreamt up – had laboured over this for many hours without coming up with anything. The Dean of Biological Sciences had suggested, taking his cue from the washing powder advertisements of the 1970s, 'High Value – Low Cost' as the phrase which summed up the present function of the university. Stephanie Kershaw from Environmental Studies had wanted something with the word 'green' in it. She had quoted the inclusion in EMU's strategic plan of the term 'campus greening' which was followed by other inanities such as 'sustainable products' and 'environmental responsibility' and by the even more baffling idea of '*curriculum* greening'. Stephanie said they should capitalize on their semi-rural location. This was seriously challenged by Lydia. 'A university for the post-modern age' had been Elliot Blankthorn's choice, but, as Jeremy Krest pointed out, the word 'post' had the unfortunate connotation of 'past'. What about something that stressed EMU's commitment to dissolving the binary divide between art and science, the marvellous idea of a university in which scholars put their heads together and came up with new methods of knowledge-production and therefore an entirely new paradigm of knowledge altogether, one which would in fact adequately mask the transition from pre-modernism to the post-modernism Elliot Blankthorn so rightly emphasized?

In the end, Callum Wormleighton had suggested what they'd all suspected from the beginning, that the meaningless challenge of framing EMU's Mission in a few choice and memorable words and then writing the text around it that rang with laudable hyperbole such as 'high-quality', 'innovative', 'grounded', 'promise', 'expertise', 'scholarship', 'international', 'strong', 'commitment', 'rigour', 'positive', 'truth' and 'justice' was yet another task that might best be handed over to the V-C's favourite team of management consultants. If a group of leading academics couldn't agree on what they were about, then perhaps they deserved to be told by someone else?

When Fern had parked her bicycle round the back of Catering Services and had struggled up the stairs with a mound of Year I essays on The Role of Government in Health and Welfare Policy, and deposited these on her desk and answered her phone, which was ringing, she walked down the corridor to collect her post from the metal rack at the other end. On the way, she glimpsed through Trent Lovett's open door the flash of his bicycle, which was chained to his desk (he, who specialized in risk theory, was taking no chances where the high rate of bicycle theft at EMU was concerned). Trent himself was not to be seen, as he was elsewhere trying to get Charlie to make him a pot of mocha brew decaffeinated coffee.

Justin had taken to shutting his door since Trent's arrival – it enabled him to sit at his desk and believe that nothing had changed: there was just him and his mind, rattling with precious gems of thoughts, if only he could collect them and put them in some sort of order. Except it wasn't just

him and his mind; there was his body as well – far too
much of it – and there was Beverley of Beverley-and-
Candida down the corridor, who wanted to fill the gaps
between her aerobics classes with something useful, and
considered that Justin as project director ought to tell her
what this should be; and there were all the burdensome
administrative duties of a PHOD, the very same as those
with which Lydia Mallinder struggled above him on the
green floor, though rather more (wo)manfully than Justin;
and then there were, as always, regrettably and intermi-
nably, the students, who flowed in and out of his room in
the form of essays and notes demanding attention, and
excuses about not doing this and that, and (less often)
apologies for doing what they shouldn't have, like painting
the statue of Sir Robert Sharpe-Palmer in stunning blue
acrylic, which Building Services couldn't find the necessary
manpower to remove. It was actually a student from
Justin's department who had committed this sin. On discovering this the day after he'd joined the department,
Trent Lovett had behaved quite overbearingly, demanding
all sorts of inappropriate retributions, and making Justin
feel as though he wasn't king of the castle after all. It was
strange, thought Justin, how the most apparently radical
of men could also be the most parochially vengeful.

At this moment, Judy Sammons was in Justin's room;
they were having a supervision. Charlie had written out a
note in surprisingly artistic italic handwriting: 'Quiet Please.
Do Not Interrupt'. This was after she'd heard the Nth moan
about the difficulty people had in having unfragmented
conversations because someone or other was always burst-
ing in on them, or the phone was always ringing. She
couldn't do much about the phone problem, because they
were all waiting (for a long time) for a new system to be
installed. The old system meant that calls couldn't be

diverted; the most you could do was leave it off the hook. A young woman with an intensely practical mind, Charlie saw clearly where and how the burdens of EMU staff could be aided by simple technology; solutions such as her nice italic notice, which now hung proclaimingly on the back of Justin's door.

The trouble was that the people inside the room couldn't read it, and in there it was, for some reason, far from quiet. Fern heard the raised voices when she went past – expletives such as 'For God's sake', and 'Jesus Christ', and even 'Fuck you'. Then the door opened with a further explosive sound, and she looked back to see Judy Sammons' green DMs coming out, striding out, in fact, with a distinctly angry air, and Judy herself, wearing a really purposive expression, clasping her clipboard like armour to her breast. After Judy lolloped Justin, looking dishevelled and apparently hitching up his trousers, and calling out, 'No, please, can't we talk about this!' and then seeing Fern, abruptly shifting breathlessly, it seemed to her, to, 'You might find Habermas useful, there's a new crib by Arrowsmith, and post-structuralism, you see . . .'

Fern stared at Justin with her penetratingly honest eyes. 'Is anything the matter?'

'Oh no, nothing, well, just a slight disagreement, that's all.'

Justin brushed his stray strands of thinning hair back on top of his forehead. Fern saw that his face was shining with sweat. 'You look as though you ought to sit down for a bit,' she said in her motherly fashion. 'Men of your age . . .'

'I know, I know, we ought to look after ourselves.'

Fern shook her head, puzzled, and so did Charlie, who yanked the 'Quiet Please' notice off Justin's door and hung it on the staff noticeboard ready for the next taker.

Fern sorted through her mail. It included a glossy appeal

for contributions to a fund for the women and children of Bosnia-Herzogovina, a memo from Pat Thwait in the Student Fees Office about an MSc student from Taiwan who hadn't paid his fees again, and a white envelope marked 'Private and Confidential'. She opened this without thinking it might contain anything confidential, since some of the most boring memos had started to come addressed like this in an attempt to evade being binned.

'Dear Mrs Meredith,' the letter inside said, 'As you know, East Midlands University is currently experiencing a degree of financial difficulties. This is due to reductions having been made in our annual grant from the Higher Education Funding Council. This is because EMU has not been operating with the necessary degree of financial stringency required by a university in this competitive age.

'As a result of this situation, difficult decisions are having to be made about how best to increase our operating efficiency. Unfortunately it has been decided that as a consequence of this process a number of staff will be released from their contracts. I am writing to let you know that your name is among these. The usual notice period of three months will apply.

'The University would like to thank you for your twelve years of committed service' (the original figure of eight had been crossed out and twelve had been written in in green ink). 'Yours sincerely, Sir Stanley Oxborrow, Vice-Chancellor.'

Fern folded the letter carefully and took it back with her into her room and shut the door. She stood in front of the window looking out over the brick edifices of the campus and beyond to the green summer fields and hills. She'd had this room ever since she came to EMU. She'd thought she'd have it for ever. Fern was quite happy for all the committees and all the arguing and all the scholarship and nonscholarship to go on around her, and just to get on with her job, in more or less the same way, year after year. EMU needed her. There was no way Justin and his ilk would have the patience for the necessary treadmill of teaching – the scene just now between Justin and Judy Sammons surely bore witness to that.

Fern's hands clenched with anger, and she bit into her nails with a masochistic schoolgirl bitterness. Presumably there was nothing she could do. It had all been decided for her. The window of her room was smaller than Justin's, but it offered the same view of the A43 with its stream of traffic that just went on and on, conveying a perhaps slightly consoling message that so would life, once Fern had got over this. But the glimpsed moment of peace after the storm passed as quickly as it had descended on her.

Jake's roots were in this part of the world, which is why he'd wanted to do his painting and have his children here, and when the job at EMU had come up and Fern had got it, the future had had the kind of brightness every young couple wants it to have. Fern's eyes were damp now with the memory of the delight of those days, when everything seemed possible and hopeful, including the renovation of the two stone farm cottages knocked into one with the paddock behind into which the cherubic Zadoc and then his brothers were born and let loose, one after the other; and the whole comfortable tessellation of her work at EMU and their family life – the routine of fetching and carrying and soothing and cleaning and feeding, of marking and instructing and talking and exchanging – the whole taken-for-granted fabric of her everyday existence, now threatened by this shameless, ungrammatical, impersonal missive. But, above and beyond everything else, they needed her job for the money; Jake's canvases hardly covered the bills.

Fern stumbled out of her room, white-faced, straight into

Tony Wiggins from EMUCS who'd been summoned to unpack Trent Lovett's computer. A new budget acronym and code had mysteriously been drawn to Phyllis's attention: SUR (Start Up Resources) for – some – new posts. Tony had been at EMU for nearly as long as Fern. He was as settled as she was and about as dynamic.

Fern clutched at him in the faded pale green light of the corridor. 'I think I've just been sacked, Tony. What am I going to do!' She showed him the letter. 'It can't be true, Tony, can it?' Her weeping brought Charlie out of the kitchen with Trent Lovett's coffee, which she promptly handed to Fern, and then Trent came out, though rather more to find out what had happened to his mocha brew, and Justin emerged from his contemplation of the agenda of next week's Council meeting on the nomenclature of honorary titles, into which he'd withdrawn after the fracas with Judy Sammons.

Although Fern's maternal absences caused her colleagues problems from time to time, people liked her: she was a kind of mother to them all. When anyone had a baby or thought of having one, Fern was there to advise and encourage, and anyone who was ill, or who thought they might be, or who had an ailing dependant, could rely on Fern's lullabies of community care.

'I'm not doing her teaching,' said Trent adamantly back in his office and on the phone to Stanley Oxborrow, who was now answering his mobile.

As HoD, Justin felt he ought to have been told about Fern's dismissal first. 'But my dear fellow,' insisted Stanley Oxborrow (who knew that this would be a day ripe with telephone calls), 'what would you have been able to do about it?'

'Forewarned is forearmed,' observed Justin. He thought

that was the phrase. 'As Head of Department,' he tried manfully . . .

'Any military strategist knows that in times of crisis the normal lines of communication have to be short-circuited,' interrupted Sir Stanley. 'It's my job as Vice-Chancellor to make this university work.' Here he came out with a list of suitable terms and phrases for misrepresenting academic inefficiency from the strategic planning document which he'd dictated from the jacuzzi of a very nice hotel in the Tyrol on a skiing holiday last November. 'There are times,' he ended, 'when decisions must come from the top.'

Tony Wiggins escorted Fern to see John Mapstone in Languages because Mapstone was the local union rep. Mapstone's repertoire of phobias gave him a concrete sense of people needing their rights protecting from the ravages of unsympathetic employers. But he was, thought Tony, rather unsympathetically over-bureaucratic himself when he cut through Fern's floods of tears with, 'I take it you are a member of the union, then?'

It was like the American habit of asking about your health insurance when you were dying of a heart attack.

'I don't know,' said Fern, sniffing. 'Does it matter? How would I know if I was?'

'You'd have paid your subscription,' retorted John pedantically. He took a large folder out of a filing cabinet and rifled through it. 'No, you haven't.'

This brought on further wailing; the more Fern wailed the less disposed John seemed to help her. Tony wondered if women crying was another of his phobias. He didn't even have a handkerchief to give her. 'Come on,' he urged John, 'we've all been at EMU forever, surely there's some advice you can give her, even if she isn't a paid-up member of the bloody union?'

John grimaced and then began to nod slowly, like a

lawyer in a courtroom drama. His head went backwards and forwards, and both Tony and Fern stared at it, mesmerized, wondering when it would stop. 'The problem is, you see, well, unfortunately, not to beat about the bush, we have of course made representations about this, but really the rot set in when Margaret Thatcher abolished tenure in 1979.'

'Yes?' said Fern expectantly.

'What rot?' asked, or exclaimed, Tony.

'There simply isn't anything you can do, Fern,' said John.

'Nothing?'

'Sod all,' he said, unusually colloquially, and showing some feeling for a change. 'Universities can sever rights like this. For everyone without tenure, that is. That's why it went. Tenure, I mean.'

'I got promoted to senior lecturer five years ago,' remembered Fern moistly. 'Because of all the teaching I do.'

'I remember. It was something of a test case, wasn't it? They turned you down at first because of your publication record.'

'How could I get any publications,' complained Fern, 'with all that teaching? And I was pregnant with Eiran at the time.'

'Yes, yes, I'm sure you were.' Pregnancy wasn't one of John's favourite topics.

'So you mean to say,' said Fern, indignation breaking through her tears, 'that *because* of my promotion I don't have any rights?'

'That's correct.'

'That's outrageous.'

'Hm.'

'Is that all you can say, "hm"?'

'Look, Fern,' John tried to sound reasonable, 'the union could do something. We could negotiate a redundancy payment for you. The letter you got doesn't mention that, does it? Typical. Although the problem there is that Council has tied the level of redundancy payments to the TRU formula, which is heavily weighted in the research rather than the teaching direction, as you know. And you would have to pay your union subscription.' John looked at Tony interrogatively. 'I don't think you've paid yours, either, have you, Tony?' John shook his head. 'Oh dear, oh dear, I think we need another subscription drive.'

Sir Stanley's list had fifteen names on it, and it had been drawn up in consultation with the deans of the six Schools of EMU. They'd gone on a nice retreat in order to discuss the list, to an eighteenth-century hotel in Wales with a tree growing through the middle of the dining room. Not everyone on the list received their letters on the same day because the postroom was short-staffed, as usual. But Gaynor Scudamore in the library got hers, and Tony Wiggins' net-surfing colleague got his, and the offending letters were also opened by two lecturers in the history department with a zero publication rate, and one of the porters, a Roy somebody who'd had a stroke when they renamed him a Domestic Service Officer, so he hadn't after that been able to carry anything, and three floating secretaries who, infected with Phyllis's total cynicism, but lacking her personal commitment to certain individuals, spent more time floating than secretarying. Under instruction from the V-C, who was himself under instruction by Richard Winkett of Winkett and Bacon, John Mapstone was summoned by his HoD, Dr Kaur Taupman, a specialist in early Icelandic, and told firmly that it would henceforth be part of his job to spend 0.3 of his time soliciting new students in far-off places such as Korea, Taiwan, the Cayman Islands, Kuwait, Manila and Bangkok.

It was a sad day for EMU. '"EMU Threatened with Extinction". Headline in the *THES* don't you think, Lydia?' invited Elliot Blankthorn's e-mail. 'Or to put it more bluntly, who's next for the chop? Why don't you and I put our heads together and plan some strategy? Fancy an evening in The Country Pie? I hear it's one of the V-C's favourite watering holes. We might pick up a rumour or two along with the beer. What do you think? We could even put more than our heads together!'

These e-mails of Elliot were getting worse. Lydia pressed the delete key.

'Have you heard the latest news?' trailed the next message from Disa Loring across Lydia's screen. 'Fern Meredith has been made redundant. Danny says I should go back to Helsingör. Did you get anywhere finding out about my readership?'

'Don't panic, Disa,' replied Lydia, thinking how unhelpful in this situation being married to a long-distance lorry driver probably was.

Roscoe Proudfoot merely nodded when he got the news about Fern's redundancy. His TRU exercise wasn't mere theory, he'd tested it out by running through the list of the 230 staff at EMU, so he had a good idea of the order of dispensability.

The temperature on the campus rose with the inflamed sentiments of those who felt hard done by and with an unexpected heatwave, which provoked a crisis in three of the lecture rooms, whose windows had been sealed rather than repaired the previous autumn.

One result of the cuts was an increase in the general level of efficiency. Jeff, the Building Services manager, a quiet, religious man who bred angora rabbits for a hobby, answered all requests for his services extremely promptly, thinking he might be next. People who'd not been at work on time for years suddenly managed to be at their desks with a smile a good hour before the coffee trolley came round, except that it didn't any more, as a memo had been circulated explaining that this was no longer cost-effective, and staff would have to go to the canteen to fetch their coffee and biscuits instead. An ominous note at the bottom warned that: 'As a further measure of economy, all such memoranda will in future be circulated using electronic mail.' This was alright for those who had it, but not for those who didn't, or for those who did, but didn't know how to use it.

While everything heated up around him, Justin switched his PC on one day and decided to turn himself into an e-mailer. He would start by sending a message to Lydia about Judy Sammons. Tony Wiggins had given him a bit of paper with his user name on it and a skeleton set of instructions, and Justin had already chosen a password, which was, unimaginatively, the licence number of his car. Tony had said this wasn't a good idea, as people commonly chose the licence numbers of their cars if they could remember them, but Justin had objected that how else was he going to remember it? The air, or wherever it was that e-mail messages went, must be full of the unread communications of those who'd forgotten their passwords. He typed in Lydia's e-mail address slowly, after a painful search for the @ sign. Then the message: 'Saw Judy today and agreed her workplan. She hasn't got a reply from the V-C yet. Will you chase it or shall I?' Then, following Tony's instructions, he clicked on a little icon with the word 'send' below it. After a bit of whirring, a little box appeared in the middle of the screen. It said 'unresolvable mail address'. He clicked on it (he was learning you had to click on most things), and it elaborated thus: 'A copy of your message is being returned to you because one or more of the addresses you specified could not be recognized as addresses that are understood by, or reachable from, this system.'

'There you are,' said Justin triumphantly, 'nothing works. Who said it was easy!' He reached for the phone to ask Tony, but there was no answer from his extension. He tried Martin Pippard, but Martin was presently on the Net, deep in Project Armageddon, a FREEWARE real-time-strategy, next-generation computer game. Martin's own redundancy letter lay unread in his real mailbox, which he rarely bothered to look in these days.

While Lydia debated whether to tell Disa the truth about the probable prospects for her readership (zero – according to what Sir Stanley had said during her uncomfortable interview with him), Fern went home to Jake and Eiran and Zadoc and Magnus and Karl, and broke the news to them, and rewrapped herself in domesticity, and Jake and she escaped to The Three Swallows, and after a few half pints of real ale, she began to feel that life might really be alright after all. 'It was only a job,' she said pleadingly to Jake, 'wasn't it?' I used them, didn't I? Even if they used me, she reflected, thinking of all those hours of treating lazy first-year students to her modestly unexciting but true perorations on the theme of Fundamental Social Policy, the Origins of the Welfare State, etc, etc, and then trying to read their ghastly handwritten or poorly word-processed essays (with fatigued printing due to worn-out printer ribbons), requiring one to surmise what should have been in the gaps between the letters. 'There are far too many publications, anyway. What's the point of publishing when you've got nothing to say? What do you think, Jake? Jake, are you listening to me?'

'Shush,' said Jake. 'We'll be alright. I've got two pictures in an exhibition of animals in art next month. You never know, our luck might turn.'

Fern had floated on the tide of Jake's optimism for years. There were very few people blessed with such unflinchingly irrational cheerfulness. She loved him for it. It was his biggest asset. 'I'll have to find something else,' she said. 'I mean some other way of earning money.'

'You could have another baby,' he suggested. 'After all, Karl's not one any more.'

That was the other side of the coin, his supreme lack of realism. 'Get me another pint,' she ordered crossly.

'This isn't a good time for this interview, you know,' remarked Lydia to Judy Sammons the next day. 'Given what's going on, we're all finding it hard to concentrate.'

'But life has to go on,' affirmed Judy, 'and that includes my PhD. This part of the study, the qualitative interviews with women academics, is really very important. It's part of the workplan we agreed. And so did Professor Leopard the other day.'

'I know,' sighed Lydia. Sometimes she wished the term 'woman academic' couldn't be attached to her; this was definitely one of those times.

'Do you think,' inquired Judy, with all the pretended naivety of a trained interrogator, 'that these cuts are falling disproportionately on women?'

'I expect they are,' remarked Lydia. 'But' (remembering her role as a woman academic) 'that's a testable hypothesis, isn't it? Perhaps your research could test it.'

'I've already got too many of those,' complained Judy. 'How many testable hypotheses does any PhD thesis need?'

'Shall we get on with the interview? Why don't you put the machine on?'

Judy pressed the button and the little green light on the tape-recorder came on. 'The first questions are all about your social background,' explained Judy.

'So they should be. I hope you've piloted this on a few unsuspecting women. I'll get going, shall I? We don't want to waste time, do we?

'I was born in 1960. My father's occupation put us in social class II. He left school at eighteen, but my mother went to university. I haven't got any siblings. I went to a comprehensive school and then to Bristol University, where I did joint honours in English and French and Sociology. I went to UEA after that and did a taught MA in Sociology and then another in Women's Studies. I got an ESRC studentship for a PhD on metaphors of gender in the world of the French classical writers – Molière, Rabelais, and so forth. Then I got a job at LSE. The rest you know.'

'Interesting,' commented Judy. 'At what point,' she asked next, consulting a list of questions on her clipboard, 'did you decide to become an academic?'

'There are two answers to that. Never, and when I did my PhD. I don't think many people do *decide* in that sense what to do. Life just happens. Like a flower unfolding.' The metaphor caught Lydia unawares; she glanced out of the window, but there was only a mottled, cloudy sky to be seen. Jeremy Krest and his metaphors were within her. 'But I do also remember,' (wasn't there a line of T. S. Eliot's about the proper use of memory being to overcome desire?) 'I also remember really *enjoying* the intellectual work I did for my PhD and thinking how splendid it'd be if I could find someone or somewhere that'd *pay* me to think!' She laughed at the folly of this particular desire.

'And to what extent,' continued Judy, casting a careful glance at the tape recorder to make sure it was still working, 'were you aware at that time of any problems that might be attendant on this dual status of being a woman *and* an academic?'

'I think that's a bit of a leading question,' observed Lydia academically. 'You shouldn't suggest to your interviewees that there *are* problems. Some of them mightn't agree.' She was thinking here especially of Stephanie Kershaw.

'Point taken.' Judy scribbled on the clipboard.

'But I'll tell you what I think the problems are,' offered Lydia. And she did.

When she'd finished, Judy handed her a stapled set of pages headed The McMaster-Cunningham Inventory of Sex-role Attitudes. 'Would you mind completing this? I found it yesterday on the Internet. I thought it might be useful.'

'Has it been validated?' asked Lydia sharply. 'You can't just pick these things up and expect them to be meaningful, you know. A lot of work goes into good instruments. This surprises me, Judy, I thought you were more intelligent than that.'

'You don't *have* to fill it in. And I am very intelligent.'

It seemed an odd remark to make. Lydia agreed to take The McMaster-Cunningham Inventory of Sex-role Attitudes home with her and study it, so she could make an informed decision about its utility as an instrument for measuring what it purported to, or, indeed, for measuring anything at all.

But if it was a bad time for some, it was a good time for others. After all, had there been no names on Sir Stanley's list, there'd have been no money to pay Trent Lovett's salary or to buy his flashy new Pentium, or to pay for the re-partitioning of offices, or to fund the new press officer's job that was about to be created, or to pay for the European centre that had been another of Professor Proudfoot's post-conference brainwaves. 'Cuts here, expansion there,' the train had sung over the Italian Alps, and Proudfoot, high on the conference debate and a bottle of Orvieto Secco, not to mention the Italian scenery, had said to himself, quite so, and what can we do to make sure that the stimulation of international conferencing is available to every man?

Both the European office and the press job were theoretically open to internal competition; Phyllis had already drafted the job details for *On Campus*, the monthly EMU publication, and taken them over to Shepley Harrod in Room Bookings, who doubled up as *On Campus* editor with a resulting loss of efficiency to both functions. Shepley was depressed by a memo he'd had announcing that *On Campus* would shortly cease as a paper publication. That, too, was going the way of the e-mail. Then he would have nothing to show for all his labours. When Room Bookings went wrong, as they often did, only partly because of a bug in the software, he'd always been able to console himself by holding *On Campus* in his hand, and saying to himself, 'I did that'. But no longer, because nothing would ever be the same again.

CHAPTER 7

Honorary Titles

Huneyball was watching two pigeons copulating on the kitchen roof. His mouth dropped open in a noiseless protest. Ever since they'd moved to the country he'd had to get used to this sort of thing. They might live in Motley, but Motley was an urban oasis in a desert of misbehaving wildlife.

Lydia was inside the house, on the sofa with Jeremy Krest. A bottle of red wine stood uncorked on the mosaic coffee table, next to a dish of fat black olives. No sane man would ever bring Lydia flowers, but Jeremy had bought her a new book called *Feminisms and the Death of Positivism* by her friend Dagmar Folsen at the University of Rotterdam, which had more or less the same effect.

'Some things die and others just go on and on,' he'd said, handing it to her, gift-wrapped in silver ribbon. 'Please, Lydia,' pleaded Jeremy, 'let's at least be friends.'

Lydia's discovery of herself in Judy Sammons' Inventory of Sex-role Attitudes hadn't been quite what she expected. She turned out to be high on liberalism, but high on traditionalism, too. She looked at Jeremy as suspiciously as Huneyball did the pigeons. Push and pull; love and hate; where do these ideological stands get us, anyway? Huneyball suspected there would soon be misbehaving wildlife inside the house as well as outside it.

The threat of loss may either paralyse or activate. In Jeremy's case, it had certainly spurred him to realize that he wasn't ready to let Lydia go. Jeremy knew it was all too easy for others to see him as a man who wanted to have his cake and eat it: his family in London, a mistress in Motley; the multiple DNA liaisons of the bougainvillaea-draped conferences of Lydia's imagination. But in truth – and Jeremy, being a scientist, knew what this was – he'd been trapped by an accident of birth – that of his daughter Claudine, with cerebral palsy. He was a man living out a very Victorian moral destiny of commitment to the family he'd created when he married Claudine's mother for better, or, as in this case it had turned out, for worse.

He and Erica had long ago ceased to have anything in common apart from Claudine. He admired her dedication to doing as much with those relentless regimes of exercise as she could; his dedication to remaining a family man was intended to be a gesture in the same direction. A lesser man would have abandoned Erica and Claudine; a greater one would have remained faithful in deed as well as in word. But Jeremy did the best he could, and this included Lydia. Sometimes he dreamed of living with Lydia, not in his tiny rented cottage, and certainly not in her awful Wates house, but perhaps in some glass-fronted penthouse condominium overlooking the Thames in London, which would satisfy her dislike of rurality and the appeal untrammelled spaces held for him – a visual respite, at least, from the unceasing factory of thought that ground away inside his head. His dream was as much about integration as about Lydia. He longed to bring the two sides of his life together – the domestic and the familial with the romantic and the intellectual.

While Huneyball continued to watch the pigeons with his bad eye, his one good eye followed Lydia and Jeremy as they left the room and went upstairs to the comfort of

Lydia's wooden-slatted bed and superior, mite-free, foam mattress. Jeremy kissed Lydia's ears and unleashed her hair, and then the ordinary, extraordinary fire of desire within her, somewhere close to her vulnerable core, though not quite there, because that would have been too much. All their arguings were now like sweet applewood, scenting a long autumn evening with slowly licking flames, orange and yellow and a fiery red, emitting green odours left over from a fertile summer when the apples had hung heavy with juice just above the emerald grass.

When Jeremy stroked Lydia's cheeks and ran his finger down her neck and into the dip between her breasts, and then round the unbelievable soft firmness of them, when he touched his tongue with hers, all the time he was just there in front of or beside her, inviting her to see and take what she already knew and had; his unique but ordinary biology. All the while she fought against the knowledge of the delights this and he invariably offered to her. Unfortunately for Lydia, the sex was always good. She was attuned to Jeremy's body; she knew in her sleep all its white curves and pits; she knew the places where the skin was smooth, the dark furry places, the little brown Smarties of the moles on his back, and even and especially the turkey-gizzard skin of his dangling testicles, and the angle to which his penis would rise as she teased it with her fingers or merely watched it as he used her body to excite his, as he was doing now.

Her resistance was the measure of her desire. It was a battle, and Jeremy knew it. He moved his tongue down and across the raspberry sorbet nipples – such a perfect body! The flat of her stomach, the lush tangle between her legs. He loved to lay his head there; it reminded him of being born.

Like most of the men at EMU, Jeremy harboured various

distorted stereotypes about women and about feminism. He really couldn't stop himself believing that feminism was a sanctuary for unattractive women – those who couldn't get men or who wanted to be like them (which, although also reprehensible, was at least understandable, since a man was such a good thing to be). Of course he never would have admitted such thoughts to Lydia. Men's hidden thoughts about women (which they will only share with other men in repartees of macho jokes) glue the social order of patriarchy together, and ensure its longevity in the face of attacks from the likes of Lydia and her sisters. Or so Lydia would have said. For, despite his secrecy, she knew well what Jeremy Krest thought of women inside himself, in that place where no women were allowed to go; and he knew she knew.

They had their secrets, and he had his life, but the life of the body went on. She watched him watching her, and this was a source of excitement to both of them. The penis was such an extraordinary bit of biology, she always thought: a limb with a life and a mind of its own, with a blue-purple ugliness that could transmute in an instant into beauty, the beauty of silk stretched tight over the pulsating engorgement of desire. Sometimes Jeremy's was so hard she felt it could be a stick to beat her with, a truncheon kept inside a policeman's trousers, but then it could have the soft tactile curve of a lily, or be transformed into a most innocuous and incommensurate piece of flesh, like too much fat on the hips, or the unexercised fingers of a baby.

Lydia put it in her mouth and a lovely saltiness ran out of it, and Jeremy moaned and placed a grasping warning hand on her breast. For a while it seemed as if she wanted to take rather than be taken, and they were caught in a messy, exciting contusion of limbs like the pigeons' wings.

Then the feathers settled and Lydia lay beneath him in that familiar pose that enabled him to look into those steadfast, luminous green eyes again, and feel himself to be where, in essence, he belonged, in the place to which he always felt he needed to return – from all the bougainvillaea-scented haunts of her imagination, and the more mundane ones of his real world experience. 'I need you,' he insisted, sweatily. 'I love you.'

He well knew the effect of such declarations on her. Letting her mind and her anxieties and all her political preoccupations just go somewhere else for a while, Lydia melted beneath him like KY jelly, and became, for a moment, the same as her body – an absolutely unusual achievement for most of us, and for Lydia and Jeremy in particular, given the rift between biology and culture exemplified in their professional lives. The exaltation of orgasm was wordless, but the light that passed between Lydia and Jeremy's eyes would have powered enough books to fill any ARQ exercise.

'Love and need ought not to be the same,' she remarked afterwards.

'I know.' He slipped out of her and folded one of her arms beneath his head in another familiar gesture. There was a silence during which they both noticed that a wind had arisen during their coupling, and the TV aerial, and external electric cables and grubby washing lines of Motley were dancing in it, as probably were the trees and the shrubs, though there were few glimpses of these from Lydia's bedroom window. 'But leaving love aside, it does seem clear that *you* don't really need *me*. Or so you claim.'

Lydia smoothed his thick hair against the purple pillow, and fingered his beard, as a child would a box of toys. His pink cheeks were red with the exertion of love. 'If I convinced myself that I did need you, would it be alright then?

Would we be able to go on? I mean, would *I* be able to see a way of continuing?'

'I don't really know what all this is about, Lydia,' he confessed. 'I love you, you love me; you don't want to live with me, I can't live with you. Anyone would have thought we were rather well matched. It's not as though you've got somebody else lined up, is it? Why don't you just hang onto me for a bit? I'm enough for you, aren't I?' He grinned with the self-complacency of the satiated lover.

'Sex is addictive. But we shouldn't use it for bonding purposes.'

'You sound like a builder. It's not the act, Lydia, it's what it means.' Jeremy wanted Lydia back but he didn't really want her to go on talking about it. He sat up. 'Let's go out for an Indian. There's a new one I noticed the other day behind the police station.'

'That won't solve anything.'

'Yes it will, it'll solve the problem of my hunger.'

'I want to talk to you, anyway,' she said. 'Not about us, but university stuff. Apparently I'm to be reviewed. And apparently our V-C has things to hide.'

The next day, when Giles Tingey of Winkett and Bacon stepped into Lydia's office and held out his business-like hand for a good shake of hers, he definitely thought he could smell lamb pasanda and chicken dansak and even something else in the air. Jeremy had stayed the night and there had been more sex this morning. She'd even left him to feed Huneyball, which hadn't gone down well, and Huneyball had retreated to a spot on the wall next to the neighbour's satellite dish and only come in to eat when Jeremy was safely out of the house.

So Lydia glowed and smelled, and Giles Tingey wondered what kind of woman he'd come to meet.

She assumed he'd be metaphorically rubbing his manage-ment-consultancy hands with glee, but this was both an overestimate of Giles Tingey's professionalism, and an underestimate of his intelligence. It was true he'd been looking forward to starting the ball rolling on the whole programme of reviews Richard Winkett had agreed with the V-C, and this review of the Department of Cultural Studies was top of the list. But it was a first for both Lydia and him. He'd never reviewed anyone before.

If he was nervous, it didn't show. He sat down in one of Lydia's old chairs (the new ones were still in stores, and this would be something Lydia would find the opportunity to complain about to Giles) and snapped open his cowhide briefcase. Lydia slipped some spearmint chewing gum into her mouth. She held in her hand a green Pentel pen and with this she added to the doodles that were already engraved in the cheap wood of the chair's arm.

'Dr Mallinder,' started Giles.

'It's Professor Mallinder,' she reprimanded him.

'Oh is it? I must apologize.'

She reached behind her and handed Giles Tingey a bundle of papers. 'I got these ready for you, *Mr* Tingey. You'll find a copy of our current staff list – grades, salary points, FTEs; the courses we teach and numbers of students, part-time and full-time, whether from here or overseas; our publications over the last five years; conferences attended and papers given by staff; and last, but by no means least, our record of research grants and current research portfolio.'

'Thank you very much, Dr, Professor Mallinder. That will undoubtedly be very helpful. Now, I wonder whether I could just run through with you the topics I'd like to cover in the review and how we might go about it?'

Lydia smiled politely, deliberately giving Giles Tingey the

impression that she might be a good woman after all. He relaxed in the sunshine of her smile. His father always said the main point of having the kind of background the Tingeys had was for men to enjoy the work they did. He was silent on the question of what should happen to the women, but Giles' mother, a natural blonde who dabbled in astrology and *pétanque*, had always seemed perfectly happy being the wife of a businessman, the mother of three blonde children and the keeper of a large comfortable home (with a good *pétanque* lawn). Giles and his brother had gone to a well-known boys' public school in Leicestershire, and then to Cambridge. Giles had read English and Edward Archeology. Their sister, Olivia, did a *cordon bleu* cookery course and then married a man who ran a stud farm. When the time came for Giles to leave Cambridge, he tried the BBC, but didn't get in, like thousands of others, and then he had a faintly dissolute phase none of them ever spoke about any more, and then his father had a word with Richard Winkett, with whom he himself had been at school, and Winkett took Giles on as a trainee. The classics of English literature were about as relevant to management consultancy as the Mission statements of universities are to anything at all, and Giles had had to take a crash course in Economics and Business Management. But it all fitted nicely into place – he into Winkett and Bacon, and Winkett and Bacon into the exciting new world of cost-cutting (liability-reducing) corporate management consultancy.

The firm had its eye on universities, because these were in trouble. Last year spending by the university sector on people like Winkett and Bacon had hit nearly £2 million. The consequences of government policy – the progressive withdrawal of central funding for higher education, as from the other essentials of a civilized life, sound health care and welfare services – spelled tragedy for the likes of EMU, which had had to enter what had effectively become a marketplace instead of a cathedral of learning. Everything had a price and a cost, if not a value. The cultural dereliction of the time propped up the myth that monetary 'value' was the only relevant currency for assessing the value of anything (a book, a course, an idea, a person). Students had stopped being students and become customers or clients, just like passengers on British Rail or candidates for by-pass heart surgery. The ARQ was invented, but it wasn't about quality, and people didn't go in two by two like Noah's animals, but individually and sword-in-hand. In the wake of the Nolan Committee on Standards in Public Life, a new Higher Education Quality Committee was looking at ways of assessing teaching quality so that in future only good teaching institutions would be rewarded, and students would have a league table to help them choose. (Exactly the same sort of thing was happening in the health service, but the avoidance of mortality was a bit easier to measure than the production of knowledge.) Students were getting more fussy; many universities had charted a 300-per-cent rise in student complaints over the last three years, and the cost of this was rising at £50k per institution per year.

These were the kinds of figures that made Winkett and Bacon and their rapidly multiplying clones very happy indeed. Since they spent some of their time designing logos and icons and publicity material for other people – glossily coloured acres of words designed to impress and obfuscate – it wasn't difficult to produce their own. This was liberally dotted with words such as 'audit', 'enterprise culture', 'organizational transparency', 'accreditation', 'rationaliz-ation' and 'mission drift'.

Winkett and Bacon's aim – though this was more Richard Winkett's than Conway Bacon's – was to set its own con-sultancy centres up within universities, thus providing on-site and on-going management services, without which universities would soon not be able to do. The newspapers were full of advertisements for higher education managers, who were people very like health service managers, with essentially the same mindless interest in profit rather than people – and the language of management was the techno-speak of the millennium. According to Winkett and Bacon's vision, all these individuals would in future be attached to their own consultancy centres. It was a process of progress-ive colonization – some would say infection – by the virus of the profit motive.

The path of transmission for the EMU infection was easy to trace, and would hardly challenge even the most junior epidemiologist. Giles Tingey's mother and Stanley Oxbor-row were siblings, which made Giles Sir Stanley's nephew. He had the same periwinkle eyes and straw-coloured hair – they all had. But unlike his uncle, Giles eschewed the sun, covering himself with total-protection suncream at the slightest sign of yellow stuff in the heavens.

Right from his freshly washed blonde hair down to his recently polished, elegant black shoes, Giles presented the image of a polite, thoroughbred Englishman, a little on the young side, perhaps, thought Lydia, looked at him as criti-cally as she could, a little wet behind the ears, but nothing that time and experience wouldn't easily take care of. His air of innocence, hidden behind the façade of management-consultancy pseudo-wisdom, could even be regarded as slightly appealing.

'Before you start, Mr Tingey,' said Lydia severely (remembering the speech she'd written in her head), 'I'd like to say a bit about how I see this review in the context of my own role at EMU.' Giles nodded. 'My job, as I'm sure you know, as a Professor of Gender Studies here' (she hoped he thought of the words as having capitals), 'is primarily to advance scholarship and make a contribution to knowledge in my own area of expertise.' She studied his reaction, but his face was disappointingly blank. Was he pretending, or what? 'Let me say, Mr Tingey, if you regard Gender Studies as a non-subject, then there are gaps in your own education which badly need to be filled.'

Giles frowned slightly. There was a knock at the door. The small weasel-like head of Frank Flusfleder appeared round it. 'Excuse me, Lydia, I'm sorry to disturb you, but I thought you ought to know that my hard disk has gone. So has Lesley's. So has Malcolm's. So has . . .'

'Alright, thank you, Frank. Have you reported the thefts to security? I'll deal with it later.'

'Such a common problem in universities these days,' remarked Giles, shaking his head sadly, relieved that the subject had moved on from his ignorance of Gender Studies. He looked sideways at Lydia's desk.

'I've got a laptop,' she said. 'I keep it locked up when I'm not using it.'

'Very sensible.'

'Now, where was I?' He had hoped to stem the tide of her prepared monologue, but she was more single-minded than he gave her credit for. She went on to say that she hadn't asked for this review and she didn't welcome it, but she would, nonetheless, co-operate with it, because she was in favour of accountability, and she thought the only institutions that would survive the current constraints in higher education were those that had the capacity to take a critical, honest look at themselves. 'But the difference between you and me,' she added quickly, 'is that I believe the measure of outcome, of success, can't be quantified in financial terms alone.'

Her style, reflected Giles, was odd, but clever. Out would come the bullet point and then there would be a slight retreat, a coy suggestion of solidarity with him, and then she'd be on the offensive again. There was also something terribly fetching about her long neck, with the hair pulled away from it, just like Emma Thompson in *Sense and Sensibility*; and there was undoubtedly also something touchingly fragile about the thinness of the wrist encircled by the bright plastic watch, an emblem of childhood which appealed to his hidden side, and even hinted that Lydia might have one too. He stared at the watch, hypnotized, as the hand to which it was attached made gestures in the tense air between them.

'Mr Tingey.' It was a reprimand.

'Please call me Giles.' He smiled at her gently, and there was nothing the least insinuating about his smile.

'I don't think you were listening to what I was saying. I was making a point about the new Council policy on research overheads. I said I hoped that you would look at the disenfranchising effect of that on the contract research culture.'

'Oh yes, indeed. Of course.' He needed a glossary. What was 'the contract research culture'?

'Now, shall we start on your questions? I've got an hour before lunch. This afternoon there's a Council meeting I must go to. But I would suggest that you talk to some of my staff. I've made some tentative appointments for you.' She handed him another sheet of paper. 'You can have my room, I think you'll find it's reasonably quiet.' She laughed suddenly; it was like a ray of the sun from which Giles was always trying to protect himself. 'Actually, it's not very noisy today, because the telephone system's down. The man in charge of telephones was sacked last year – and Telephones were merged with Building Services. Between eleven and one and again from three to four, when people make most of their phone calls, there's a fifty per cent chance the entire system will be down. That's something else you ought to look at.'

What Giles couldn't tell from Lydia's performance was how carefully rehearsed it was. She was very anxious about this review. As she'd said to him, resisting it would have been pointless; coming on top of her difficult encounter with Sir Stanley, such a move might also be deeply counter-productive in a personal sense. But the review was out of her control, and there was nothing Lydia hated more than not having control. Had she learned there was nothing that appealed to Giles Tingey more than a woman who appeared to have it, she wouldn't have needed to have spent so much time writing speeches in her head.

Lydia had sounded quite like Trent Lovett, whose impression of EMU's efficiency had not been improved by finding that his own newly acquired hard disk had gone the same way as those of his colleagues – down the fire escape at 2 AM in the arms of a gang of teenage boys who'd become remarkably adept at recognizing a good hard disk when they saw one.

To Justin's relief, the thieves hadn't bothered with his computer because it was too old and its hard disk was insignificant. He was still having trouble with his e-mail. He'd composed this long message the other day to Lydia about Judy's Chapter One, which she'd produced remarkably quickly, and he'd decided to be a bit sophisticated and save the message first to something which he had gathered was called the Drafts Folder so he could read it carefully before sending it. (It was terribly important not to get anything about Judy Sammons wrong.) But the machine refused to save the message. When it asked him to agree with this decision, it said it would delete the message unless he wanted to save it to the Drafts Folder. When he said yes, obviously he did want to do that because he'd already said so, it said 'cannot open Drafts Folder to save message' all over again.

The Council meeting at 2 o'clock was in the pretentiously grand Committee room of the main EMU building – the Senate, where the V-C had his office, and a small-ish flat for the occasions when he wasn't able to cover the fifteen miles back to Keynes Hall. The colour-coding architect who'd been let loose on Motley Polytechnic's reincarnation as a university had given way to delusions of grandeur in the Senate building. In redesigning the Committee room, he'd had in mind the Great Hall at Castle Ashby in North-ampton, an early-seventeenth-century panelled and galleried affair (the gallery had been borrowed from the French). The words 'University of the East Midlands Senate' had been inscribed on the front of the building over the older legend, 'Motley Polytechnic', but on a bright day the original words could still be seen faintly.

Sir Stanley Oxborrow was chairing the meeting. Round the quite superfluously enormous polished table were ranged the deans of the six Schools; EMU's secretary and registrar, Graham Piper (there used to be two separate posts, but these had been merged, like a lot of other things); Bill Budgen, EMU's accountant, a stout ex-bank manager from Derbyshire; ten appointed teachers of the university; five PHODs; one representative of SAR (Phyllis); one from Domestic and Building Services (Jeff); one from the library (Gaynor Scudamore – Martin Pippard from EMUCS was also supposed to be there, but he never was); one from Student Affairs (Vicky Withers, the opthalmologist's daugh-ter); one from the Research Committee (Beverley, in time off from her aerobics class); and one from the Degrees Board (Roscoe Proudfoot). There were also four representatives from the City of Motley and Motley District Council representing the local environment and industry.

In theory, Council meetings decided University policy, but in practice their size and the diversity of members' interests rendered this unlikely. The important decisions were taken in the V-C's room on the first Monday in every month, by a much smaller and more consensual coterie, the Policy and Resources Implementation Committee (PRIC). So this meeting was mainly for show.

Sir Stanley Oxborrow enjoyed it. He beamed at them all, fresh from a weekend with Trent in Prague, and treated them first to a discursive narrative full of shipping metaphors on the theme of his captaincy of the liner EMU during a force-nine gale in a part of the ocean known to be strewn with treacherous rocks and currents capable of pulling and threatening even the most experienced and seaworthy captain like him. The point of this narrative was to instil confidence that the fiscal crisis was under control. It was thus less impressive for those who were part of the controlling. These included Gaynor Scudamore, whose redundancy letter had now arrived, Fern Meredith, whose weeping had shifted into a disputative attitude, Jeff from Building Services, whose post was next for the chop, Vicky Smithers, who had a litany of complaints from dissatisfied students in her capacious Calvin Klein bag, and Phyllis, whom it took a great deal to impress these days. But there were some around the table who *were* on Sir Stanley's side, especially the Deans of Business Studies and History, Proudfoot, and both Graham Piper and Bill Budgen, who all laughed in the right places.

'Now we come to the gladsome business of honorary titles,' announced Sir Stanley. 'Jevon has prepared a short paper on the issue which he will hand round.'

Sheets of pink paper navigated the table. 'Sorry about

the colour,' remarked Jevon. 'We seem to have run out of white.'

'Thank you, Jevon. Now the question is: why does EMU have seven categories of academic visitors – Visiting Professors, Visiting Fellows, Visiting Lecturers, Honorary Fellows, Honorary Professors, Research Associates and Honorary Research Fellows – when most of these probably mean the same thing, and who are they, and do we want them anyway?'

'History,' said Alan Livingstone, who was Dean of the School of Modern History.

'Yes, I thought you might say that, Livingstone.'

'I'm not sure they do all mean the same thing, actually,' observed Graham Piper, stroking his goatee beard meticulously.

Sitting next to Jevon Tricker, Sir Stanley's right-hand man, Phyllis noted that Jevon was taking the minutes very inefficiently using a debased form of shorthand. She moved her head sideways in an effort to catch exactly what Jevon was writing down.

'You see, if I might be allowed a word of explanation, Vice-Chancellor,' intoned Graham Piper pompously, 'two of the Visiting Professors are actually paid for on fixed-term contracts. These were designed to develop new areas of activity without having to go through the usual procedures. But we have other Visiting Professors who are merely people with some sort of honorary attachment to EMU. For example, representatives of industry and commerce. Visiting Fellows, on the other hand, are for visitors of academic standing.'

'What *are* Visiting Professors, then?' interrupted Fern Meredith, who'd never been known to speak at a Council meeting before, but who now had nothing to lose by saying what she thought. 'If they aren't visitors of academic standing, then what the hell are they?'

'Thank you, er . . .'

'Mrs Meredith,' she supplied, knowing full well that although she'd been here for ever, Graham Piper hadn't a clue who she was.

'Well, yes, of course they are, too. In fact, Visiting Fellows are also professors, that is, not here, but where they come from.'

'Why don't they go back there, then?' murmured Gaynor Scudamore, who was feeling a bit mutinous as well.

Phyllis stood on Gaynor's foot and passed her a note which said, 'It's *Howard's End* on TV tonight. Do you want to come round and watch it at my house? I've got a lasagne that needs eating.'

'I've got a bottle of wine that needs drinking,' Gaynor scrawled back, 'and someone gave me a bottle of that new drink called Tabu.'

'Whereas,' went on Graham Piper, raising his voice to cover these insurgencies, 'EMU has only a relatively small number of Visiting Professors, there are a much larger number of Visiting Fellows.'

'How many?' asked Bill Budgen.

'Well,' said Graham, looking uncomfortable. 'Seventy or eighty. Or perhaps ninety.'

'Don't we know?'

'We did send round a brief questionnaire,' interjected Jevon in his Christopher Robin voice, 'but there wasn't a very high response rate.'

'You got twenty-five per cent of them back, didn't you?' said Phyllis baldly. 'It wasn't very well designed. You didn't have "don't know" as a consistent option. And it looked to me as though you'd had some trouble with the coding. The nines and the ninety-nines were quite inconsistently used.'

'Twenty-eight per cent actually.'

'But isn't there a central list somewhere? How do these people get here, and what do they do when they are here?'

'If we don't know who they are,' replied Graham acidly, 'it's a little hard to know what they do.'

'I know one of them,' said Gaynor Scudamore thoughtfully. 'I've always been a bit puzzled by him actually. He seems to live mainly in St-Rémy-en-Provence. Every now and then he phones me up and asks me to look up a reference for him. He rings from a local post office and he always asks me to phone him back. Of course,' she added quickly, 'I can't do that since the phones were re-programmed for local calls only. He used to ask me to post him the books out there, but of course I didn't do that.'

'No, of course not.' Sir Stanley looked startled. 'What did you do then?'

'I put them in the pigeonhole in Languages with "G" on it.'

'Why did you do anything for this chap,' asked Fern, 'if he couldn't even be bothered to come here?' They looked at her in amazement.

'Well, I don't know. I suppose I thought it was my job.' Gaynor suddenly started crying quietly, thinking that whatever she'd done because she thought it was her job was all in vain really, because she didn't have a job any more.

'This is getting a bit out of hand,' reflected Sir Stanley.

Fern started to say something about victim-blaming, but she thought better of it.

'If we come to Honorary Fellows,' Graham stuck to the (his) main theme, studying the pink paper in his hand, 'then those are rather different as well, because Honorary Fellows have fellowships.'

'They're paid, you mean?' asked Bill Budgen.

'Yes. Well, usually.'

'It all seems a bit of a shambles to me,' observed Jon

Pitton from Environmental Sciences. His narcolepsy was catching up with him; he'd felt himself dropping over the edge, and so had said something to wake himself up.

'Anyway,' said Sir Stanley brightly, determined to get the show on the road again, 'we have some proposals, don't we, Graham, for rationalizing the system. Perhaps you'd like to run through them briefly?'

Pitton fell into a deep slumber. Next to him, Vicky Withers took a Twix out of her bag and unwrapped it noisily. Mrs Carruthers from the Motley branch of Supporting Parenthood, who'd been pushed onto this Committee because Head Office said it was good for their image to get involved in community affairs, reflected that if an organization like theirs were run by a bunch of idiots like this, it would collapse in no time. She had a lot of sympathy for Fern Meredith, whom she knew slightly, because in between Zadoc and Magnus Fern had tried to fit in a bit of voluntary work for Supporting Parenthood, going out to befriend other members who were having a difficult time. But some of them had actually ended up befriending her, which wasn't the point.

Justin watched and listened but said nothing, and so did Lydia. They were both elsewhere, although they would both have hotly denied it. Justin was floating in a cloud of unpremeditated lust for Judy Sammons, and Lydia was staring at the muslin curtains with the EMU logo embroidered on their bottoms, wondering whether she was in love with Jeremy Krest or with his genitals. She thought he was using her, but perhaps she was also using him? If only we didn't have bodies, the life of the mind would be so much simpler. If only academics didn't have universities, they'd just be able to get on with the job. Intellectual and biological capital; that's all it was.

The life of an academic, thought Justin poetically, is dark, brutish and short. Probably shorter now than it ever used to be. If I had my time again, I'd be a lawyer if I could stand it, or even a Winkett and Bacon-er, but life's not a rehearsal: the drama is now, and if mine's not dramatic enough, I'll only have myself to blame.

He didn't know why he'd been so suddenly overcome by the spectre of Judy with her clipboard and dark green boots, because he'd never allowed himself to indulge in fancying a student before. Rosemary said he was behaving meno-pausally. He'd been collecting cures for baldness recently; people didn't understand how traumatic it was to lose your hair. Charles the Bald had been King of France for thirty-four years, but we remember him not as the great warrior or the great intellectual he was, but because he didn't have any hair. Where was all the research on the psychological effects of male baldness to parallel all the stuff about women's reactions to not having periods any more, won-dered Justin. Curry paste, smelly cheese, dead mice: all these had been the desperate remedies of desperate men. The Labour MP Bryan Gould had reportedly tried hanging upside down and considered this promising. Last month Justin had sent for a new hair-restoring compound called Regenesis 3, but Carey had mistaken it for the dog's worm tablets. The dog couldn't get much furrier. Justin put his balding head in his hands; and the mirage of Judy Sammons naked except for her green DMs rose beckoningly before him once again. After his noisy meeting with her the other day, he'd gone home and demanded sex with Rosemary. 'You've been odd ever since that Spanish holiday, Justin,' she'd observed. 'Can't you settle down? I've got half a book on the social life of moles to get finished before the end of the week.'

'I expect they have a wilder time than I do,' Justin had moaned.

'Oh, do shut up.' She'd looked at him crossly. 'Oh alright, if it'll keep you quiet, I'll go and put my cap in.'

The old diaphragm, faithful servant of their conjugations for fifteen years. It probably wasn't the same one, but Justin thought of it as their permanent sexual companion, a true *ménage à trois*. It got closer to Rosemary's soft womanly centre than he did. It was always in the way, blocking the journey his sperm ought to take. What did Judy do to prevent babies? He knew nothing about the sexual habits of the young, though he'd soon be finding out the hard way from the nubile Moon-and-Sixpence-attending Carey. As he'd fucked Rosemary with a momentary renewal of youthful virility he'd imagined himself doing it with Judy instead on the tigerskin rug he didn't have on the floor of his office under the windows that didn't open and with the newly discovered territory of e-mail flashing its global error messages up behind the two of them. Judy would be as wet as the ceiling of the exam hall in wintertime. With another extraordinary short-circuit of the imagination, he saw Rosemary and Phyllis and the young secretary, Charlie, and the moon-faced Disa Loring and his undedicated team of part-time ROs and even the redoubtable Lydia watching him from the doorway as he moved in and out of Judy, in and out . . .

The real Lydia was now staring at him from the other side of the table. 'In other words,' chanted Graham Piper, apparently near the end of whatever drivel he'd been pronouncing, 'what we recommend is the creation of an Honorary Appointments Committee, HAC for short. This would be responsible for conferring four titles only: Visiting Professor, Visiting Fellow, Honorary Research Fellow and Visiting Academic. The first three would be non-stipendiary. The last one, that is, the title of Visiting Academic, would be conferred by the V-C on the advice of

HAC and such visitors would be required to pay a bench fee of a hundred pounds a week. This fee would be divided ninety per cent to central funds and ten per cent to the department concerned. We estimate,' here Graham licked his lips, as though anticipating a culinary treat of some kind – a dish of profiteroles or cherry ice-cream, perhaps – 'we estimate that approximately two thirds of our current Visiting Fellows could be converted into Visiting Academics with a consequent addition to the University purse of some thirty k annually.'

What was the sting in the tail for some was the bees' knees for others. Gaynor Scudamore wondered what would happen to her book-orderer in St-Rémy-en-Provence. Jon Pitton woke up and went to sleep again. Lydia thought that Giles Tingey would approve of Graham's saliva-inducing calculations. The air in the room was stuffy with the perspiration of boredom, anger and anxiety. She moved her chair away from the table a little, to allow herself to breathe. The altered position gave her a view under the table, where one of the V-C's hands was lightly brushing Jevon Tricker's leg. It was there and then it was gone. On the surface of the table, on another pink sheet, Jevon's pen continued its unintelligible scribble. An orange butterfly had landed on the window, its wings neatly folded like a pair of praying hands. Not like Sir Stanley's, which wandered, or her own, which never prayed, though she almost wished they could, because she didn't like either what was happening all around her at EMU or the dissonant tone of the psychic shifts inside her head.

CHAPTER 8

Unholy Alliances

Sidony Wormleighton rested her hip against the Aga. Facing her on the Welsh pine dresser was a large pottery jug of pale purple lavatera. The plant by the kitchen window had grown massively so it was almost as tall as Callum himself, and Sidony enjoyed cutting it down. The results of her labours were everywhere in the house, not only on the dresser.

She was in what Callum called her battle position. They'd been composing the SSACS five-year business plan at the kitchen table in an affable mode when Mrs Scarsdale, the cleaning woman, bustled in to collect the bucket from under the sink and had spilt the beans to Sidony about what was happening in St Nicholas's churchyard.

The church of St Nicholas in the district of Kingham Deeping was mainly seventeenth century with a large nave and a roof of Collyweston slate. The wooden stalls bore misericords of an angel and a pelican and Father Time with a scythe and an hourglass. In the chancel, two angels' heads, probably early sixteenth century and either French or German, looked down with stony disdain on the few inhabitants of the twentieth century who still came to St Nicholas's for whatever purpose. And therein lay the rub; for it appeared that St Nicholas's, with its angels, had become an unofficial meeting place for the gay community.

The church itself was no longer used, except three times a year, at Christmas, Easter and for a Harvest Festival to which the local children brought tins of economy baked beans and Sprite lemonade rather than the sheaves of corn and glowing jars of farm-made jam that the vicar and his angels were more used to. So although the church had fallen into disuse and was not well repaired, and no band of brisk middle-aged matrons signed their names on a list to decorate it with pruned lavatera and other country pickings, it had not been deconsecrated. It was still, as Mrs Scarsdale rampaged to Sidony, a sacred place. Mrs Scarsdale had been marched there as a child by her father in the days when this was one of the things childhood meant. 'I was glad of it, I learnt my morals there, we all need morals, don't we, but where this lot gets theirs from, I'm sure I don't know.' Neither did Sidony.

According to Mrs Scarsdale, whose ears lay very close to the ground in this no-longer close-knit community, the men met mostly in the churchyard which had the usual spread of grey lichen-covered tombstones set at rakish angles in the soil, marking bodies long dead and almost as long forgotten. At the back was a copse of Whitebeam trees, which gave shelter from the sky and the watching eye of God and the people in the village houses not very far away, and it was here, and in the undergrowth around the trees that the men who met in St Nick's did what they came to do. The church was between the village and the local primary school, and the children and their parents who still walked rather than drove the journey couldn't help but notice the effluent of these activities: pieces of sticky toilet paper; a few green beer bottles; fly-decorated faeces which hadn't come from any fox or horse's bottom; used condoms glistening in the afternoon light amidst the clover and the buttercups.

It was impossible to explain to the children what all this was about, especially since the Tories in their wisdom had displaced AIDS education from the primary school curriculum. The local outrage was understandable. 'We all do what we have to do,' insisted Mrs Scarsdale darkly in the Wormleightons' kitchen, 'but some of us keep it to ourselves. Why can't *they*, that's what I want to know! And do you know, Mrs Worms, *cottaging* is what they call it! Why *cottaging*, of all things? Some of us *lives* in cottages! Downright insulting, I call it!'

A local AIDS trust had been apprised of the activities at St Nick's and was launching a safe-sex campaign for the churchyard users. A poster had therefore appeared by the church door: SAFE SEX IS HAPPY SEX with a telephone helpline number underneath. Such literature had become an unremarkable feature on the walls of many public buildings since the beginning of the AIDS epidemic. But the END AIDS Trust was now proposing to install containers of free condoms in the environs of the churchyard, if not actually in it; the containers, moreover, would be coated in luminous paint so they would glow in the dark, and could easily be dipped into by men in a hurry to do what they had to do.

It was hard to tell, reflected Callum, listening to all this, instead of getting on with the five-year business plan, what the real cause of the offence was. The fact that the condom bins would glow? The likely addition to the volume of discarded condoms which no-one was proposing to deal with? The desecration of a sacred place by a profane human activity? Or the profanity to some of such acts of physical congress between consenting adults of the same sex? He rubbed his head in anguish as Sidony ranted on by the Aga, not only because he wouldn't now get the business plan finished in time for the PRIC meeting next week, but because it had suddenly hit him that Sidony's involvement in a Clean Up

St Nick's Campaign wouldn't endear him to the V-C. Not that he needed endearing; the two men got on well enough. Nonetheless, in such precipitous times one needed to watch one's step. But he knew it'd be useless saying anything to her. He'd just have to wait for her to cool down.

He took himself off into the cooler spaces of his study, which he rarely used for studying, and sat down in his favourite red leather armchair, with the folder from K and K about the Bayreuth festival on his knees. He turned the evocative pages, bent on filling his head with pleasing alternative images. *Tristan and Isolde* swam into view: the storm-tossed deck of Tristan's ship in Act One, with Brangäne vainly consoling Isolde about her future life as a Cornish queen; King Marke's palace garden in Act Two, the rhapsodic love duet: *'O sink' hernieder/Nacht der Liebe/gieb vergessen, dass ich lebe'* – 'O sink down upon us/night of love/make me forget I live'; the orgasmic strains of Isolde's *Liebestod*, the triumph of death, love's transfiguration. It was just as well Callum knew he couldn't sing. He and Sidony would be off to Bayreuth soon. They would see not only *Tristan and Isolde*, but *Tannhäuser*. It was the climax of any opera-lover's career; it had taken Callum three years to get the tickets.

'Hadn't you better be going?' Sidony appeared in the doorway with her handbag. 'You can give me a lift to the garage; my car's ready.'

They drove in a silence quite as stony as that of the angels in St Nicholas's church.

'I'll be home late tonight, dear,' he said in what he intended to be a mollifying tone. 'I've got a RIPS meeting and then a course accreditation meeting and then . . .'

'Yes, yes,' she said impatiently, with other things on her mind.

When he got to work he found Lydia Mallinder waiting

for him. Phyllis said Justin also wanted to see him. Frank Flusfeder had an appointment at 1.30, and Graham Piper one at 4, inbetween the RIPS and the other meetings, and a seminar by Richard Winkett on 'The Audit Explosion: Enough of a good thing?' which was designed to inveigle management-consultancy doctrines into the hearts and minds of any EMU staff who could be bothered or forced to attend.

Lydia looked tired. Yesterday she'd had a trying session with Judy Sammons on the subject of what could be done (nothing) about the V-C's refusal to let her study EMU.

'There's a lot I can do *without* permission,' Judy had observed threateningly.

'Oh sure.' Much as Lydia warmed to the subject of Judy's thesis, she was beginning to wish she'd never taken it on. Wasn't Justin supposed to be doing some of the work? She'd have to talk to him about it. And then this morning she'd had another one of Elliot's e-mail soliloquys. This time she'd replied: 'I'm very busy at the moment, and I really don't have the time for any social life.' Not true, really, but she was striving to work out what kind of social life she wanted to have. 'So please don't send any more invitations.' (Proper or improper, she might, and perhaps should, have added.)

Then she'd had a row with Disa. It had started off with a tense but equable exchange about Disa's promotion.

'I'm doing my best,' Lydia had said.

'In Denmark,' Disa had responded, 'we have proper procedures for these things. It is all open and above board. Danny says . . .'

'I don't care what Danny says!'

Disa's face had gone white. 'I think,' she'd said carefully, 'that maybe you do not want any other woman to be happy when you yourself are not.'

'Oh fuck,' Lydia had said uncharacteristically. 'I can do without your cheap psychologizing.'

'I beg your pardon?'

'You should.' But Lydia was getting ground down by her own unhappiness. It wasn't simply (or complicatedly) a question of whether to go on with Jeremy Krest or not. She felt there was something Jeremy wasn't telling her. And she continued to be seized by a certain restlessness that was so global she couldn't put her finger on any one cause. She wondered if she might be ill, and stuck her tongue out in front of the mirror, but it looked alright, and then she pulled down her lower eyelids as she remembered her mother doing when she was a child, to see if she should eat more spinach or not, but the bottoms of her eyes seemed pink enough, which was good, because she hated spinach. Mirrors never lied, did they?

Callum didn't notice Lydia's tiredness now because he wasn't in the habit of looking at people directly. 'Yes,' he said brusquely, 'what is it, then?'

'It's this review,' she said, trying hard to forget the argument with Disa, 'that Winkett and Bacon are doing of my department.'

'Ah yes.'

'I want to know what will happen as a result of it. Will there be a report, and who will read it? Will it make recommendations, and what force will these have? You will appreciate,' she paused to allow him time to do so, 'that in the present financial climate I have some very real concerns about the process and its consequences.'

'Hmm.' Why did women ask so many questions and expect you to appreciate so much? 'Well, Lydia, the truth is that you are by way of being an experiment. By that I mean that this is the first time EMU has embarked on a management review, and I don't suppose the ground rules have been quite, well, laid down yet. They're being worked out as we, they, go along.'

'That's exactly what I'm worried about,' said she. 'Rules that are being invented are dangerous things. The procedures should all be discussed, agreed and written down: we should all know where we stand.' This was what Disa had said to her about promotion procedures, and Disa was quite right.

But Callum knew enough about university life to know that discussing and agreeing and writing things down didn't mean that anyone knew where they were any better than they had before. The myth that articulation was all was a sinuously creeping miasma. The currency of academia laid a great premium on turning things into words; and in putting words on paper. Words were supposed to have a value of their own and a life of their own, but it was a bit like the disconnected relationship between men and their penises – the rest of the body politic lived its own life with only the faintest cross-reference to the oceans of words that surged across desks and littered the insides of filing cabinets and got lost in the interstellar spaces of electronic mail. Callum thought for a moment about the weighty greenish octagonal shape of the old threepenny bit; now there was a metaphor for you. It had seemed so solid at the time, a prince among coins, so easily found by the fingers in the pocket or the purse. But it was worthless now, and no child alive would remember it.

Callum's angular profile was turned towards the window. In the space between the buildings, students were carrying books if they were lucky, and complaining to one another if they weren't, and Judy Sammons was meeting Ola and Veronica and Miriam and Fern Meredith, no doubt to plan some sort of revenge, and a large van marked Triggs' Meat Products was trying to deliver three kinds of sausages to

Catering Services, but the door was locked because the staff had all gone to a union meeting. And above all this, in a rectangle of blue sky with a few baby clouds like bits of mashed potato, the black curl of smoke from Biological Sciences was wiggling its way up to the ozone layer. Callum looked vague and depressed, thought Lydia, who did make a habit of looking at people. The lines on his face which were usually animated, drooped downwards.

'Can we have them written down?' she asked again. 'Please? There isn't even an agreed remit for the review. It leaves me in a very awkward position with Giles Tingey. You must see that.'

Callum got rid of Lydia with promises about letting her have a draft document by Tuesday, and excuses about his very full timetable of meetings that day. Professors of Gender Studies in the present era of a backlash against anything that smacked of radical politics had to expect a hard time.

Justin, it transpired, had come to see Callum about two things: the new policy on overheads; and the letter Judy Sammons had now had from the V-C refusing her access to EMU for her PhD, which had been copied to him as joint supervisor. Whereas Justin formulated his opinion on both these points with an appropriately righteous indignation, Callum felt his heart wasn't in it, which was just as well because there wasn't anything he proposed to do about either of them. Sir Stanley had mentioned the Judy Sammons business in the bar of The Country Pie the other night. 'I shall say no, of course,' he'd observed suavely, with a flick of his silver hair, 'problems of ethics and confidentiality, you know.'

Callum did. He asked Phyllis to get him a sandwich. Munching a horrible concoction of chicken tikka and coleslaw, he next saw Frank Flusfeder, a little man whom he heartily despised, as did most people who came into contact with him. Frank had come to complain about Lydia. 'The truth is, and I'm sorry I have to say this, Professor Worm-leighton, I really don't think Professor Mallinder is up to the job.' Frank had a list of wrong-doings on Lydia's part: failing to take the recent epidemic of computer thefts seriously; not organizing the retrieval of the new office furniture from stores; a dilatory attitude to the new round of staff appraisals; allowing Veronica Waaheed, an RO with pelvic inflammatory disease, too much time off to attend clinics, when he, Frank, had this bad knee and had even had to cancel an operation he'd been waiting for for six months because he'd had to chair an important departmental meeting instead of Lydia. The list went on and on. Frank's little eyes burned with passion, his lips grew thinner and meaner before Callum's eyes, and his characteristic habit of jabbing the palm of one hand with a finger of the other approached the staccato rhythm of certain passages from *Tristan and Isolde*.

'I've heard what you've been saying,' commented Callum, finally, knowing that hearing wasn't the same as listening, but confident that Frank wouldn't notice the difference. 'Professor Mallinder is an elected HoD and she's serving a three-year term. When she gets to the end of it, I'm sure she'll be delighted to let someone else take over. And now you must excuse me, I have a RIPS meeting.

'Give my apologies,' he said to Phyllis, grabbing his brief-case, and a new biography of Wagner to read on the train.

Phyllis nodded and lit a cigarette, knowing that, as this was against EMU policy (no smoking except in single-use offices with the door closed), someone would be bound to complain. But they couldn't have it both ways; not both open-plan offices and a smoke-free environment. Everyone knew it was the secretaries who smoked the most. They had the lowest salaries and the most stress, what with lying for people like Callum Wormleighton and typing memos for people like Frank Flusfeder, and it was either nicotine or something worse. That was why people sacking staff were advised to do it in an office where smoking was allowed. There'd been a piece about it in the *THES* the other week. The middle of the day and the middle of the week were the ideal times for sacking people. Just before teaching was the worst. Phyllis always read the *THES* from cover to cover. She inhaled deeply and thought about the call she'd just had from Sidony about the Clean Up St Nick's campaign. She laughed quietly. Disa Loring had told her that Trent Lovett had been spotted there. Phyllis wondered idly if the V-C knew. Or perhaps he went there as well? She laughed out loud at the picture of them all messing around in the bushes, trying to disengage themselves from their smart suits and their tight trousers; and the vision of their profane nakedness successfully reduced them all to the level of mere sad human beings on a par with the rest of us.

Frank Flusfeder's list of people and their wrong-doings expanded slightly when he saw Callum fitting himself into a station taxi. Justin and Lydia, seated in the Students' Union with half a pint of low-alcohol lager (him) and a bloody Mary (her) also witnessed Callum's flight.

'That man spends more and more time travelling,' observed Justin.

'Well, wouldn't you, if you had his job?'

'Things are going from bad to worse around here, don't you think, Lydia?'

'I need your help.'

'You always say that.'

'Okay, before I get onto that subject yet again, will you please get off your backside and do something about Judy

Sammons? Joint supervision means you do half the work, remember?'

A swathe of cigarette smoke moved in their direction – no amount of health education awareness could convince the students to ban smoking here. A new brand of cigarettes featuring a skull and crossbones was selling particularly well. Justin waved the smoke away, trained by Rosemary to be sensitive to women's sensitivities about smoking, but to his surprise Lydia was breathing it in deeply.

'I used to smoke once,' she said. 'As a matter of fact, I think I still do. I'll be back in a minute.'

She looked quite different with a cigarette between her fingers.

'I'm sorry about Judy Sammons,' he admitted. She looked at him quizzically. 'I mean I'm sorry I haven't been pulling my weight.' He pulled his stomach in as he said it.

'I've suggested a division of labour here.' She took a piece of paper out of the pocket of her skirt and pushed it towards him. 'You can do chapters two, five and six, and I'll do one, three and four. After that we'll work out what to do next.'

'Do you feel peckish?' he asked. 'I'll be back in a minute.'

Lydia waited for him while he ate most of his chips. It was fairly disgusting to watch, but then so, probably, was her smoking. She laughed. 'Look at what this place is reducing us to, Justin,' she said. 'Over-eating and tobacco poisoning.'

Justin belched. Lydia blew smoke in his face. 'This Giles Tingey,' she said, 'have you met him?'

'Briefly.'

'What did you think?'

Justin ate his last chip and tried to remember. 'Well, I don't think he said very much.'

'What would *you* do if you were being reviewed?'

'Over-eat some more, probably.' Justin took his coat off.

'It's warm in here, isn't it? The way I see it, Lydia, we haven't got much of a choice. We can decide to go along with it, or we can decide to go along with it.'

'That's very defeatist.'

'Don't you want an easy life, Lydia?'

'No.'

'Ah. Neither do I, really. Well, I don't know. Do I? When you were a child, Lydia, didn't you equate being grown up with knowing what you wanted to do in life?' She stared at him. 'It's depressing, isn't it?'

'Not that depressing. We've both got jobs and somewhere decent to live. And you've got Rosie and the children.'

'And you've got . . . how's it going, Lydia?'

'Badly.'

'By the way, Neal Burnell got his readership.'

'Oh no. That means Disa won't.'

'I'm afraid so. But she won't go back to Denmark, that's only a threat.' Justin finished his beer. 'Think of it like this.' He put his hands palm-down on the table. 'In the broad span of human history, or even,' he paused, 'the somewhat shorter span of higher-education policy in Britain in the late 1990s, what's happening at EMU is only what's happening everywhere. *We* can't stop it happening. It's history.'

'History is what people make it.'

'Most people don't.'

'Resistance is important. If you don't resist, you don't have control.'

'You shouldn't be such a control freak, Lydia. Look, who's that over there?'

Sitting by the remains of Catering Services' disgusting sandwiches were Elliot Blankthorn and Judy Sammons. There were a number of empty beer bottles on the table between them. Under the table, their knees were clearly touching.

CHAPTER 9

Thunderflies

Giles Tingey worked through the list of interviews Lydia had set up for him: Disa Loring and Frank Flusfeder from among the lecturers; Veronica Waaheed and Miriam Curd representing the contract research staff; Marion, a solid grey-eyed administrative assistant who maintained she didn't know anything about anything, which Giles thought was unlikely, but the more he pushed, the less she gave. Frank Flusfeder later told him that Marion was very overactive in the union.

Lydia's department also had a few of the visiting academics whose status would in future be subjected to the bureaucratic scrutiny of the newly formed HAC. Grudgingly, Marion gave him a list: Bronwen Relf from Evans University in Pittsburgh, a professor of women's studies (or a Professor of Women's Studies, as Lydia would have put it); Dr Dagmar Folsen, a specialist in media studies from the women's university at Rotterdam in the Netherlands; Ms Pat Wright-Manley, who was called an Honorary Research Fellow; and a Mr Craig Morgan, a Research Associate, whose specialism was the culture of satellite television. 'What do they do for EMU, these people?' asked Giles.

'You'll have to ask them that, Mr Tingey, I'm only an administrator.'

He caught Lydia emerging from a meeting with the

Women and Leisure Study research team. 'Just a few questions,' he said, 'if you can spare me a minute.'

He followed Lydia into her room. She had a hangover because of the drinking session with Justin last night. But her mood was improved; fraternal solidarity – the sort of support Jeremy Krest never gave her – was exactly what she'd needed. She ripped open a brown internal envelope and read the contents quickly, then tipped them into the bin with an irritated expression. 'I don't know what those people do over there,' she complained. 'Personnel, and their bloody – wretched databases. I've *given* them this information about a hundred times already. You don't mind waiting a minute, do you, while I just find the file and print it out again?' Lydia clicked on the mouse and a printer in the corner started whirring away.

She turned to face him. 'I've got far too much to do, I hope you can see that,' she shouted above the noise of the printer. He looked at it pointedly, but of course she said: 'It's six years old, we can't afford to replace it. We have got a new one down the corridor – we bought it on a research grant,' she added quickly. 'We don't get any money for computing from central funds – but it's only ever printed on the right-hand side of the page. Tony Wiggins from EMUCS has been over nine times, but he says he can't fix it, and it seems they've lost the guarantee, so we're stuck with it. As I said before, you want to ask some burning questions about efficiency in *other* departments around here, Mr Tingey. Giles,' she added, before he did.

If he hadn't been slightly offended at having to wait while she transacted this business and affirmed again what an enormously busy person she was, he might have felt more sympathy for her having to listen to the noise of that dreadful printer all the time. 'I wanted to ask you about this list of honorary attachments to the department.'

'Yes.'

'Could you tell me what the relationship is?'

'Between who and whom?' Lydia smiled suddenly at the thought that Giles Tingey might have a subterranean gossipy interest in private amours, and that this was what he was *really* finding out about. A spy of the heart, not a management spiv, after all.

'I meant,' he corrected, 'the *material* relationship. Why are they here, and what do they do, and to be blunt, who pays for it?'

'It varies. Bronwen, Professor Relf, is here on a six-month sabbatical doing some research on women and electricity.'

'Women and electricity?'

'The new biological evidence about the differences between men and women suggests that the effects of low-level radiation may also be sex-differentiated. Women may be more affected.' She only said this to distract Giles into thinking that Bronwen's research was important, in the sense in which he would have used that word. 'But Professor Relf is mainly interested in the social uses of electricity: electricity as an aspect of domestic and workplace technology.'

'Why is she doing this here?'

'Motley may not be the centre of the academic universe, but the research we're doing here in DCS has both a national and an international reputation. Believe it or not, people think they can profit from an association with us. Professor Relf and I are, of course, working on several joint research grant applications.'

'Ah, I see.'

'We're going for European Science Foundation money.'

'But Professor Relf isn't European.'

'With a name like Bronwen, she might as well be.'

He shook his head to clear it, and looked at the next

name on the list Marion had given him: Dagmar Folsen from Rotterdam.

'That *is* a European research project,' said Lydia. 'It's co-ordinated from Athens. Six countries are involved. There have been various exchanges. There's money in the project grant to cover those.'

'And Miss Wright-Manley?'

'*Mizz*,' she corrected. 'We give her a desk because she's writing up some research data.'

'From a project conducted here.'

'Yes.'

'Why isn't she on the payroll then?'

'She was, until five years ago.'

'Five *years*?' He said it in the same tone as he had said, '*Women and electricity?*'

'I'll explain. Pat had a brother who had a tumour on his spine. He was a very talented scientist, actually. For the army. Pat gave up work to look after him. He died last year and she came back here to write up the research she'd been doing when he became ill. We thought it was the least we could do.'

Giles was taking notes in a large black notebook.

'You think people have always got to pay their way, don't you?' remarked Lydia, over-sensitive as always to other people's thoughts. 'There's no room for altruism in your way of thinking, is there? But, you see, the real world doesn't fit your model. People have other quite sound motives for doing things apart from making money. If you don't understand that, you can't understand anything.'

He closed his notebook and looked at her. Why was she so argumentative? And why did she assume their opinions would always be so different? There were some black and white photographs on the wall behind her of children blowing bubbles in a garden. There was also a colour photo of a large orange cat sitting on top of a garden wall. The photos were the only personal objects in the room: there were no plants, or rugs, or candles, or any of the other kinds of things women use to humanize their work environments. A dark pink cotton jacket hung on the back of the door, and a white mug with the face of Emily Dickinson on it stood on the floor by her desk. There was some brown liquid in it, with a few patches of greenish-white floating on top, like lilies on a pond.

'Are they yours?' he asked, referring to the photos of the children. He wanted to find out more about her.

'A friend's. The cat's mine. I expect you've got a lot to do, haven't you?'

He looked at his watch again. 'Yes, I suppose I have.'

'Well, then.'

When Giles came out of Lydia's room, he passed Charlie from Public Policy who'd come to use DCS's photocopier because theirs had broken down. Trent Lovett had given her a research application on disaster theory and life-cycle transitions to photocopy: twenty-five copies in the mail by twelve PM or else. Their life in your hands, thought Charlie, smugly.

'Well, what do you know?' she said to Phyllis, leaning over the photocopier. 'Who would have thought it?'

'I would,' said Phyllis. 'You shouldn't have any illusions about this place. If it's not one thing, it's another. Mind you, I don't suppose it's any different elsewhere.' She sniffed with a disapproving air. 'I think the chemical in here's leaking again. I'd call the engineer, but Mr Clever Accountant's gone and cancelled our servicing contract.'

Charlie's youthful disbelief was at the news that Callum Wormleighton had been arrested for having sex with an opera singer on the M25. The performance of *Das Rheingold* had been quite glorious, a modernist production with the Rhine maidens in hot pants and skimpy tops, and the giants dressed up as bikers in black leather gear. Ulla Ljungström was the youngest Rhine maiden. She was from the oldest town in Sweden, Sigtuna, which was poised above Lake Mälaren, and on which, in the wintertime, people could skate all the way to Stockholm, though local men preferred the solitary splendour of fishing, which they did by boring holes in the ice.

The pace of life in Sigtuna was hardly momentous, even in summer, when small droves of tourists would perambulate past the pastel-painted wooden houses, and skirmish round the squat modern museum, which celebrated the exploits of a monk from Wallingford who'd first revealed the mysteries of minting money to the Swedes. Ulla sang to get away from all this. She had the solid baroque figure of Wagnerian fantasy and majestic Scandinavian good looks, and was about the same height as Callum – rather tall.

As Chairman of the British Opera Board, Callum had the opportunity to meet quite a lot of female opera singers. Their technique of producing heavy Germanic sounds by drawing in their diaphragms beneath what Callum, ever since a popular 1970s comedy sketch, had always thought of as 'busty substances', seemed to him quite irresistibly sexual: deeply suggestive of the whole genital repertoire.

Ulla was currently renting a flat in Chertsey, which is how she and Callum had come to be on the M25. A reporter from *Newsnight* had unfortunately passed Ulla's Fiat on the hard shoulder just after the police patrol car had stopped to find out what was going on. The reporter had mistaken Callum's height and authoritative bearing for those of an already infamous MP. Further research on his part revealed that, although Callum wasn't a political figure in that sense, he wasn't nobody. Not only was he Chairman of the British Opera Board, but in the eighties he'd chaired a fairly news-worthy public inquiry on standards in broadcasting, and he was known to be a director of one of the new privatized rail companies, all of which made it worth the young man from *Newsnight*'s while to spread the news of Callum's arrest among his media colleagues.

Most people at EMU couldn't have cared less, but there were a few, like Lydia Mallinder and Disa Loring, for whom the incident confirmed all they already knew about men behaving badly, and some, such as Justin Leopard, who wouldn't admit to a sting of admiration for Callum's envi-able risk-taking, and also some, for example Stephanie Ker-shaw and Elliot Blankthorn, who sympathetically said that a man shouldn't be punished for such a common fall from grace. As Lydia said to Disa, Stephanie could always be relied on to take a patriarchal point of view. Elliot was clearly quirky sexually, and the more Lydia learnt about him, the more she vowed to stay away from him and his e-mails.

It was clear what the Rhine maiden had been doing to Callum, but it was less clear to those at EMU, who were ignorant about opera and culture, which was most of them, what Callum had been doing with the Rhine maiden. 'Most men who pay for sex are married,' Elliot Blankthorn had said knowledgeably, and assuming, of course, that what Callum had got on the hard shoulder of the M25 he'd paid for, one way or another. Elliot had read an article about prostitution in the *British Journal of Sociology* recently and proceeded to quote from it. 'Oral sex is very popular, but a hand-job gets a higher rating. The average prostitute has vaginal sex 2.2 times a night, and oral sex three times, and she masturbates clients 0.9 times every night.'

Charlie had stared very hard at Elliot Blankthorn at this

point (a group of them were standing in the corridor). It was the concept of 0.9 times that she found hard to grasp – Motley comprehensive wasn't renowned for its excellence in maths. 'If it's less than once, does that mean . . .'

'They don't come?' Elliot had said coarsely. Charlie had giggled loudly.

It was the end of July, and the countryside round Motley was still and golden and heavy with rape beetles and thunderflies when Sidony Wormleighton got the news about her husband. She knew that the world – their small world – would be waiting to see how she reacted, so she went on gardening while she thought carefully about it, methodically extracting plantains from the rather bald area round the roots of the apple tree, which in spring hosted crowds of miniature daffodils, and where she planned to plant some pansies as soon as she could fit in a trip to the garden centre. When she straightened up, she felt the sharp pain on the left of her lower back which she sometimes got if she didn't watch her posture when gardening, and it was this, rather than Callum's misdemeanour, that had her on the verge of tears when Lydia Mallinder came in by the garden gate.

'Mrs Wormleighton,' began Lydia tentatively. 'I'm sorry to intrude like this. I did ring the bell but nobody answered.'

Lydia stood there in front of the ample remains of the wonderfully blooming lavatera, a pert figure in a neat white broderie anglaise blouse and a short green skirt with a chain of coloured beads round her neck. She looked fresh, contained, sure of herself, a pure, chiselled specimen of modern womanhood.

The contrast with Sidony herself was unflattering: a large woman, thickset, with grey hair cut short and pinned back any old how with a clip; she'd never bothered much about her appearance, having been brought up in a high Anglican family which taught her that the only proper adornment for female bodies is the loving gaze of God.

The pain in Sidony's back slackened somewhat. She looked at her watch. It was the one her father had given her; she'd had it for fifty years and it had never gone wrong. 'You'd better come inside. I could do with a drink.'

Lydia was glad to get away from the thunderflies. Although the air was full of them, you couldn't see them, they just landed on you in their thousands, and then, when you started to itch, you could see the microscopic specks, not more than a millimetre or so long, having a grand old time at your expense. They even penetrated the EMU campus, where she'd discussed with various of her colleagues the correct political response to Callum's adventure. Jeremy Krest had laughed, which was perhaps only to be expected. In Jeremy's eyes the tragedy was not what Callum had done, but that he'd got caught doing it. 'Projection,' Lydia had advised resentfully.

'Of course we don't know what *meaning* this has,' Disa had murmured. 'I mean, how it fits in with the kind of marital relationship Callum has with Mrs Wormleighton.' Nonetheless, she and Lydia had agreed that Sidony deserved some acknowledgement from the women at EMU that they themselves didn't necessarily countenance the way many men at the top used and abused power.

'Gin? Vodka? Whisky? Wine? Or would you like something softer? I'm going to have a G and T myself. It's my only peccadillo.' Sidony smiled sardonically, thinking in an almost feminist way of how peccadilloes seemed to be shared out in that distributive (in)justice system called marriage.

'You may think it's strange that I called. I hope you don't mind.'

'I don't mind, dear,' said Sidony, pouring two substantial gins. 'Though I can't say I know why you've come.'

'To express sisterly solidarity, I suppose,' ventured Lydia. 'To say how sorry I – we – are that you should have to suffer this kind of indignity. It can't be easy for you in this – this situation. I'm sorry, I'm not expressing myself very well.'

Sidony took a gulp of her gin and flung the French windows of the sitting room open to the whole of her dear, golden, insect-infested garden. 'That's better. It gets so stuffy in here.' She stood with her back to the garden and looked across the room at Lydia, who wished she'd brought a jacket to protect her arms from the thunderflies.

Sidony had sorted out what to do about Callum – she'd known when she married him that what to do about Callum would always be part of her life. But she didn't need unwarranted interventions of this sort. She stopped wandering around the room, refilled her glass, and sat down opposite Lydia. She leaned forward, clasped her hands together firmly, and looked straight into those clear green eyes. 'I hear things haven't been going too well for you at EMU recently, dear. Callum has told me about this management review business. And then there's the little matter of overheads, isn't there? We thought you'd be upset about that.'

Sidony was either blocking off or deliberately presenting a united front. Lydia didn't know her well enough to tell which.

'I said I didn't mind you coming, but I think I might do, after all. What do you know about anything? What is this sisterly solidarity? You're no sister of mine. You feminists are full of high-sounding precepts, but it's all a load of bunkum really. Are you married? Have you got the faintest idea what it's like to share your life with someone for years and years and years, through thick and thin, and more thin than thick? Would you even be *able* to do it if you tried? What kind of morals do you have? Oh yes, I know about you and that biologist. The whole world knows, and some of us have been saying for a long time what does a girl like you see in a man like him?'

She knocked back the gin again. 'I don't suppose you like me calling you a girl, but that's what you are to me. If I had a daughter, she'd be your age. Callum and I had a son when we were first married. Few people know that. We don't foist our troubles on other people the way everyone seems to these days. Emotional prostitution I call it. It's just as bad as the other sort.' She laughed harshly. 'He was a mongol and we put him in a home. He's fat and he dribbles and he smells and I find it hard to think of him as my child. He was one of the worst affected. Some of them are almost normal, and they are happy – they can give happiness – but ours wasn't like that. I decided not to risk it again, so to all intents and purposes we're a childless couple. But we've stayed together, and it's certainly not all been plain sailing even without Down's syndrome and Miss Swedish Opera Singer. Callum's not a bad man really – he's kind and he's generous and we've had some marvellous times together. Did you know we're going to Bayreuth soon?' Sidony's eyes glazed over. 'We shall stay in the Bayrische Hof, where all the best people stay, and then at five o'clock we shall walk up the Green Hill in our evening clothes – Callum is a fine figure of a man in his dinner jacket and his tuxedo – and we'll see the opera house like a jewel awaiting us, and it will be magic, believe me, and quite worth going through thick and thin for. But I don't suppose you can understand that.

'I'm not about to leave him now because of whatever he did last night. We pay far too much attention to sex in modern society, if you ask me. I suppose that's what glues you and the biologist together. You like the fucking, don't you? Just wait till you're my age. You'll see it in perspective then.' Sidony sat back, her face flushed against the blue of the sofa. She smiled at Lydia, a light, bright smile, with the relief of having spilt it all out. 'Sorry, my dear. But I wonder what you expected me to say?'

Lydia felt awed by the coherence of Sidony's position, the way it all hung together, the fact that she knew what she thought and what she would do, and that behind it was what could only be called a *moral* structure. She suddenly saw that she, Lydia, lacked that. Yes, that was exactly why she felt so adrift these days. 'I don't know what I expected,' she admitted.

'Have another gin: I'm going to. I don't suppose Callum'll be home this evening. He'll come back tomorrow, his tail and everything else between his legs and a big bunch of flowers in his hands, as though I hadn't got enough of those in my garden.

'You look troubled, child. You see, you're getting younger all the time. A minute ago you were a girl, now you're a child.' Sidony laughed. 'I think you're making me feel better. Perhaps I *am* glad you came. Now, I propose that we forget about Callum. You know how I feel about it. It's my business, mine and his, to sort out. There must be much more interesting things going on.'

Sidony was right. There was no such thing as sisterly solidarity. Women were not united against men. Men weren't all the same. Callum Wormleighton was quite a different kettle of fish from Jeremy Krest. Lydia found herself telling Sidony all about her troubles with Jeremy. Given Sidony's earlier mention of the topic, she also talked about the difficulties she was having with the university over overheads and other aspects of the new policy; she didn't mean to complain about Callum ('Don't worry, my dear,' said Sidony, 'they all do'); and then this led onto how she felt, well, there was no other word for it, *discriminated* against, could Sidony understand that? You see, it all seemed to be such an awful repeat of what happened to her at the LSE. In her dark moments she thought the problem must be her, but she knew it wasn't. What could be done about it? What could or should she do next?

'I'm going to put the duck in the oven,' Sidony announced. 'You'll stay and have supper with me, won't you?'

Callum rang from his mobile phone when the two women were merrily rooting around the remains of the duck and two bottles of wine stood empty by the side of the Aga. The honeyed smell of beeswax candles flickered gently in the air. The thunderflies had gone to bed and a dish of peaches in brandy lay waiting on the table. Sidony had put *Die Meistersinger* on the CD player when the phone rang.

'Sidony? What's going on?' Callum was in a corner of the dark mock-Tudor bar of a Best Western on the outskirts of Birmingham. He was shouting because the reception wasn't very good.

'Lydia Mallinder's come to supper,' said Sidony gaily. 'We've just eaten the duck.'

'What?'

'Duck, Callum. What did you think I said?'

'I'm glad you're having a good time,' he shouted. Sidony laughed, and put the phone down.

Lydia stayed the night. Sidony gave her a strangely old-fashioned nightdress and a toothbrush and she slept like a child or a girl in a guest room overlooking the garden. She woke to the scent of blossom through the open window, and the sound of the church clock chiming ten. Sidony came in with a cup of Earl Grey. 'I've phoned Phyllis, dear, and she's cancelled your ten o'clock class. She said it would have been very poorly attended anyway as apparently there's a demo today. Against the cuts, you know.' Lydia groaned. 'There's some paracetamol in the bathroom.'

Lydia sipped her tea and looked at the dreadful country-side through the window. The garden of the Wormleigh-tons' house sloped gently downwards to a river, and then rose up again the other side in a paddock enclosed by haw-thorn hedges which was let to a farmer for summer grazing. Five brown cows contentedly cropped the thistles.

She'd had a strange dream. She'd been with Giles Tingey in a wood somewhere, and in between the tall black trees they could see the flashes of torches trying to seek them out. But she and Giles had been running hand-in-hand, sweating and exulted, and then they had come to a clearing in the forest and a still, round pool with a hundred orange fishes, the colour of Huneyball's fur in the sunlight, charg-ing around its depths. Still holding hands, she and Giles had looked down into the mirror of the water and looking up at them had been the faces of Jeremy Krest and Sidony Wormleighton. Jeremy had been a small boy in a school uniform. Lydia had turned to Giles to say something, and Giles had kissed her, and when she looked again, the faces in the pool had gone.

'Where were you last night?' interrogated Jeremy's e-mail when Lydia got to work and switched the machine on. 'I phoned and phoned and then I went round but all I could hear was Huneyball howling for his supper.'

'Stay away from me and my cat,' typed Lydia fiercely. The evening with Sidony had shown her how women had to take the lead in this business of relationships, whether this meant insisting that newsworthy oral sex with an opera singer meant nothing in the long rich tapestry of a marriage, or that a man's playing around with a double life in the name of Victorian values really could not be countenanced in this modern age.

'You see what counts, my dear,' Sidony had said authoritatively, as the last quarter inch of the beeswax candles had burnt itself out in the cool flower-filled kitchen of Haddon House, 'what *really* matters is everyday life. It's who calls out to you when you come home at night; how homes themselves are made by two people joining their tastes together to build a retreat from that noisy old world out there.' Sidony had cast her wise eyes around the soothing cream walls of the kitchen, the lavatera in its jug on the dresser, the silkily painted door standing open to the regency sitting room with her glorious garden displayed through the French windows. 'It's all this,' she'd said simply. 'Everything that's done every day. The getting up, the making of tea, who picks up the post from the mat, sitting reading the paper, eating together, sharing friendships, accepting the silence as well as the words between you. Seeing the future as a path down which you'll both walk side by side, if not exactly hand in hand. In God's love, His compassion – which I don't expect you to understand, my dear, and I don't mean that in any patronizing sense – it's all this, not the sex and romantic love that counts in the end.'

Lydia buried herself thankfully in more ordinary mail. An invitation to a conference in Kristiansand next spring; a letter from Sheffield University Press about a chapter she'd written for a book, *Post-critical Feminist Pedagogies*; some reprints of a paper she'd ordered on cybercultural texts; a conciliatory reply from Callum to her memo about the falling quality of Domestic Services; guidelines to the conferment of titles as Professor or Reader from Marcia in Personnel; a draft paper for Council on EMU's policy on consultancies; another dire memo from Frank Flusfeder, which she binned. Frank Flusfeder's tedious memoranda were well known outside the department because he headed the Sub-committee on the Operation of the Inter-departmental Structure (SOIDS). It was a position no-one else had wanted; indeed, no-one apart from the V-C had wanted the new IDS in the first place. But there was nothing Frank enjoyed more than a meaningless committee.

By mid-afternoon, the emotions and the alcohol of the previous evening had caught up with her. She felt suddenly dreadfully tired, so she packed up and prepared to go home to bed. She planned to have a nap and then come back in later, when things were quiet, and get some more work done.

But it didn't prove to be as simple as that. Jeremy Krest was waiting for her in the car park. He was sitting on the grey-brick boundary wall staring at the weeds growing through the cracks in the concrete. The sky was full of storm clouds, and the wind was lifting Jeremy's hair from the high dome of his forehead. When he saw Lydia, he stood up and put his hands in his pockets. 'I got your message,' he said, 'again. I want us to stop this, Lydia.'

She felt emotionally disconnected, exhausted. 'Oh, for God's sake,' she shouted, as she piled papers into the back of her car. He took her by the arm. 'Please get out of my way. You don't get it, do you? You've got to face it, Jeremy, sometimes a woman *can* reject you!' The look of paralytic fury in his eyes was one she'd never seen before. She was suddenly frightened.

A car drew up in the space alongside, a smooth petrol-green Volvo. Giles Tingey wound the window down. 'Do you need any help, Professor Mallinder?'

'Like hell she does!' screamed Jeremy. 'This is between the two of us. You stay out of it!'

Giles got quietly out of his car.

Lydia said, 'I would be grateful if you got out of my way, Jeremy, so I can get into my car and go home.'

'I'm coming with you.'

'You are not coming with me!'

Jeremy opened the passenger door and got in, filling the small space with his angry, bulky presence, and staring straight ahead at the countryside beyond the car park in just the same manner as he'd been looking at the weeds a few minutes ago. It began to rain. Lydia shivered and wiped a hand across her face in a gesture meant both to remove any moisture and help her see more clearly what to do.

Giles Tingey looked at her over the rain-spotted roof of her car. He tapped on the passenger window. Lydia leaned in on the driver's side and pressed the button which lowered the passenger window. She kept her finger on the button so the window would stay down. It'd become a collusion between Giles and her.

'I think,' began Giles carefully, addressing Jeremy's stubborn profile, 'that Professor Mallinder would like you to leave her alone.'

'I told you to stay out of this!' Jeremy went on staring straight ahead of him.

'This is a university campus,' observed Giles quietly, 'not the set of a television soap opera. Professor Mallinder would like you to get out of her car. If you don't do it, I shall call the security staff.' To show that he meant it, he drew a mobile phone out of his jacket pocket and held it in front of the window in Jeremy's direct line of vision.

Jeremy gave a snappy laugh. 'They won't answer. They're all in the bar.'

'Or the police,' affirmed Giles. 'So what's it to be? You move, or I call them?'

'This is ridiculous,' said Lydia, as much to herself as to the two men. 'I don't believe this is happening.'

Giles moved round to the front of the car and pulled the aerial out of his phone.

'Alright, alright.' Jeremy got out of the car and slammed the door. 'But you haven't heard the end of this, either of you.'

'I should get in, Lydia,' advised Giles, 'and go.'

At home she fell instantly into a deep sleep. In it Giles Tingey recurred, again in a forest with his long pale legs moving suggestively between the trees. She woke suddenly, in a pool of sweat.

It was much later in the evening, when she was sitting in front of her computer with Huneyball in his ordinary position on top, having decided not to bother going back into the university again, when she thought she saw a shadow on the patio. But when she went out, she decided it must have been a cloud passing over the face of the moon. The moon was unusually large and soft tonight, the melting white of a ripe goat's cheese.

How strange everything was. Her own inner struggles; Sidony Wormleighton's moral certainty; Callum's sinking into his night of love (or something) with Ulla Ljungström; the immaculate Sir Stanley Oxborrow and the less immaculate activities in the churchyard to which his name was linked. It did all seem so sordid. And in the middle of all this, she, Lydia, was apparently the involuntary subject of not one, but two experiments: Judy Sammons' survey of the position of women in academia, and Winkett and Bacon's of her efficiency, however (misleadingly) defined. Being the subject of other people's experiments definitely did not contribute to a feeling of being in charge of one's own life. But, strangely, Lydia was now feeling more disturbed by the interrogatory gaze Judy Sammons was turning on her, especially when combined with the mystery of those knees touching Elliot Blankthorn's in the Students' Union, than by the superficially much more threatening invasion of Winkett and Bacon's management-consultancy review.

In Suckley Green, six miles away, Justin Leopard stood trembling in the garden of the Thatch Palace looking at the same moon, hanging low over the half-harvested fields. The silos in the nearby farm were sending their low whirring noise over the countryside, a comforting mechanical sound, more reliable and quieter than the graceless mooing of cows or the shrieking of baby sheep. Justin held in his hand a letter from the personnel office informing him that Miss Judith Sammons had made a formal complaint of sexual harassment against him. There was a grievance procedure to be followed. A copy would be sent in due course.

'Justin!' called Rosemary from the kitchen. 'I've made the tea!'

'Coming,' he called. He tucked the letter in his pocket and turned his back on the moon, but he carried its look of whitened outrage with him as he stepped back into the kitchen.

CHAPTER 10

Topsy-turvy World

The campus was quiet in August, with most of the students away and the academic staff taking their holidays in a series of overlapping chunks, so the chances of the likes of Frank Flusfeder getting people together to have meetings were more remote than usual. Room Bookings had jubilantly acquired a conference on Aviation Studies with an attendance of 150 and another smaller affair, on cellular toxicology, following a mailing of flyers advertising EMU's attractive conference rates – a mere £49.50 per person per night, not including VAT, for a single room plus all meals. 'Top-class catering,' it boasted, 'full English breakfast, a buffet lunch and a three-course dinner with coffee and wine extra.' There was a colour picture of a white plate groaning with cholesterol-laden sausages, bacon, fried bread, mushrooms, eggs and tomatoes, which had been taken by Kelly Bloom in the Art Department, using a series of plastic props. 'Full conference facilities,' noted the brochure, depicting one of the three overhead projectors that still worked.

So there were other people, outsiders, stalking the campus, and peppering the thundery air with tales of indigestion, blocked toilets, missing flip charts and blown overhead projector bulbs. It was a dry August, which made it worse, what with the thunderflies and the rape beetles and the fact that the nearest swimming pool, in Motley city centre, between Tesco's and a discount clothing store, was one of those 'leisure' ones which meant that mechanically produced waves stimulated the local children to peals of excited laughter and even more pee-ing than was normal, and got in the way of anyone doing any serious swimming.

So far as Lydia was concerned, August was a time for serious work. The data from her project on Women and Leisure had been collected by her hardworking team in room 307, and Tony Wiggins from EMUCS had helped them to construct a computer database. Ola was cleaning them (in accord with the way the women in the study itself occupied most of their time) and soon they would be ready to analyse – for that delicious moment when the keys could be pushed and the ergonomic mice clicked and hey presto there would be the answer facing you on the screen. Sometimes it'd be the answer you wanted and sometimes not. But that, for Lydia, was what it was all about: the excitement of finding something out, of making what various earlier versions of EMU's mission statement rather vacuously described, despite the onset of the monetarist culture, as 'a contribution to knowledge'.

It had been difficult breaking the news to the team in room 307 that they wouldn't be able to have their promised new computer after all. The overheads – the money which would have financed this and other goodies – had gone, and there appeared to be nothing Lydia could do to get them back. A further squabble had broken out about lamps; Miriam, who had the darkest desk, wanted a third anglepoise to make up for it, but Lydia had to tell her that she'd have to buy her own if it was that important. The next time Lydia went into the room, Miriam's corner resembled a floodlit football stadium and the label tied to the neck of a new emerald lamp base bore the legend, 'This is the personal property of Mrs Curd, DO NOT REMOVE.'

The end-of-term fracas about the dean's doings on the M25 had settled down. Sidony Wormleighton's vision of Bayreuth – one of the more trivial reasons why the odd encounter with a Swedish opera singer would not persuade her to disrupt her marriage – had come true. To Bayreuth the Wormleightons had gone, and at this very moment were pleasantly ensconced in the Steigenberger Festspiel restaurant enjoying an extremely expensive seasonal dish of Frische Pfifferlinge in Kräutersahnesauce mit Semmel-knödel, and a carafe of 1991 Bourgogne Chardonnay.

A meeting had taken place between Callum and Sir Stanley in the bar of The Country Pie where all such serious extracurricular discussions took place. Callum had offered to resign, but Sir Stanley had laughed in his face. 'Nonsense, dear chap, your private life is no concern of the university. We must defend our private lives against the rabidly inquisitional excesses of those who set themselves up as our moral judges.' Callum admired the choice of words. 'By the way,' Sir Stanley had continued, in a carefully casual tone, 'I expect rumours have reached you about the business in the church?' He'd paused. Callum had said nothing. Sir Stanley had made a slightly dismissive sideways gesture with his hand. 'Very fine roof, of course, or it would be if it was repaired. Twenty five k. I think we're well on the way to reaching the target.' He'd paused again. 'Your wife,' he'd gone on, a bit more obviously, 'Mrs Wormleighton . . .'

'Yes? Oh yes. Yes.' The penny dropped. In return for ignoring the episode with Ulla, Sir Stanley wanted him to stop the Clean Up St Nick's Campaign. It made perfect sense. Callum had hunched his shoulders, unhappily but resolutely. It was going to be a difficult one. 'Leave it with me. That's right, I'll see what I can do.'

'Good, good.' Sir Stanley had rubbed his hands. Callum had ground his teeth together more or less silently. Once

Sidony got an idea into her head it could be difficult to shift it. But if anywhere could do it, it'd be Bayreuth.

They climbed the hill to the Opera House three nights in a row, and processed down it afterwards, along with all the other ladies in their long silk dresses and the gentlemen in their stuffed penguin suits, passing like vestiges of another age through the ordered summer-hung spaces of the clean little German town, breathing in light flowery scents to counterpoint the lusty singing on top of the hill. German opera, reflected Callum, was this extraordinary mixture of rock-like order and besieging tides of romanticism. There was something so structured, but also so unbridled about it. The sucking diaphragms of the singers still turned him on, but with Sidony's rapt attention beside him, it was merely, fortunately, a cerebral sensation he felt.

'Marvellous,' said Sidony repeatedly, putting her arm through his. 'Quite, quite wonderful.' She lay awake longer than he in their neat white beds in the Bayerische Hof. He knew because she told him in the morning. He did try to talk to her about the need for circumspection in relation to anything reeking of university affairs, but his episode with Ulla had clearly given her the upper hand here. Sidony was a woman of few words, and all she'd said to Callum about Ulla was that she expected Callum to conduct whatever he had to conduct well out of the limelight in future. At any rate, a comfortable atmosphere of harmony was re-established between them.

Callum wasn't the only one in trouble that summer. Justin Leopard drove around the countryside thinking about Judy Sammons and the grievance procedure, and also to get away from Rosemary and Carey's shouting matches. Sometimes he took Amos with him and they went to the butterfly park, which Amos didn't like very much, and once to a garden centre to buy some wasp repellent; Amos liked this better because there were two peacocks braying and strutting there, and he ran after them, whooping joyfully. They also went to a number of car boot sales, where Justin rifled through the second-hand books, buying copies of several things he already had.

One Sunday he took the boy to a local fête. A brass band was playing the Pink Panther theme, and a car alarm had been going ooh-eh ooh-eh ooh-eh all afternoon. He gave Amos £2 and told him not to leave the field without telling him. Justin wandered between the people wondering whether he had the energy to make some resolutions about his life and then how other people did this. He'd never been sure how different he was from other people. He *felt* very different most of the time, but that could have been either arrogance or ignorance. He felt he ought to resolve to be a better husband, a better PHOD, and of course a better father. He passed two women holding some runner bean seedlings and talking about the murder of little Sophie Hook, taken from her uncle's tent in the middle of the night; and the beating and killing of a mother and her daughter in a quiet Kent lane; and the rape and murder of a teenage girl on a school holiday in France. Both the women had pushchairs with infants tied into them, placid and unable to wander. Justin, suddenly alarmed, looked round for Amos and couldn't see him, and ran all over the field and then finally into the tent where teas were being served, and where Amos was removing the pink icing from trays of fairy cakes.

'You'll have to pay for those,' a stout village matron was saying, and then, seeing Justin approaching, 'Is that your boy? You want to keep him under control. That's how boys go wrong, you know.' It was a menacing suggestion, coming as it did on top of all these items of bad adult male behaviour. Justin touched Amos's soft marmalade hair as cherishingly as any father could.

Opinion on campus was divided about Justin's culpability in the Judy Sammons case. The women who knew Justin and those who didn't but who weren't feminists plumped for his innocence; the other women thought him guilty. Most of the men sat on the fence with a there-but-for-the-grace-of-God-go-I attitude. It was rather like their attitudes to Callum's indiscretion. The question, of course, was what had *really* happened between Justin and Judy. Judy told Lydia that she had been there talking to Justin about her disappointment at being turned down by the V-C, and Justin had tried to console her by putting a fatherly arm round her, and then a nonfatherly pair of lips on the side of her face, which he had rapidly eased round until they were in a more compromising position. As a feminist, Lydia wished to believe Judy's story, but as a professor, she got Judy's file out, and looked to see if there was anything in her background to suggest that she might have reason to invent it. But Judy proved to have the normal divorced parents, and a normal younger sibling, still at school in Hampshire, and her own educational and personal record was startingly blameless. Her medical examination said '?anorexic', but then so did those of most female students these days.

Justin's story started out the same as Judy's, but omitted the last part. He said she was upset at being turned down, and his gesture was simply one of fatherly consolation, through and through. It would be a good test of the new grievance procedures that Personnel had hastily assembled, thought Lydia.

She felt more and more alone. She tried to talk to Disa about the truth of the matter between Justin and Judy, but

Disa was having none of it. According to her, there was no question but that Judy had to be believed. Every word of it.

As to more academic matters, Justin had managed to write his first research grant application for five years, a modest idea to a charity for spending £70k a year for two years researching students' views on higher education. But when he'd passed it across Graham Piper's desk for an administrative signature, he'd been astonished to get a stormy, handwritten response (Graham's secretary was on maternity leave, and at a meeting Graham had missed because he'd had to take his Jack Russell to the vet, PRIC had decided not to pay for temporary cover). 'NO OVER-HEADS!' Graham's note had screamed. 'Charities do not pay overheads! Following the recently introduced Procedures for Recovering the True Cost of Funded Research, your departmental grant will be top-sliced by £.4k for every £1k of the proposed grant.'

The strength of Lydia's objection to the new overheads system finally dawned on Justin. He wrote Graham Piper a note asking for it to be discussed at the next meeting of PRIC, and copied the note to Callum and to Sir Stanley. He would have done this by e-mail, but he still hadn't anything like mastered this. He'd done his best – he'd even gone over to EMUCS to seek help, but Tony hadn't been there and Martin Pippard was deep in an Internet news-group on Literacy in Virtual Reality, learning how information design and concept development could help one to escape flatland and infiniteland. He'd even tried explaining these concepts to Justin, but Justin only wanted an explanation of the mysteries of his Draft Mail Folder.

When he'd got the grant proposal off (with a small adjustment to the overheads) he took Rosemary and Carey and Amos for a fortnight's holiday to Iceland, where the sun didn't shine once, let alone at midnight, and beer cost £4 a pint. He'd managed to keep the sexual harassment case from Rosemary, as he fancied she couldn't be relied on to respond with the same sound judgement as Sidony Worm-leighton. In any case, Carey was harassing them both to an extraordinary degree, and only Justin's inherent laziness and Rosemary's inherent motherliness prevented the whole family from erupting like one of the scenic Icelandic geysers.

While Justin succeeded in getting his research proposal in, Trent Lovett didn't. His, on disaster theory and life-cycle transitions, had failed to make the deadline. He'd blamed Charlie, in whose youthful and possibly sabotaging hands he'd left it, but Charlie had said it was the fault of the post-room staff who'd been on a go-slow at the time. 'But if you knew that, why didn't you take it to the post office yourself?' Trent had screamed.

'It's not part of my job description,' Charlie had explained calmly. Personnel were under instruction from Sir Stanley who was under instruction from Richard Winkett to issue everyone with new job descriptions. In many cases these were the first that staff at EMU had ever had, and so they were amazed to find out what they were expected to do, especially when Personnel got some of the job descriptions mixed up, and sent them to the wrong people.

It all gave everyone a lot to think about, and this included Giles Tingey, who prowled the EMU campus with all the athletic acumen of the wild puma which the local community claimed to glimpse from time to time. The legend of the Motley puma, or lynx, or panther, or possibly very large fox, had been endemic to the region for some years. Housewives on Studfall Road estate had seen it while hanging out their washing; quarry workers had caught it in the headlights of their lorries. There were regular reports in *The*

Motley Mercury. Far more sightings of the animal had been recorded in the town than in the countryside, which a local psychologist, called in by a journalist desperate to fill his column spaces, had unscientifically attributed to the repressed desires of those who live in towns to have some contact with Mother Earth. At any rate, those who saw the puma definitely believed they had, while those who hadn't contented themselves with other explanations.

Giles Tingey, like the puma, if it existed, was well aware that conditions were perfect for prowling that summer. On the bisected EMU campus, the key players came and went, like articulated lorries on the A43. Some could be nailed down in sharp question-and-answer sessions in between their wet family weeks in Cornwall or Dorset (particularly wet that year), their ambitious home-maintenance programmes, weekends abroad, operatic festivals, and even spa holidays (Sir Stanley and his friends). The ones who stayed behind, like Lydia, were clearly the hardest workers, though this didn't apply to John Mapstone, who stayed because going on holiday couldn't be contemplated – it would have tapped into a veritable army of phobias (being trapped outside/inside, other people, lavatories used by other people, things with more than two legs, etc, etc). Mapstone was in any case entirely occupied with the medical impossibility of his new mission to recruit third-world students. He was seeing a psychiatrist in an attempt to get a medical certificate about his phobias which would let him off the hook. He thought Proudfoot ought to go instead. Proudfoot might as well, since he spent most of his time travelling anyway.

The more prowling Giles Tingey did, the more complicated things became. He'd started out with a simple brief: how cost-effective an exercise was the Department of Cultural Studies? It had a staff of ten FTEs and a hundred and twelve students taking courses either on their own or in combination with other departments in the new IDS that had been designed to make such combined courses easier. The department had eight research grants, making a contribution last year of £247k to the cost of funded research. It occupied fourteen rooms and used a calculable share of other university resources including EMUCS, the library, catering, administration, domestic services, etc. It should have been child's play to work out the cost-benefit ratio. You put the output in one column and the input in another; what DCS brought in and how much this cost were the two halves of an equation that would be most unlikely to balance. Then you could say what ought to be done. If DCS was performing well, there might be a case for additional resources; for Disa Loring's readership; for a new senior lecturer to spread the teaching load more evenly; for a full-time administrator (or even upgrading Marion); for more reading lamps to lighten everyone's dark corners, and more computers to be incompetently looked after by EMUCS. But if DCS wasn't performing well, then these things wouldn't happen. What was much more sinister, and Giles Tingey knew that Lydia Mallinder knew this, was that there might have to be cuts, or what Callum would have called liability-reducing activities.

But, as Callum had acknowledged to Lydia, this was the first academic financial review Winkett and Bacon had done. Not only was Lydia an experiment, but EMU itself was an experiment, a shaky stepping stone in Winkett and Bacon's own pathway to success as the leading light in academic management consultancy.

Giles Tingey's shoulders bore the weight of all this experimentation increasingly heavily as the summer wore on, as the farmers around Motley got the harvest in, as yet another factory (making new pine furniture) on the industrial estate closed down, as the hanging baskets outside the police station dried out, as another child was murdered in the undergrowth behind the army recruitment centre, and as the local refuse collectors went on strike at the prospect of privatization. The piles of rubbish grew and maggots took to the streets, keeping some potential juvenile offenders off them. A man was arrested for having sex with his Ford Fiesta in broad daylight, and, as this was one of the same men who claimed to have spotted the puma taking an evening walk through Motley to the new housing estate by the roundabout, the credibility of the puma story took an abrupt downwards plunge.

Giles Tingey read the local news in his suite in The Country Pie Hotel. It was hardly a suite, actually; more two rooms joined together by a door, and one bed made up to look like a sofa. But it was convenient, and it stopped Giles having to go back to his flat in South Kensington every night of the week. The firm paid for it; they paid Giles handsomely. Money was not something he, personally, had to worry about.

But something strange started to happen to Giles that summer. He grew more and more depressed by it all; by the poverty of Motley, and the drabness of the university, and the unceasingly humid heat, with the overcast skies and those wretched little flies which kept crawling up his nostrils and into his ears and his mouth, so that even if they weren't there he thought they were, and he was reduced to frenzied episodes of scratching quite worthy of the clientele of Victorian lunatic asylums. Sometimes he'd labour on about them in the public bar of The Country Pie, where a few of the more prosperous local farmers met to swap stories about falling prices for wheat straw, and the pros and cons of castrating the new intake of calves to meet the changed specification of supermarkets for less bull beef. The farmers, it seemed to Giles, were having to confront essentially the same problems as the universities: the need to cover the costs of an unwarrantably expensive infrastructure; dependence on the vagaries of the political and physical climate; a public scepticism about low-quality products. But the farming industry probably did better out of a central grant than the academic one, and there was little evidence (as yet) that what universities produced actually drove people mad.

The more depressed Giles got, the more he laboured over the figures in the pink cretonne squareness of his rooms in The Country Pie, and the more confused he became about the answers that came out, and the questions he was being asked to answer in the first place. For example, he had to admit he'd been impressed by the honesty of the people he'd interviewed in DCS. Disa Loring was a nice woman, a hard worker, a true European. Everything she said in her lilting Danish accent sounded reasonable. The two research officers, Veronica and Miriam, had complained bitterly about the exploitation of contract researchers, but had recognized that wasn't EMU's fault – it happened everywhere. It amazed Giles that they were so committed to such lousy jobs – part-time and only for eighteen months. The odd one out was Frank Flusfeder, but his weasel eyes flickered and darted all over the place, and Giles would have been an idiot if he'd been taken in by anything Frank said. Whatever else it was, DCS was clearly a place where people worked hard, did their teaching and did their research and were nice to students, and produced publications, and what more could you want? A little more accessibility in the publications themselves, perhaps, a little more commitment to the University's Mission (once this had been determined by Giles' colleagues in Winkett and Bacon's Kensington office), a little less of the them-and-us attitude, but . . .

Sometimes he just sat staring into space, like Jeremy Krest

facing the rain-spattered windscreen of Lydia Mallinder's car when they'd had that weird set-to in the car park. Giles' suite in The Country Pie overlooked another car park, and so he would sit by the window as the blue Vauxhall Novas and the red Ford Mondeos and the green Range Rovers came and went.

As the present was rendered more problematic, the past beckoned him. 'There was a time,' he would murmur: 'when meadow, grove, and stream/The earth, and every common sight/To me did seem/Apparell'd in celestial light/The glory and the freshness of a dream/It is not now as it hath been of yore/Turn wheresoe'er I may/By night or day/The things which I have seen I now can see no more.' Had Giles been a social scientist like Lydia or like Elliot or Justin or even Dennis Rudgewick, he would have understood what was happening to him: he was 'going native'. This phrase, originally coined by anthropologists, meant, in Giles' case, that the more he found out about DCS the more he was absorbing their point of view. This process was hastened by the presence and persona of Lydia Mallinder. Had Giles had more experience of doing management reviews, he might have been more detached. But equally, had Lydia not been the person she was, everything might have gone according to Sir Stanley and Richard Winkett's plan. It was partly a problem of ethics, as Sir Stanley would have put it.

When Giles went home for the weekend to his parents' house in Taunton at the end of August, his mother was quite worried about him. He seemed so self-absorbed, so unresponsive to what was going on around him. 'Leave the boy alone,' said his father. 'He's got a tough job on just now, he'll be alright.'

This suave disregard for human distress was characteristic

of the kind of classic Englishman Boyde Tingey was and expected his sons to be; educated to a brand of classism and nationalism which would be incompatible with anyone's notion of equal opportunities; and brought up to such a firm belief in the eugenic superiority of white male power that a world without it was literally inconceivable. Such men were unplagued by self-doubt, and a sense of their own self-worth shone out of their eyes, along with their inherited good sight; myopia would strike much later, but was curable, along with most other minor misfortunes. The peculiar repression of sentiment which accompanied the core values Giles had been reared to hold was also unremarkable. It was partly for this reason that his encounter with Jeremy Krest in the EMU car park had upset him. The raw excesses of Jeremy Krest's emotion had disturbed Giles more than he would admit.

As he drove back to Motley early on the Monday morning, the sky was streaked with pale orange light and the summer landscape seemed more than usually colourful. The sparking electrons in his mind threw up some more lines of poetry he hadn't read since Cambridge: 'I saw the beating of the world/Before me like a flag unfurled/The splendour of the moving sky/And all the stars in company/I thought how beautiful it is!/My soul said, There is more than this.' Giles struggled to remember the rest of the poem: 'I saw the generation of the earth, and love as wide as heaven is round', he chanted, and then he believed he'd found another line: 'Sometimes I have a useful thought that bids me do the thing I ought.'

He turned off the road and into a service station. Directory enquiries gave him Lydia's number, and she answered on the fourth ring. 'It's Giles Tingey,' he explained. 'Something's come up. Can I see you later today? Not at the university, if possible. It's confidential, you see.'

When they met in the Black Cat wine bar, Lydia complained gently about the hour at which he'd phoned her: 8.15 AM. 'I'm sorry. I didn't realize the time. But I'd been trying to piece things together over the weekend and I realized I needed some help.'

She looked quizzically at him in the musty atmosphere. Behind them a man, whistling Rod Stewart's 'Sailing', was lugging crates of beer and soda water around. Lydia had her hair down today, Giles noticed. Over her shoulders. Like a shampoo advertisement, it shone the colour of honey in the weak light from the mullioned window at the back of the wine bar. A pearl necklace encircled her throat, though perhaps they weren't real pearls. Her whole appearance made him catch his breath. She didn't seem to him to be Professor Mallinder of Gender Studies with capital letters any more. The miserable muddle of EMU faded along with Lydia's proper designation. As in the poem, his soul was telling him something. He felt it strongly.

'Do you mind if I take my jacket off?'

'Of course not.'

Giles wiped his sticky brow with the back of his hand. 'It goes like this, you see.' He sighed.

'Yes?'

'I did take to heart what you said about Gender Studies.'

'Yes?'

'Well, perhaps I should begin the other end. Do you understand the TRU formula?'

'Broadly. Not the details. But I understand the purpose of the formula.'

'Hmm.' He paused.

'Can I help you with this?' she offered. 'I mean, you do seem to be finding it difficult to say what's on your mind. Have you finished the review of my department? What are your findings? We never discussed this when we met before,' she went on, seizing her opportunity, 'but I hope you'll give me a chance to see a draft of your report before it's finalized. So I can correct any factual errors, you know,' she finished quickly. She was trying hard to separate the professional issues from any feelings she might have about this curious man who, like the Motley puma, loped in and out of her life and her dreams.

'There won't be any report,' said Giles. 'I won't be writing a report after all.' He waited. She stared at him. He thought her face had taken on the pale silvery look of the pearls round her throat. 'It surprises you, doesn't it!' he exclaimed. 'You want to know why. Well, there are six Schools in this university, and twenty-two departments,' he went on quantitatively. 'So why has yours been singled out for a review? According to what criteria? I'm sure you've asked yourself and others that. Even if I can decide how to define "cost" and "effectiveness", no-one will have the faintest idea how the findings for DCS would compare with those of any other department. I've been given some figures,' he reached down and unsnapped his briefcase, 'which I'd like to share with you. But you must promise to keep them to yourself.'

In the smoky alcoholic darkness, Lydia leant eagerly towards Giles' handsome pale face to receive what he had for her. There were two sets of figures. He explained that the first set showed the payroll costs of centrally funded academic and support staff by school, department and gender; and separately for the V-C's office. 'I asked for these so I could get an idea of how to attribute the input to TRUs from central funds across the university, and also in order to calculate the percentage of the salary infrastructure that needs to be carried by contract research staff.'

Lydia stared at the figures. It was obvious that some people at EMU got much larger salaries than others, but that wasn't really news. Giles had also calculated the average salary for each grade of staff for men and women separately. There were differences; predictable, again.

'You see how seriously I've taken your tuition on the topic of gender, Lydia?' He said her name very slowly, with the tip of his pink tongue touching his white teeth. 'The figures might not all be correct, but I got them from the payroll database.' Lydia continued to stare at them, wondering what this was all about. 'Some moments in history are more transitional than others,' he remarked darkly.

'Sorry?'

'I think you know what I mean.'

Lydia cleared her throat, and shuffled the sheets of figures. 'I thought the payroll database was limited access,' she observed, buying time.

'Oh yes, but they gave me the password.'

'I can't use these figures, Giles,' said Lydia. 'Did you know that I've got a student who's doing a PhD on equal opportunities? She wanted to do a case study here, but your dear uncle wouldn't let her. I can see why. This is dynamite.'

'He's not my "dear uncle",' said Giles.

'Isn't he?'

'You know what I mean,' he said again.

'I'm not sure I do. In fact I don't know why you've shown me all this, given that I can't acknowledge the information in any way. I don't even know why you dug it out in the first place.'

'As I said, Lydia, I'm not too old to learn.' He leaned forward now and grabbed her hands and held them for a moment very tightly and then let them go. 'I'm sorry. I'm really sorry.' He moved away from her. 'Do you by any chance know a poem of Edward Lear's called "Topsy-turvy World"?' he asked.

She shook her head.

'It begins: "If the butterfly courted the bee/And the owl

the porcupine/If churches were built in the sea/And three times one was nine"' and ends ' "If a gentleman's son was a lady/The world would be Upside-Down!/If any or all of these wonders/Should ever come about/I should not consider. them blunders/For I should be Inside-Out!"'

Lydia blinked. 'You're not making an awful lot of sense this morning.'

'It depends on your point of view.' There was a short silence. 'You haven't seen the second lot of figures yet.'

These showed teaching hours and numbers of students and contract research income by school, department and gender. In the teaching domain, the women clearly worked harder than the men. The figures for research were less clear, as there were some male stars in other schools, especially Jeremy Krest in Biological Sciences, who got substantial funding from the MRC and Wellcome and a tobacco company or two (about which he and Lydia had had many arguments), and Proudfoot in Business Studies, who had a close friend on the Economic and Social Research Council's Research Grants Board.

'Can you get the figures for promotions?' asked Lydia suddenly. 'You know, applications for promotion for lecturers to senior lecturers and readers and professors and so forth?'

'I don't see why not.' His face was flushed with excitement. Lydia thought quickly. 'Look, Giles,' she said simply, 'I don't know quite what's going on here, and I've got a meeting with one of my research teams in about twenty minutes, so I've got to go. But I think we need to continue this discussion.' She took a deep breath, and hoped this wasn't something she was going to regret. 'Why don't you come round to my house this evening and we can talk more about it all then. That is, if you're free,' she added, conscious that it would be impolite for her to consider him to be automatically at her disposal just because of whatever crisis of conscience had struck him in relation to his task of reviewing DCS.

'I don't see why not,' said Giles, again.

He really was an odd fellow. She ruminated on this while Ola and Veronica and Miriam showed her the first printout of data from the Women and Leisure project, and presented her with a list of articles they'd decided they wanted to write to improve their own chances of promotion. Frank appeared (did he never go on holiday?) to complain that Lydia really must do something to enforce the no-smoking policy, otherwise EMU would have a case of wilful negligence and lung cancer or fatal asthma or somesuch on their hands, sooner or later.

'Don't worry, Frank, I expect I'll have passed on by then,' said Lydia irreverently. 'Oh, I don't mean I'll be dead,' she added, seeing the grin on his face. 'I meant I'll be somewhere else. I'm not staying in this dump for ever, you know.'

Frank went away and wrote down what she'd said in his red exercise book. He'd thought of having an encrypted file on his computer, but you never knew who could hack their way into there. A lot of his e-mail had gone missing recently, and when he'd asked Martin Pippard about it, Martin had said airily that yes, they in EMUCS had known for some time that someone was using Martin's password to get access to the system. But where had all the messages gone? It wasn't good enough! 'Look in your mailbox,' advised Martin. But Frank's mailbox was empty, so the hacker had obviously been there too.

Lydia went home via Tesco's, where she bought a nice piece of hopefully uncontaminated beef and some frozen French fries, the wherewithall for a green salad, and some raspberries and crème fraiche. Nothing complicated. Huneyball could have the fat off the beef.

The cat sat watching her as she prepared everything. He perched on the kitchen surface between the cooker and the sink, which was one of his favourite spots. From there he could easily dip his chin into any interesting looking saucepans, and then, if he wanted a drink, it was only a short stroll to the sink where, due to a faulty washer, the tap would be dripping at a steady rate and he could do his trick of tucking his head sideways underneath it and catching the drips as they fell.

Lydia was listening to the news on the radio. Huneyball hated the news. Giles came promptly at 7.30 with a bottle of good Bordeaux. He wore a new shirt of an intense blue with a darker blue tie. He looked very handsome. Huneyball glared at him with his one seeing green eye and then flung himself at Giles' neck as he bent with the first bottle of wine between his legs to pull the cork out using Lydia's old-fashioned bottle opener.

'Good God!'

'No, it's only my cat. I'm sorry, I should have warned you.'

'So we both have something to apologize to each other about,' commented Giles. They took their wine and Giles took the orange fur collar of Huneyball out on to the patio.

'There's no view of the setting sun,' apologized Lydia further and companionably, 'but we do a nice line in satellite dishes and underclothes which would flap in the wind if there was one.'

The wine and the setting and the unacknowledged possibility of things being different in future relaxed them both. 'I was sorry about that scene in the car park,' he said.

'So was I.'

'I didn't ask you,' he said, 'but I suppose you and Professor Krest have been having A Relationship?'

'I suppose we have.'

'If I may say so, I liked you the first time I met you,' he confessed suddenly, Huneyball's tail waving excitedly in front of his mouth at the prospect of a bit of beef. 'That's part of the explanation, of course,' he went on quickly.

'What explanation?'

'The explanation of my apparent change of mind.'

'We come from two different worlds, you and I,' she responded, sipping his gift of the Bordeaux. 'What I think is mad is the world you come from, not you. What my world knows and what yours does are different. We have different sets of values. You judge quality by quantity, I judge it by the characteristics inherent to itself. One way of knowing is deductive, the other inductive. But you do seem to have had some sort of change of heart, to have altered your position radically. I *am* interested in why that happened. I'm curious, I admit that.'

It was a very professorial speech, thought Giles. Swallows swept across the small square of silver blue above the patio, and the pigeon whose sexual antics Huneyball had watched the evening Jeremy Krest came round returned to look for his lady. But the television aerial was bare, and after a few coo-coos, which made Huneyball's mouth drop open in its normal way, the pigeon flew off to look for another companion.

A large ladybird landed on Lydia's skirt. She watched it as it waddled its fat red-spotted way across her lap. She touched it delicately with the tip of her little finger. 'Ladybird, ladybird, fly away home!' quoted Giles. He leaned over it and touched it too, and then her, feeling the presence of muscle and bone and moving blood and silky skin beneath the fine linen of her skirt.

'Do you want to eat?' she asked.

'Food's never been one of my appetites,' he answered. Huneyball, who'd fallen off Giles' neck during the ladybird watching, went and sat determinedly in the kitchen. He sensed it might be a long wait.

Lydia put the bottle of wine down on the bedside table. 'I hope we aren't making a big mistake.'

He took his clothes off down to his underpants, and folded them carefully and put them on the chair. Curiouser and curiouser, she thought. Then he took her in his arms and kissed her sweetly, while the swallows circled and dived in the twilight sky outside the window. 'We won't know whether it is or not until afterwards.'

He was quite the slowest and most hesitant lover she'd had, but the nature of the structural relationship between them – that he was her reviewer and she the object of his sartorial attention – combined with her dilemma about Jeremy Krest, seemed to create a great sensitivity between them. As Giles explored her body, carefully with the same thorough attention he seemed to give to everything, she allowed her hands and her mouth to explore this new biological terrain that life had presented to her. There was a tiny moment of regret for Jeremy Krest when she thought of the word 'biological', but the tide of newness – discovering all over again with Giles Tingey what bodies can do – carried her over it. Giles' body was altogether different from Jeremy's – almost hairless, and very thin. His ribs could almost be counted.

'My love,' said Giles, 'you are my love, aren't you?'

It would do for the moment. She had to help him into her, but then all women are different from one another. At first he was completely motionless inside her. 'Amazing,' he said, 'amazing!' in much the same tone of voice as Sidony Wormleighton had admired the opera in Bayreuth. Giles seemed lost in some private disclosure inside his head; it was as though he wasn't sharing these moments with her at all. But before she had time to give way to disappointment, he came back to her again. Every movement of his body, every interior sensation, showed on the screen of his eyes.

A few minutes later it was over. Lydia managed to catch up with him just in time. Giles lay back and sighed. She sensed some great sadness about him. 'I don't suppose that was very good for you, was it?'

'It was our first time,' she said.

He sat up and pulled the duvet up to his waist and bent his knees and put his arms round them and his head down. The sound was muffled, but she thought he was crying.

'Let me help you, Giles.' She sat up too, and put her arms round him. 'What is it? Tell me. Please.'

'When you said it was the first time, I know what you meant, but you were right in another sense. You see, Lydia, I am – was – a virgin.'

She'd only thought of women being virgins, not men. Women were supposed to be virgins, but men weren't. He raised his head and looked at her and then laid his head on her breast and said, 'Oh Lydia!' quietly, several times. For some reason she thought of a George Eliot novel and the sex scenes that were only alluded to in it. There was something deeply Victorian about Giles Tingey.

'I expect you think that's very strange,' he invited.

'Unusual. Statistically unusual.'

'I'm not gay or anything like that. I like women. It's just that it's always seemed so difficult to be in the right situation with a woman to make love to her. I do think of it as making love, you see, not as having sex. I used to see animals doing it on the farm and on our estate, and I thought it looked such a violent thing, I couldn't see how any man would do that to a woman he loved.'

'Not to, but with,' observed Lydia.

'I know that now. Oh Lydia. Can we do it again?'

She was delighted by his naive ardour, and also by the thought that hers was the first body he'd known like this. She thought how much she'd have to teach him, but only over time, with time on their side, with the sensuous time-lessness and wonder of the way Giles was touching her now, wanting to find out about her very soul. He made her realize that her soul had never been of much concern to Jeremy Krest.

'The sky's so full of stars,' he remarked, much later, 'I envy you being able to lie here and look at them.'

'Oh, I don't much,' said Lydia. 'The stars just twinkle at you in an annoying way. They don't answer the questions you want them to.' She turned onto her side and fitted herself into the curves of Giles' body. Of course she wanted to know why he'd never made love to a woman before, but she had this overwhelming sense that for the moment all the questions could wait. So could the future: what they would both do next. What she would do about him, and about the unfinished saga of Jeremy Krest; and about the running stream of innuendoes of various kinds that seemed to make up her life at the moment; and about Judy Sammons' study of her and others as academic women in an era of both apparently equal but also significantly lost opportunities; what he would do about the report on DCS and his commitment, or lack of it, to the Mission of Winkett and Bacon, as well as whatever family loyalty he felt – and she didn't entirely believe Sir Stanley wasn't his dear uncle. But it could all wait. Time was at a standstill. They were wrapped in intimations of eternity.

She got out of bed to close the curtains, and thought she saw something move in the area of wasteland beyond the patio. It wasn't Huneyball, because he was still in the kitchen waiting for his dinner. Perhaps it was the puma,

whose sighting would be more believable away from anyone's perverted erotic gaze, or perhaps it was some other
stalking creature. She put it out of her mind. Giles Tingey
was a much more interesting subject for study than the
flatland and infiniteland of Motley.

CHAPTER 11

The Sociologist's Warning

'The notion of reflexive modernization takes us usefully away from older evolutionary ideas about the nature of modern society,' proclaimed Trent Lovett from the platform of the Robert Sharpe-Palmer lecture theatre. 'But modernity itself imposes constraints of a not-dissimilar kind. The central theme here derives from the icon of science. I say "icon" because science in this sense is not simply knowledge, for nothing is simply knowledge; a belief in science has elements in common with religion. Science gives rise to what Ulrich Beck has called "the risk society". But the central problem of modernity is the relation between science, risk and social relations. The risk society puts in place new mechanisms of social control, and the modernization of intimate relations equates intimacy with democracy. Here the modernist project is the realization of autonomy: I am who I am with you, but who I am leaves you free to be who you are. It is a fine principle, but is of course rather less easily attained.' Trent paused to allow the note of confident sarcasm to sink in. 'And here we have one of the tensions at the heart of modern personal relationships, for, as Anthony Giddens has put it, "democracy is dull, sex is exciting"; there is for most of us an impulse towards risk, and the point about risk is that it discriminates in ways which defeat the egalitarian ideal of the reflexive project of the self.'

He reached out for the glass of water strategically placed on the podium, and took a sip, flashing the bright scarlet wings of his academic gown as he did so. There was always something impressive about the scholar in action, thought the V-C affectionately from the front row. Callum Worm-leighton, on the platform next to Trent, curled and uncurled his long legs, and wondered what Trent was talking about. It was hot in the hall; the air conditioning had broken down. Male and female sweat rose and mingled in the sickly atmosphere, engaging in that same risky project of democracy about which Trent was speaking. Sensibly, Trent had decided not to use any audio-visual aids apart from himself. His golden hair was freshly cropped and the two small earrings in his right ear sparkled in the reflected reading light of the podium. This was Trent's inaugural lecture as a professor, and he wanted to make it good. He knew there had been opposition to his coming to EMU, and so he was making it his project to impress on people that, despite the manner in which he'd arrived, he was a serious scholar after all.

'Phew!' said Lydia afterwards, expressing a reaction both to what Trent had said and the atmosphere in the hall. 'What did you think of that, then?'

'I must admit I was impressed,' said Disa. 'Ulrich Beck is worth reading, although the translation could be improved.' Disa was a fluent linguist. 'And I am not sure about the links between the risks of modernization and the transformation of personal life.'

Lydia reflected. 'I'm not sure whether this was what he was saying, but perhaps the decay of modern culture and the declining usefulness of the old paradigm of knowledge are two sides of the same coin. A new culture is arising out of the ashes of the old. The change in personal life also challenges old ideas about risk. It makes people think differently.'

She herself continued to think differently about Giles Tingey. The evening in her house had affirmed the theme of Giles' oddities. When she'd finally started cooking the steak, much to Huneyball's satisfaction, Giles had announced he was a vegetarian. 'I'm sorry, I should have warned you.'

'All the more for me and the cat, then. I'll make you an egg.'

He'd only toyed with his food. He'd moved it round his plate like the statistics he'd dug up and given her about EMU, but he'd evinced a good deal more enthusiasm for the figures than for the food.

He'd sent her a note afterwards, on one of those old-fashioned notelets with a flower, a honeysuckle in this case, on the front, and with an inside, 'Blank for Your Personal Message'. His said, 'Thank you for a most wonderful evening. I hope we can repeat it soon.' This was followed by four lines of poetry: 'And the sunlight clasps the earth/ And the moonbeams kiss the sea/What are all these kissings worth/If thou kiss not me?' Underneath this Giles had written, 'From "Love's Philosophy" by Percy Bysshe Shelley'.

Lydia and Disa made their way upstairs to the yellow meeting room where there was to be a reception. Khadeeja of Catering had downgraded the wine order when Jeff from Building Services had got his redundancy letter. He'd taken it particularly hard, although he was putting a brave face on it, and was going round telling everyone that it'd give him more time with his rabbits. Khadeeja had heard the widely circulating story of Trent Lovett's position vis-à-vis the V-C, and she said, 'Well, if they can find the money to pay him, then what's the harm in keeping Jeff on till he's ready to go? A man who's worked all his life won't find it easy to make do with rabbits.'

So instead of the Pouilly-Fumé the V-C had ordered,

Khadeeja had de-crated a nasty Hungarian Riesling. She hadn't been as inventive as the budget would allow with the nibbles either, sticking to cheese squares and gherkins on rye and one prawn in a casket of mayonnaise on each savoury biscuit.

Justin had been sitting next to Stephanie Kershaw, who'd been sitting next to Jon Pitton, who'd fallen asleep as usual, and Stephanie had had to wake him up when people started leaving the hall. Jon had started to do it to the students now, and they were complaining. Justin got Stephanie and Jon a drink, and he saw Elliot Blankthorn doing the same for Lydia and Disa. Trent Lovett's mother and father were there, talking to the V-C. Mrs Lovett, a gaily decorated brunette who taught martial arts, was berating the V-C for the quality of the EMU wine. Mr Lovett, a fishmonger, was looking rather out of place.

Trent's lecture took place in the first week of term. The splendid August weather had held almost into October, and the lawns of Motley and the fields round the EMU campus were now bleached to approximately the same colour as Trent Lovett's hair. The barley harvest was right down, with nitrogen levels running at an unacceptable two per cent. A water shortage leading to a hose-pipe ban was proving quite a deprivation to the likes of the Wormleightons and Stanley Oxborrow in their country mansions, but Callum watered the garden late at night when he hoped no-one would notice, and Stanley Oxborrow's gardener was deaf and never read the newspapers. In Suckley Green, Rosemary Leopard had perfected a means of preserving the bathwater so the Leopards' few shrubs could have a drink. Justin did wonder about the effect of the noxious substances their daughter Carey put in her bath, but Rosemary said if Carey came out of her bath alive, so would the plants.

There was a general atmosphere of 'Oh God here we go again, have we got the energy?' but this was normal at the start of a new academic year. Fern Meredith was going at the end of October, but Gaynor Scudamore had negotiated a reprieve on the grounds that her husband had been unable to work for twenty years, and she needed a pension for both of them. There must be a slight vein of charity in Sir Stanley after all. Fern had been egged on to challenge the decision by Tony Wiggins (himself glad to see the imminent end of Martin Pippard), and by Lydia and other women who thought they could see in Stanley Oxborrow's list a more-than-faint hint of discrimination. But she'd decided to take what life had dealt her and make the best of it. They would have less money, but she would be less tired. Gone would be the guilt about missing a seminar or a class because one of the boys was ill; gone would be the misery of leaving one of them, pale-faced and languishing, on the sofa for the tense cycle ride and the even tenser few hours at EMU.

Sitting there listening to Trent Lovett's lecture, Fern had reflected that the impression of being a scholar Trent was trying to create was really rather far removed from ordinary life. What would Bridget, her comfortable rural childminder, for example, say about it? Or the farming couple who rented Jake his studio overlooking the bird sanctuary? If you couldn't explain it to them, was it worth having – were the likes of Trent Lovett and herself worth paying for? She, Fern, never used words like 'modernity' and 'deradicalization' and 'eschatological' or even 'socio-historical'. She used ordinary words, because most of the students were quite ordinary. They didn't come to EMU with gigantic technical vocabularies, and Fern didn't see why they needed to acquire them.

Giles Tingey, who had a technical vocabulary of his own,

had had a frank encounter with the V-C only the previous week about the review he was doing of DCS. Uncle Stanley had been glad to see him; unlike some of his appointments, this piece of nepotism was at least grounded in affection. Giles was the nearest Sir Stanley would ever have to a son, and he would have seen a mirror image of his own in Giles' face even if it hadn't been there. Stanley was especially keen to hear Giles coming to the right conclusions about Lydia Mallinder, because of this new business involving one of her and Justin Leopard's students.

Giles had opened with: 'I may not be going to say what you want me to'. He'd gone on to confirm this by indicating the general lack of evidence pointing to Lydia's department being out of line, and his inability to recommend anything other than that it should perhaps receive more resources rather than fewer. This was all backed up with figures. In Giles' view, he'd told Sir Stanley, it was impossible to answer the question as to whether DCS was cost effective without asking the same question of other departments. 'Then there's the question of outcome measures.'

'What questions? I thought it was all pretty simple.' Sir Stanley's suntanned fingers had drummed impatiently on his desk. 'Student numbers, research overheads, publications, consultancy, perhaps important government committees. You can forget the international stuff.' He thought of that disgusting man Proudfoot wending his way round all the conferences in the world and now, moreover, trying to sell EMU plc at the same time.

'Well, no, actually,' Giles had said. 'I don't want to disagree with you, Uncle, but I've been thinking that it is, well, a question of quality as well as quantity.'

'And how on earth do you measure quality?' Sir Stanley had barked.

'I admit it's difficult. It's a subjective question, I can fully see that. But I've suggested to Richard that we commission some work on quality measures. After all, this question is likely to come up again, isn't it?'

'Not if I have anything to do with it, dear boy. But that's between you and Richard. My only concern is what you're doing here, and what we do about this Mallinder woman.'

'I haven't found her particularly difficult,' Giles had observed honestly. He swallowed. 'She's been very co-operative, in fact.'

'I'm glad to hear that. Perhaps she's finally learning what side her bread is buttered on. But she's a troublemaker. I should never have listened to Venetia. We should have stayed away from this dreadful gender business. How's Olivia, by the way?'

'Fine, fine. Why is Lyd – Professor Mallinder – a trouble-maker?'

'Read this, dear boy.' Sir Stanley had pushed a book with a colourful red and blue cover across the desk towards him.

Giles picked it up. It was called *The Witch in History*. He decided to change the subject, or rather go back to one of Sir Stanley's favourites. 'There are some interesting parallels with farming.'

Sir Stanley's eyebrows had shot up his bronzed forehead towards his elegantly waved silver hair.

'No, not with witches, with overheads. You see, farmers have learnt a lesson over the last few years about the impor-tance of "whole farm management". Inputs need to be targeted to the specific needs of individual fields and crops. It matters most when the weather's bad and there isn't enough rain to go round. Because of the vulnerability to world crop prices, overheads need to be spread over as wide an area as possible. And the other thing,' Sir Stanley wondered if the boy was mad or just onto something, 'they've also found that secure contracts for staff reduce administrative costs, and re-claiming farm-saved seed boosts gross profit margins. Rather than buying new seed, you understand.'

'I think you've rather lost me there.' Sir Stanley had looked at his watch.

But Giles had really got going now. 'You see the central question is, what are universities for?'

'Well, I know that,' Sir Stanley had said equably, 'I'm the Vice-Chancellor of one. If I don't know what they're for, who does? But if I may say so, that's hardly your concern. It's like asking what railways are for. Or hospitals. In fact, it's very much the same kind of question. Especially these days.'

'Yes, it is.'

'Well, there! No need to be so confrontational about it, dear boy. We all have to get on with our jobs, and that includes you. Whether you like it or not. I can see you don't, but I propose to ignore that. You know you need to make a success of this, don't you, Giles? You haven't exactly got a star-studded past. You should pay attention to that.'

Giles had flushed. 'I don't need to be reminded.'

'Good. So a bit more of doing what you're told wouldn't come amiss.' Particularly as Sir Stanley wanted Giles to review Building and Domestic and Catering Services next. Richard Winkett knew this was what Sir Stanley had in mind, and had negotiated a very fair price for the whole package, which would form the beginning of the new Management Consultancy Centre PRIC would shortly agree would be established at EMU.

Sir Stanley had been left in rather a quandary. EMU was paying Winkett and Bacon a considerable sum of money for this review (about which, naturally, questions had been asked in PRIC and RIPS), and the money was for a product which it now appeared might not be delivered.

He'd rung up his friend, Richard Winkett. 'I'm fond of the boy,' he'd said, 'but do you have a feel for what he's up to? He's talking a lot of nonsense about seeds and so forth. We've got two alternatives, as I see it. Either you make him toe the line or I do. You could get him going on another review in the hope he'll see some sense. But in that case, it might be as well if you put somebody on the job with him. Just to be on the safe side, if you understand me.'

'Leave it with me, Stan. I'll get back to you.'

Richard Winkett had considered the situation. The firm had taken a blow when the contract for sorting out what to do about the farmers and BSE had gone to Coopers & Lybrand. Richard had reflected that Giles' immersion in the mysteries of farming accounts would have well qualified him for undertaking the BSE business. Even a bit of insanity could be useful in the right place. But then it had come to him. In Edwardian times, when young people had fallen unsuitably in love, their parents sent them round the world to get over it. By the time they got back, the sights of Florence, the wonders of Rome, the Egyptian pyramids, the temples of Luxor, had all worn the craze away. Richard didn't think Giles was in love – in fact, love had hardly ever been mentioned in connection with him – but he preferred to turn his back on a problem rather than look it in the face. So moving Giles out of the orbit of EMU for a bit could well be the answer. There was an educational management conference coming up in Japan shortly. Giles could go to that. It'd kill two birds with one stone.

The conference was in a chrome and white-leather hotel in the middle of Tokyo. There was much expensive jollification, and a lot of what was politely called cross-cultural networking. Giles sent Lydia a series of postcards indicating his growing disaffection from this way of life. But as the distance between them expanded, Lydia's memory and incomplete understanding of Giles and his relationship to women and other things had faded a little; it became another aspect of her life over which she had no control.

In another era, Lydia might well have been a romantic, like Elizabeth Barrett Browning or Mrs Gaskell; but in the present one her desire to find in love the answer to all her problems was habitually strangled by the weed of her political understanding that, as Trent Lovett had said in his inaugural lecture, the flower of autonomy grows best on a democratic soil. The enduring hubris of love was that it appeared to transform the world, making everything sparkle anew; but every vision would fade in time to reveal only the old world shimmering with unchallengeably reactionary light. The revolutions that love seemed to accomplish were basically self-serving; their purpose was the survival of love itself. That greater understanding which, for some, including Lydia, was the purpose of life, was obscured by love rather than nourished by it. And so love – the democracy intimacy promised but rarely delivered, the exciting sex that lured you into the web and kept you glued there – was to be avoided in the interests of the mind.

Callum came up to her at the reception. Ever since the M25 incident he'd been distinctly less ebullient than normal. Some people even speculated that his fall from grace had made him more sympathetic to other people's problems. 'I gather the sentence has been lifted,' he said now to Lydia, 'and your review isn't quite the straightforward affair Giles Tingey thought it would be. You must be pleased.' He remembered her bristling with indignation in his office and laying down all sorts of impossible conditions about it. He didn't blame her, one wanted staff to show such gumption, but it didn't mean they'd get their way, and Lydia was too green to have learnt this lesson yet. On the contrary, it seemed that she'd been able to achieve a *volte face*; and Giles had solved the problem for her. Callum held his glass of cheap wine up to the light, and thought he saw a few atoms of cork despoiling it, if such a thing were possible. He fished them out and licked his finger.

'It wasn't me, you know,' Lydia told him. 'I was very co-operative; I told Giles Tingey what he needed to know.'

Callum nodded, and wondered what Lydia meant by 'needed'. Sidony had confided little of her evening with Lydia except about Lydia's problems with Jeremy Krest. Sidony had hinted that Lydia was in some distress and needed a friend. His vision of Lydia began to shift slightly (EMU during this era did seem to be a landscape of generally shifting visions), and under Sidony's influence Callum started to see Lydia as, perhaps, in some way, the daughter they might have had. In this new light, her annoying effrontery became an admirable determination; and Callum felt almost sorry for the way Sir Stanley had picked on her.

He could have done with a friend himself with whom to discuss his own predicament. Ulla had vanished to Sigtuna. But after Bayreuth they'd be in Salzburg, and after that Verona. Magic of Italy had a good deal – *Aida* and three other operas plus lodging in a winery run by Count Alighieri, a descendant of Dante's.

Lydia and Callum were standing in front of an unlikely portrait of Sir Stanley, its unlikelihood enhanced by the gilt frame Sir Stanley had insisted went round it. The picture showed him sitting on what looked like a throne, wearing a vehemently blue suit and an academic gown with a screaming orange hood. Not much was known about Stanley's academic background, except that he'd started out as a medieval historian, and then worked for the British Council, and after that become the MD of an electronic goods conglomerate, which had made a great deal of money out of cheap Cambodian labour. The portrait was flattering on the position of his hairline and the Dulux whiteness of his teeth; less so on the quality of his expression, which was somewhat fixed, if not exactly inanimate. The portrait would have hung there in a distinguished gallery of others, but there weren't any others, as EMU had only been a university since 1992.

Callum spotted Jon Pitton asleep on a chair in the corner underneath a pile of coats over by the trestle tables which had been laid with cheap paper cloths left over from the staff Christmas party; but what was more disturbing was that Jeremy Krest and Stephanie Kershaw were conversing with one another very animatedly on the other side of the room. Jeremy had been on television last night giving a magnetic performance in a rather striking red and green tartan shirt. Callum had been going to ask Lydia if she'd seen him, but now he thought better of it. There was something about the posture of those two which put him off.

When Sidony had referred to Lydia's problem, Callum had assumed she meant Jeremy Krest – it was so long ago, he'd forgotten who'd told him about it. He'd not been interested at the time, he rarely was in other people's romantic entanglements; it was only his newly discovered protectiveness towards Lydia that made him interested now. What could he do to prevent Lydia noticing the way Stephanie's bejewelled wrist was now lying happily on Jeremy's tartan shoulder? What could he do to block out the insinuatingly tinkling laughter that was at this very moment coming out of Stephanie's carefully contoured mouth?

One of the students from Sports and Turf Management hired by Khadeeja to help with the catering (the budget for outside help had been axed) passed by with a scratched enamel tray of drinks. Lydia reached out for a reconstituted orange juice, and Callum for more of the nasty Riesling. Happily, or unhappily, just then Elliot Blankthorn came up to them with a foil plate of Twiglets.

'Not a bad investment package after all,' said Elliot darkly, a couple of bits of Twiglets stuck between his teeth, referring to Trent's lecture. 'And there we all were wondering what had got into the V-C! It only goes to show, doesn't it!'

Lydia thought the phrase 'got into the V-C' was a bit close to the bone, or something. She seemed to shiver when Elliot came up, although the room was hot. 'Someone walking over your grave?' enquired Callum kindly.

'Not exactly.'

'You're lucky to get me at this thing,' started Elliot with his usual rabid insensitivity. 'My boys have been over. Millie – that's my ex-wife – sent them on one of those low-cost jets to New York. I would have told her not to, but I've had enough of her lectures about child support. Thankfully she booked them on BA from New York, and that was before the strike. A friend of Millie's was on the TWA Boeing that went down over Long Island, so you can imagine the state she was in. Anyway, these two boys landed on me. They're as bright as hell and it's been great to have them, but they didn't half take some entertaining. What we haven't done is nobody's business. Buck House, Windsor Castle, the Tower of London, the Science Museum, the dinosaurs in the Natural History Museum, the Hard Rock Café, the Regent's Park zoo and that other one where the monkeys climb all over your car, only we had a couple of lion cubs that were a bit too friendly for my taste, and that's only the start. I took them to York to see the Viking Museum but Jethro fell over a paving stone and we spent six hours in the A and E department, and I tried to bribe the kid not to tell Millie. She said they weren't to have any British hamburgers but I figure those kids are so full of junk food they're probably immune to anything it can do to you.' He guffawed and took his glasses off to remove the steam from them.

Callum and Lydia just stood there. 'I must go,' said Callum, 'soon.'

'So must I,' said Lydia. 'I've got some phone calls to make.'

'There's something I've been meaning to say to you Lydia,' observed Elliot, as though he hadn't said enough already.

'There's something I've been meaning to say to you, Elliot.'

Callum couldn't think of anything else to do except to wave and stride off.

'Okay, okay, you go first.'

'Sexual harassment,' she said.

'Sexual what?'

'Don't be an idiot. You know what I mean. Stop it, Elliot, or I'll have to do something about it.'

He looked at her for a minute. 'You know your problem, Lydia, you take yourself too seriously. Life's a ball really. I'll make a clean breast of it. I fancy you like hell. But with three disasters under my belt I've kinda resolved not to walk into a fourth. I don't know, though, their names all begin with M, and yours is next to theirs in the alphabet.' He looked at her to see if she, too, was amused, which she wasn't, of course, and he tugged his tie, which bore a repeat emblem of pandas on it, presumably from one of the recently visited zoos.

'Besides, it's clear that you're otherwise involved. So, not to beat about the bush, I want to do you a coupla favours instead. I mean Eros is okay for a time, isn't he, but who'd choose him as a recipe for being nice to one another? Yes,

I thought you'd be of the same mind. Well, here are the favours: one, be warned, Mr Giles Tingey of Winkett and Bacon is not what he seems to be; and, two, none of us is exempt from the political retributions of the times, and that includes you. With your title, you have to be a beneficiary of the feminist revolution, though I know there's a respected body of opinion that says what revolution, or this must be the longest one, etc etc, but it's as clear as hell that you got to where you are on the bandwagon of feminism, excuse me, that's probably a little harsh, I mean on its heels, or somesuch. So my advice to you is get out before they get you.'

'What?'

'Look, Lydia,' he coaxed, for all the world like some detective with twitching eyes in a creased raincoat, 'Your number is up. Take it from me.'

CHAPTER 12

To the Powder Closet

After the cheap EMU drinks, a hired bus took forty-six of them to Keynes Hall, Sir Stanley's residence. The rest had gone in private cars or were there already. Sir Stanley Oxborrow's parties were normally of the private kind, but he judged that most of EMU knew that Trent Lovett was a friend of his and the achievements of friends needed to be honoured. He'd been counting on Trent to give a blisteringly impressive lecture, and Trent hadn't let him down.

A marquee had been set up in the grounds because bad weather had been forecast, and the minibus did, in fact, pass through a band of misty light rain on its way to the house, fortunately just as it climbed the hill by St Nick's.

Jevon had been left in charge. The champagne was all chilled; the local salmon, poached in a lemon bouillon, rested with sad eyes and sprigs of dill on delicate silver filigree dishes; buttered baby potatoes awaited a rapid warming in the two Miele microwaves; and bowls of radicchio and curly endive anticipated fatiguing in puddles of raspberry-flavoured vinaigrette. For the vegetarians, there were quiches of red pepper and goat's cheese and dishes of chargrilled baby aubergines. For the teetotallers, there was a fruit punch with a base of elderflowers and local blackberries. For afters, there was vanilla and almond mousse, blueberry sorbet, and little cakes filled with cream after a

Swedish Easter recipe. Jevon's ex-lover ran the catering firm that supplied all this, and he'd just popped in to make sure there were no hitches in time for the two of them to have a quick soak in the Jacobean jacuzzi before the guests arrived.

'I must say,' said Roscoe Proudfoot to Dennis Rudgewick – Proudfoot had missed the lecture because of a conference in Tallinn on the Economics of Deep-Sea Fishing in the Millennium, but had flown in specially to take a look at Keynes Hall, 'I'd be surprised if a V-C's salary could pay for all this.'

Rosemary Leopard overheard his remark. Justin was hanging onto her, petrified that, if he didn't, someone would tell her about his sexual harassment case. 'Well, he's got a private income, hasn't he? He probably doesn't need a salary at all,' said Rosemary. She hadn't wanted to come, but had changed her mind at the last minute, because Justin seemed oddly keen to go without her.

Their eyes were out on stalks at the lavishness of the place – the polished Stuart parquetry of the floor, the glossy wood panelling, the carved cornices, the entablature supported by Ionic pilasters, the gilded ceiling with allegorical scenes of flowers and fruit, the Italian marble fireplaces, the marquetry on the walnut furniture – it all spoke of an indulgent elegance beyond most of their wildest dreams. 'I wonder who cleans this lot,' remarked Rosemary, running her finger across one of the protuberances in the wood panelling, to see if there was any dust on it. A tall Afro-Caribbean waiter with hollow cheeks appeared, and the silver tray he carried with the crystal glasses holding the Moët et Chandon bore no resemblance to the paltry implements of the sallow-faced students paid £2.50 an hour to service EMU receptions, who, at this very moment, were bundling the undrunk bottles of Hungarian Riesling into their lockers before Khadeeja emerged from her smoky kitchen gossip with the men from Building Services.

Rhena Malik from sociology was inflamed by the presence of a black waiter, and said so. 'Stuart households always had one black servant for show,' said Alan Livingstone, 'although they used to have a habit of escaping. It's a private house, Rhena, equal opportunities don't apply.'

'There was even,' put in Dennis Rudgewick, 'a peculiarly eighteenth-century form of insanity which was nothing more or less than slaves running away from their masters.'

The black waiter overheard this and gave them all a broad grin, which filled out his cheeks no end. 'Don't worry, my friends,' he counselled, 'I'm an actor the rest of the time. You may have seen me in *The Bill*. Joseph Padda's the name. I'd shake hands with you but I'd drop the Moët.'

'So why do you do this?' asked Rhena crossly.

'This is a fun house, darling, I have a fun time, lots of my friends are here.' He cast his flashing eyes a good deal further than the immediate net of EMU staff and their spouses, as far as the green-and-white striped marquee, whose flap was pinned open, giving an unimpeded vista all the way from the great front hall of the house to the lawns which stretched as smooth as a baby's bottom down to the artificial lake with its folly, modelled on an Alpine castle.

'The Oxborrow estate,' pronounced Lydia. 'What do you bet neither of us will achieve anything like this ever, Disa?'

'Marry a millionaire,' advised Bill Budgen, emboldened by the Moët, 'that's where you girls go wrong – you don't find enough rich men.'

'Give us a break, Bill. He never loses an opportunity, does he?'

It would be trite to say that everybody who was anybody was there at Stanley Oxborrow's party, because they weren't, although some of Sir Stanley's industrialist friends threw their corporate weight around: the head of the British office of Lingman's Bank could be glimpsed from time to time among the bushes of blackthorn that flanked the rose garden, and a couple of chaps from the Foreign Office conversed guardedly with a man resembling a bulldog who took care of the British Council's links with industry. Sir Stanley had sufficient experience of office parties to know that you needed outside blood at them or the in-fighting could be painful. Joseph Padda wasn't the only actor there. Also, several local landowners, carefully selected, and mostly wifeless, had been invited, and Sir Stanley's doctor, the usual silver-haired man from Wimpole Street, was to be observed popping open a classy bottle of water by the lake in the company of the Director of the END AIDS charity. Other than that, it was EMUs or others like them from elsewhere. The new head of Total Quality Management from EMU's competitor, the University of South Derbyshire, was a cut above the rest, and so was his friend who held the Münster Chair in Accountancy, funded by a European mobile phone company.

It was on Sir Stanley's agenda to get more industrial money into EMU. He was currently mounting a plan for a McDonald's Chair in Eating Disorders which he knew was hardly likely to go down well, so, to make it more palatable, he was hoping to induce his third cousin, who'd made a fortune in South Africa with a computer programme for anti-racism training, to endow another chair, in Hermeneutics and Post-modernism or Continental European Philosophy. It would look good in the EMU prospectus, and no doubt there'd be some students who'd find it exactly their cup of tea. After all, the words reeked of the very intellectual obscurantism which had made British universities what they were.

Looking around him, Sir Stanley wasn't dissatisfied. All this had been created by him; it was his estate, it had been paid for, then manicured and decorated with an authentic sense of style and passion. The people who were here were here because of him. He took pride in this; that he was the king, that without him Keynes Hall would still be crumbling into the ground as it had been when he'd found it, and EMU would have remained the seventeenth-rate university it was when he had been appointed. One day his daughters would speak to him again; but he wasn't that old, and he was in fine health (the silver-haired doctor from Wimpole Street checked him over twice a year), and he could wait. Meanwhile, it was consoling to get visits from Venetia, his granddaughter, a solicitor working with battered women. Venetia kept him up to date with radical politics, and it was to her he owed the inspiration for Lydia Mallinder's chair, and the new honours and diploma course in Gender Studies combined with practically anything else a student wanted to do, provided they could find someone to teach them whatever it was. Flexibility and the importance of choice was what the brochure advertised. Once they got there, the students might discover that another word for this was chaos, but by then it was thankfully too late. As to Lydia, even Venetia would admit that sometimes women had to be restrained from taking themselves too seriously.

Sir Stanley strolled upstairs to slip out of his formal suit and into something more comfortable. Natural preference would have led him to pick his sapphire shantung caftan, but he reminded himself that this wasn't one of his ordinary parties, so a pale blue shirt and a tuxedo embroidered with peacocks over a pair of stone linen slacks would do instead. There was laughter from the powder closet as he passed it, and the door of the green bedroom, which stood ajar, emitted the sound of percale sheets rustling like sparrows in the eaves. Stanley smiled. He'd bought Keynes Hall to bring the place to life, and so sounds of life were exactly what he wanted to hear in it.

After the rain, it had turned into a fine evening, and a gentle dusk passed into a star-spangled night, but most of the people at the Keynes Hall party were too busy for star-gazing. In any case, the floodlights by the house and the marquee mercilessly blazed forth their stunning light, and rabbits, scurrying across the motorway of the Keynes Hall lawn, mistook them for the headlights of cars.

Jevon put Pavarotti on the CD and loud-speakers dis-gorged Verdi's *Otello* over the rabbits' scurrying, and the conversations about private and public lives, and the crunching of salmon bones, and the slithering of baby potatoes down greasy throats.

'Justin, you've had enough,' said Rosemary, whacking his stomach.

'I'll go back on the diet next week, Rosie,' promised Justin. 'You absolutely can't deny me some of those gorgeous-looking puddings.'

Lydia slipped a freezer bag out of her purse and pilfered a good portion of salmon for Huneyball. She thought she'd been very clever about it, but when she turned round with that guilty look worn by people unused to criminal activi-ties, Jevon Tricker was watching her with a bulging cream cake half-way to his lips. He took the cake away and put his finger there instead. 'Shush, I won't tell,' he promised.

'It's for my cat.'

'Quite so. Your secret's safe with me.'

'Hallo, Lydia.' Stephanie was dressed in a ribbon-strapped cream satin dress with a gold choker and many gold and silver bangles. Her skin was also golden, and her hair was much lighter and curlier than it used to be. The whole effect was to make her look like a poodle. Someone's expensively pampered and bird-brained pet.

'Stephanie. How was your holiday?' Lydia took the suntan as a sign she'd had one.

'Oh, we haven't got away yet. I'm admissions tutor, you know, for two of our joint MAs. It was pandemonium when the A-level results came out. Especially given the introduction of tuition fees next year. But after that we hope to get a couple of weeks in Tuscany.'

Lydia nodded without interest.

'Lydia,' said Stephanie, in the same tone of voice Jeremy had used when he wanted to call her attention to something in a patronizing way, 'there's something I think you ought to know. There's no way of breaking this news easily, I'm afraid. Jeremy and I are having A Relationship. I wanted to tell you myself, rather than you just finding out. I told Jeremy he should, but he's a coward in these matters. As I'm sure you know.' Stephanie's laughter tinkled again, part of a fugue with her bracelets.

Lydia just looked at Stephanie, and then walked away without saying anything. What was there to say? Stephanie was welcome to him. Well, she wasn't actually, because relationships don't die, they take time to fade away. It made sense. This was what Jeremy hadn't been telling her. They made a good pair. But what would happen to her? Panic, the other half of love, set in. Where was Giles? He hadn't been in touch with her since he'd got back from Japan. She had a sudden longing to talk to Sidony. Looking round the crowd in the hall and in the dining room, she couldn't see her. There was much noise and laughter from upstairs. Lydia looked up and saw the little group at the top of the stairs, and went up to see if Sidony was one of them.

The west staircase of Keynes Hall had some extremely nice acanthus scrolls on it, and Sir Stanley was pointing these out to one of the industrialists from London, who wanted to see the house. Other people eavesdropped, and began to follow the two men, and Sir Stanley soon became a kind of tour guide. 'Now, sanitation,' he explained, 'was rudimentary, of course. The waste closet had been invented by the time this wing of the house was built, but the plans included only one closet, which we find here.' He flung open a narrow door. It had been preserved as it was, and a large ivy trailed its glossy leaves round the old stone seat and the tiny window. 'But Keynes Hall is unusual among houses of this period for having a bathroom. The marble is from Italy. Water had to be heated in the kitchen and brought up here.'

Graham Piper, EMU's registrar, over-dressed in a stiff white shirt and a bow tie, flashed a short smile at Lydia from above his little beard. She gave him an equally artificial one back. They were looking in the bedrooms now; four-poster after four-poster, with each room given over to a different colour: rose, vanilla, green, dark blue, pale orange, deep purple, sandalwood yellow. 'Themed, the Americans call it,' said one of the industrialists, somewhat crassly.

Lydia couldn't see Sidony anywhere. She paused on the gallery and looked down. A fire had been lit in the chimney breast, and the huge logs spat the scent of English apples into the air. Through the enormous arched door which led into the garden she could see that the rain had returned, curtaining off Keynes Hall from the night, and painting the scene inside as an esplanade of medieval jollity. She pictured Sir Stanley Oxborrow sitting at the dark oak table that stretched the length of the hall, wearing a dark velvet doublet and cap and the primped muslin of the Elizabethan period, helping himself to a pewter tankard of spiced burnet wine, with the table in front of him piled with boars' heads and cygnets and larks and sucking pigs, and dishes of quince pie and sweetmeats and marigold cheese and medlars with cloves and eyringo jelly.

There would be ladies at the tables with pinched waists and ruffs, and an entourage of velveted courtiers at whom, in the fierce apple-light of the fire, Sir Stanley would look with lascivious intent. As the scene took place in her mind, she embroidered it with puppy dogs running around, and babies in lace caps and muslin gowns sucking at matronly breasts, and silver swords dangling on the walls, and sheaves of aromatic herbs – chamomile, comfrey, lavender, lamb mint, motherwort – hung over it all to conceal the stench of drains, perspiration, disease and death. Up here, where she was, minstrels would be playing their mandolins and wooden flutes. All of life would be here, and Keynes Hall would be famous for its feasts and its jousting and its lovemaking. When the meat dripping with blood had been eaten and the fine fruit wine and strong mead had been drunk, then the big table would be pushed back and the dancing would begin.

Brief lives – for that was what they were in those days – could nonetheless be happy ones. It was one of the most seductive dogmas of our time that reducing risk to produce longevity would also bring happiness. Quality versus quantity: the very point Lydia and Giles Tingey had discussed, and which, in some measure, though perhaps not if she were to believe Elliot Blankthorn's warning, she had succeeded in driving home. With only three or four, or at most five, decades instead of seven or eight, people would have valued the moment then more than they do now, thought Lydia, and they would have pressed it to yield as much laughter and pleasure and loving as they possibly could, just as the elderberries that went into the wine would have been crushed so that the rich red juice came running out in gushing streams. The women would have died in childbirth, unable to stop the blood flowing from them as though they themselves were elderberries, or trapped by the skeletons of fetuses too big to pass through the gateways of their inadequately nourished hips, and the diseases of love, to which we now much more mundanely attribute the acronym of STDs, would have been rife, breaking out in yellow discharges and chancres all over the place, and then seeding themselves into the hearts and brains where love comes from, the sexual organs being merely servants of mental desire. Young men would have died young, and the muslin caps of babies would have been handed down from one dead sibling to another. But such facts of life would have been unremarkable. The frame within which life is lived, like the elaborate decor of the west staircase of Keynes Hall, has been metaphorical for most of human history, and it's only our culture now that insists we remember it all the time, so that nothing we do is without reference to it. Don't eat too much of the wrong thing, or you'll get heart disease; drink water to flush the system out, and half a glass of red wine a day will burn the cholesterol out of those clogged-up arteries; smoke and you'll be damned; run and you might die; walk and you'll be saved; enclose your bodily parts in luminous condoms and see if it's love you can make like that; search for cancers everywhere with the eyes of the very rays that cause them; sleep if you can stop worrying about all of this.

Lydia rubbed her eyes and looked again at the scene below, but it had vanished, all of it; all the laughter, all the indulgences; all the denial of mortality. The apple-light of the fire still flickered on the walls and in the air; and the twentieth-century figures from Sir Stanley's party supped their Moët and their Perrier, and talked of stocks and shares and mad cow disease and plane crashes and the murders of little children and the sacking of big ones and of ARQs and TRUs and PRIC and the troubling business of over-heads, according to which the people who have, receive more, only to have it taken away from them; and they left plates with scrapings of salmon bones and curly lettuce like waves and deposits of cream on them untidily on the table and in the deep stone recesses of the windows, which held in their uneven squares the wet starry blue of the night.

Lydia left the gallery and went into the east wing. Most of the doors were ajar, and she pushed each one gingerly, not knowing what she might find, but it wasn't either Giles or Sidony. In one room, unlit except for a fat white candle, Graham Piper and Richard Winkett were sitting next to each other on the high damask mound of a bed. 'Sorry,' she said. Next door, the room was dark, but there were heavings in the bed and Lydia thought she could hear Jevon's throaty falsetto laughter, but as an owl hooted at the same time through the soaking counterpane in the open window, she couldn't be sure.

In the Italian marble bathroom, Justin Leopard was feeling distinctly ill. He had eaten too much and drunk too much, and there was a nagging pain on the left side of his body. He sat on the floor with the fastenings round his neck and his waist undone. Rosemary was somewhere else. He didn't want her here anyway, berating him for his sins of over-indulgence. He wasn't sure he wanted Lydia either, but in she tripped as light and as undrunk as a fairy. 'Don't you ever overdo things?' he groaned.

The perfect, retributive image of her clean, neat face floated in front of him and he pushed it away, but Lydia said, 'It's only a moth, Justin, they're attracted by the light.'

'Sod it,' he said.

'I'm going to get you a glass of water.'

'Don't minister to me,' he objected, 'I don't need any

bloody angels of mercy, I can look after myself, thank you very much.' He shut his eyes and felt perspiration stream down his face. He felt sick. The pain seemed to be worse. 'Go away,' he cried, 'for God's sake, go away!'

Lydia left, and went on to the library, so-called because it had books in it, although few of them had actually been read. Callum and Sir Stanley were propped up in front of a mahogany leather row of them. 'You'll like this one,' Callum was saying confidently to Sir Stanley, and not talking about a book. 'A student gave it to me, I believe he found it on the World Wide Web.' Stanley blinked: he didn't think of Callum as someone who had students.

'Why doesn't God have a PhD?' started Callum. 'He only had one publication, it had no references, the scientific community has had a hard time replicating his results, he didn't have ethics committee permission, he had his son teach his classes, his office hours were infrequent and usually held on a mountain top!' Callum roared with laughter.

Sir Stanley smiled. 'Can I talk to you about the new MCC, Callum?'

'Marylebone Cricket Club?'

'No, Management Consultancy Centre. We're going to set one up at EMU.'

'Are we?'

'The question is: where should it sit in relation to the IDS?'

'Ah.'

'As a matter of fact, I think the place of such centres isn't clear within the IDS as presently organized. Should they be free-standing, or should they be School-based, or even department-based? What do you think, Callum?'

Callum's ability to think had seen less hazy times. 'As a matter of fact,' he ventured, copying Stanley, 'I think we need to develop some research centres in EMU. I've thought so for some time. It's a separate point, of course. But a similar argument.'

Roscoe Proudfoot strolled up to them with a large wet umbrella.

'You should have left that downstairs,' reprimanded Stanley. 'Jevon! Jevon!'

'I think he's busy,' offered Lydia, but they ignored her.

'That was a plan I conceived myself,' chorused Roscoe, opening the window and shaking his umbrella out of it, which didn't make much difference, as it was raining again. 'On the train back from Groningen. A conference on the Economics of Information Technology. I made some very useful connections.'

'Where do you get the money from for all these conferences, Roscoe?' It was a question Lydia had been dying to ask for some time.

The truth was that Roscoe had been paying all his consultancy money into a private bank account which he'd opened at the Halifax building society in Motley. That's how all sorts of things in Business Studies were paid for, not just Roscoe Proudfoot's trips, but a new information technology laboratory, a reception suite for local business links, and the latest office furniture for everybody. Roscoe could hardly admit this, in view of the new policy on consultancy income (which he himself had devised on the way back from a seminar on Alternative Models of Financing Higher Education in Sardinia).

'They pay me,' he said. 'They pay my expenses, I mean.'

'Pull the other one, Roscoe,' said Lydia. Roscoe's eyebrows started to shake. His shoulders shot up and that odd epileptic sound of his started again.

'Back to the business of the MCC,' said Stanley urbanely. 'I thought perhaps linked both to Business Studies and SSACS, in view of the policy connection? There's a space between the Health Centre and the Library. I've had some plans drawn up. Winkett and Bacon would head it, of course. There are some staff who we could usefully pull out of other departments. You've got Mrs Ginger, haven't you, Roscoe, teaches on your Principles of Economic Theory course? Four hours a week only. We should have sacked – well, erhm, considered a constructive reappraisal of her duties, but well, we didn't. She might, perhaps, be regraded as an administrator. Women are terribly good at administration. And Callum, I think we might find a few branches of dead wood in SSACS if we look not all that hard, couldn't we?'

Lydia didn't believe her ears. Redundancies all round, and now this! She should have said something, for it would have been in character for her to defend her position, but the conjoined power of these men, so cosily plotting together, in wilful ignorance of such notions as justice and fair play, only made her want to escape to a black hole somewhere where she could block out this world and run another set of scenes through her head. She should have stayed at LSE. It was time she took the salmon home to Huneyball. At least he would be waiting for her with his uneven loving eyes, his wet nose lovingly poised to burrow into the hollow of her neck.

On her way out, she passed Sidony Wormleighton coming in. 'I've been looking everywhere for you,' said Lydia. 'I decided you were boycotting it.'

'I was, my dear, but then I thought what a golden opportunity to publicize the Clean Up St Nick's Campaign. Did you know that Sir Stanley *himself* has put up the money for the END AIDS charity to supply these horrendous sanitary arrangements in the churchyard?' Sidony turned round and beckoned at the ornamental shrubbery which spewed forth the figures of Phyllis and Mrs Scarsdale, both of whom carried what looked like waste-paper bins covered in fluor-escent paper. The injunction PLEASE KEEP MOTLEY CLEAN ran round the bottoms of the bins. 'Got them from the council,' explained Sidony. 'This'll teach them!'

The three women marched upstairs, with Lydia follow-ing. They bore the huge glow-worms of the bins straight to Sir Stanley's converted powder closet, where the heart-shaped jacuzzi throbbed with the pink-gold body of Trent Lovett and the whiter one of Elliot Blankthorn. They dropped the bins on the floor with a clang. Trent's mouth dropped open, and reflexively he re-pressed the jacuzzi button so that the white bubbles frothed and foamed hiding the most private bits of him and Elliot from the women's staring eyes.

'So that's where you were!' said Lydia. Elliot reached for his glasses, which were hanging on an ornate brass shelf, but they were all misted up so he still found it hard to see what was going on.

'Now,' said Mrs Scarsdale authoritatively. 'This is to learn you fun-loving chaps a lesson.' She put her hands on her ship-like hips and might as well have been wearing an apron. 'It's no use dumping your rubbers and worse for other folks to clear up, because no gentleman in 'is right mind'd do that. Didn't you learn no manners where you came from? And don't talk to me about aitch eye vee and suchlike, because we've got bovine spongiform encephalitis to contend with, 'aven't we, Mrs Worms?'

'The moral right,' pronounced Elliot from the jacuzzi, finally grasping the point.

'That's right, the moral right,' agreed Sidony, 'with a mes-sage for the immoral left. Clean up your act, or we'll do it for you.'

'It's got nothing to do with me,' protested Elliot.

'Or me,' echoed Trent.

'Well, it is just a bit more to do with you than me,' pointed out Elliot placatingly.

'Oh dear.' Callum's bulk filled the doorway. There were far too many people in the small vaporous room, and the rubbish bins didn't help. 'Oh dear, Sidony, what on earth have you been up to now?'

'Just a little demo, Callum,' she told him firmly. 'Don't worry about it.'

What happened next was quite sufficient to distract them all from their internecine conflicts.

'See the conquering hero comes,' sang someone from behind Callum. They all stopped in their tracks. 'Well, he's hardly one to talk, is he? What a hotbed of vice we have here. What a can of worms, oh dear, oh dear! I suppose you all know what WORM stands for? Write once, read many. It's one plot multiplied many times. You're all variations on a theme; you're all as bad as one another!'

Turning round, they saw in the doorway, framed like a modern painting, the modernity achieved in part by the colourful disarray of his person, yellow hair standing nearly on end above a bright red T-shirt with a faded portrait of Che Guevara on it, and blue and green plaid trousers quite worthy of one of Jeremy Krest's television appearances, but with unattractively gaping holes in the knees, Giles Tingey.

'You're off your rocker.' It was Callum who spoke first. He shook his head sadly.

'He's right, of course,' observed Sidony, meaning Giles rather than Callum.

'Well, he's right about Worms, at least,' observed Elliot.

'Modernity and intimacy,' muttered Trent, from beneath the jacuzzi bubbles.

At first Lydia had trouble recognizing Giles, and then, when she did, she stepped forward to try to take his arm and establish some contact with him, but, no sooner had she stepped forward to claim him, than off Giles ran, off down the stairs, back through the great hall with its firelit shadows and out of Keynes Hall and down the driveway to the Winkett and Bacon Volvo that he'd parked by the stone lions at the gates, finally vanishing in a burst of unleaded petrol fumes.

Inside the house, someone screamed in the marble bathroom. Callum, whose body was still blocking the powder closet door, went to investigate. He found Rosemary Leopard sobbing over the prostrate figure of Justin, who looked like a sleeping tramp on the floor. 'He's dead, he's dead!' shrieked Rosemary.

Callum stooped and felt in the heap of disarrayed clothes for Justin's pulse. 'I don't think so,' he said. Trent Lovett, an acre of fluffy white towel around him, followed, mobile phone in hand. He flicked the aerial upwards and called for an ambulance.

CHAPTER 13

Wild Life in the City

Justin Leopard stayed in the coronary care unit of Motley Regional Hospital for five days, with Rosemary mostly by his side. It wasn't a major infarct, but it wasn't a minor one, either. Justin was glad to be alone, but when he woke up with all those tubes and wires attached to him, his second thought was that he was now going to have to do all the things like lose weight and stop drinking beer that Rosemary had been going on about. Then he realized he'd probably missed the sexual harassment case, but had Rosemary?

'I'll be a reformed character, Rosie,' he promised, and hoped this would cover it.

Giles Tingey had completely disappeared. There was no trace of the Winkett and Bacon Volvo, and he'd only dropped into his suite in The Country Pie briefly to fetch some things. Richard Winkett talked to Giles' mother and his brother, who both intimated that Giles had always had a sensitive side, but there was no history of anyone going off their rocker in the Tingey or Oxborrow families. Sir Stanley confirmed that. 'We can only wait for him to turn up,' he counselled Giles' mother. 'I don't expect it'll be long before we get a sighting.'

'You make him sound like a wild animal,' complained Roberta.

Sir Stanley asked Callum to have lunch with him in The Mitre for a change. The dish of the day was pheasant breasts in green peppercorn sauce. With it they had a bottle of Cabernet Sauvignon. 'Tragic about Leopard,' said Stanley. 'Mind the shot in that, Callum, there's hardly an NHS dentist to be found in the whole of Northamptonshire any more. Now about your wife.' He refilled Callum's glass. 'I expect what happened back in August was a little hard on her, wasn't it? But maybe she doesn't have enough to do. I do think that's one of the good developments for women over the last fifty years, don't you think? More employment; the important thing in life is to keep oneself occupied.

'But,' said Stanley, running his long hands down his blue and green paisley tie in a gesture that could be interpreted as thoughtful, 'she does seem to have a problem which, well, quite frankly, perhaps you should talk to her about. In fact, I thought we'd settled it when we had a word about you and that other business. How was Bayreuth, by the way?'

Without waiting for Callum to answer this, Sir Stanley went on: 'I could put two and two together. That is, what happened in August and what happened in my home last week. Not much interested in sex, ever, was she, Callum? A trifle cold, maybe? The dear lady I married was somewhat like that. I've often thought it's something the upper classes haven't quite sorted out. What are women for? They're not supposed to work, and they are supposed to breed, but rather like racehorses – in between times the desire's got to be all bridled up. Which really means it's better if they don't have any.

'Ah well. Let's have some cheese, shall we? I fancy a nice bit of stilton. I've got a meeting with the architect this afternoon. About the MCC, you know. I'd like to get it off the ground before I go. Can you deputize for me at the Degrees Board?

'I knew you would. Now, about Sidony's problem. Homophobia. Are you coming to the Equality Committee next week? We're going to discuss the new guidelines for grievance procedures. Got to tighten up our act, you know. Part of being a modern university – towards the millennium and all that.'

Callum got the message, but Sidony was unrepentant. It seemed she, like the university, had a Mission. 'I'm going up to London next week, Callum,' she told him, 'to Charities House. I want to look up this AIDS charity Sir Stanley's involved with.'

Callum always wondered why Sidony talked about going 'up' to London when it was really down. He decided to leave it for the time being. He was knee-deep in hotel brochures for the Salzburg opera festival. He was veering towards the Schloss Mönchstein, a fairy-tale castle covered in vines with wonderful gardens and a lordly view over the city.

While Callum contemplated marital harmony and Mozart arias, Lydia talked to her cat. 'Things aren't going well for me, Huneyball. In either the men or the work department.' She was thumbing through the job ads in the *THES*. 'Something – or someone – tells me it's time to move on. "Hong-Kong Baptist University, Associate Professor in Social Studies." No, I don't think so, too far away. "Senior Lecturer in Media Studies, Thameside University." No more a proper university than this one, and a step down as well. "Nottingham Trent University, Research Programme Leader" – what on earth's that? "Considerable management experience" – oh, no. "Fellowship at Magdalene College, Cambridge", that's better. ". . . Gross stipend . . . £11,800 per annum." Impossible!

'The trouble is, Huneyball,' – the cat was asleep on the

microwave – 'I'm not going to get a chair anywhere else until I've finished this wretched book. Yes, I know, finish the wretched book then. But how can I do that with all this nonsense going on? It looks as though we're going to lose at least one lecturer post this year. There's a ten per cent increase in the intake for three of our courses and twenty per cent for the ones we do jointly with Public Policy and Environmental Studies.' (Stephanie had had to give way on Gender and Development.) 'The Dean wants us to develop this combined social welfare honours course, but Justin's heart attack has put a stop on that for the time being. I spend most of my time trying to fix Charlie's machine anyway. We never should have embarked on this Windows 95 upgrading.' The cat stirred and his tail fell sideways over the oven. 'And did I tell you the news about the library? RIPS has decided it's got to make twenty per cent more this year on fines and photocopying. It's fifty pence a day now, unless you're a friend of Gaynor's. Photo-copying's gone up to twenty pence a page. An enterprising lad in Business Studies has set up a service for the students – he takes the photocopying round to Instant Print in the City Centre, they do it for ten pence a page and he gets five pence commission.'

They had a leaving party for Fern and for Martin Pippard, and for Jeff in Building Services and for several others, all of whom threatened to boycott it. But they all came in the end, having laid down the condition (communicated informally via Phyllis) that Sir Stanley had to stay away. He was relieved. Callum could make a speech instead.

The sadness of the occasion was intensified by the unre-mitting rain, and the consequent smell of damp umbrellas, raincoats and hair, but was relieved by Fern's small boys, who were brought by their artistic father, and Rosemary

Leopard brought Justin, who was making his first appearance since his heart attack, and Amos as well, though not Carey, who wouldn't be seen dead at anything to do with EMU. Amos Leopard and Eiran Meredith made a good team. But when they started sticking toothpicks up each other's noses, Phyllis separated them forcibly, making comments of the kind Justin had heard from the matron at the village fête earlier in the summer.

Rosemary was talking to Martin Pippard in an attempt to get some advice about whether Justin should be on e-mail at home, now he needed to take life more calmly, which meant spending more time away from the office. Martin was no more interested in the technical needs of EMU staff now he was leaving than he had been when he was one of them. Lydia, passing, overheard Rosemary doggedly pursuing her enquiry. She offered the opinion that Justin needed some help with e-mail in the office first before he could be expected to make much sense of it at home. 'It can be very stressful,' she observed.

'That's right,' agreed Martin, to her surprise, 'it can. There are some shocking things going on out there on the World Wide Web.'

Lydia always envisaged it as a huge cobweb stretching right across the galaxy. But at least she knew what Martin meant, whereas the term had to be explained to Rosemary, who did her I'm-only-a-rural-housewife-and-part-time-copy-editor number, which had been unconvincing for as long as anyone could remember.

'I found something that might interest you the other day,' remarked Martin conversationally, giving Lydia a fixed, slightly malignant look. 'W-A-S-H,' he pronounced meaningfully.

Coming on top of Rosemary's comments about housewifery, it wasn't clear what he meant. 'What?'

'Women Against Sexual Harassment. It's some sort of international network. Of women who organize strategies to uncover some of what they imagine is going on.' He laid the stress on *imagine*. 'I'm surprised you don't know about it. There are some rather, well, local, connections. I think you ought to take a look at it. Here you are,' Martin took a card out of his pocket, 'I wrote the address down for you.'

'Martin Pippard, Freelance Internet Consultant,' proclaimed the card.

'That's my new life,' he explained. 'There's a huge demand for the services of people like me out there.'

'There was a huge demand for them here, too,' observed Lydia.

'I took the view,' said Martin, and it was to be quite the longest pronouncement he'd ever made in his time at EMU, 'that those of you who were stupid didn't deserve to be helped, and those who weren't would be able to work it out for themselves. There's nothing magic about computing. It's neither a science nor an art. Besides which, the World Wide Web is much more interesting than you lot, with the possible exception of some of your e-mails. I don't expect you know this, which is why I'm telling you, but when you delete an e-mail message it doesn't disappear, which is what you might think it would do. Oh, no! It stays on the server, where it can still be read by those who have the confidential password. Such as myself. Which is how,' he added, in anticipation of her possible next question, 'I know that some of the W-A-S-H newsgroup's accusations may not be all that far out.'

Lydia turned the card over: 'http://www.witch–wash.org.fi.'

'Try it,' ordered Martin.

She did. Huneyball got in the way of the list of group addresses when she got it up on the screen, and she turfed him off the desk rather harshly in her haste to read it. There, as she had suspected, was Judy Sammons's name. There were various subfiles. One of these made it clear that it'd been Judy herself who'd put forward the idea, received with much enthusiasm by women in Finland and Spain and Italy particularly, that one could easily fabricate scenarios of purported harassment in order to put the structure of patriarchy on its toes.

The rest of September had been wet, and now, in October, the climate around EMU was dry and cold. A lemon sun staggered up the sky each day, and proceeded to shine weakly on the crimson and gold crispy curls of fallen leaves and on the bright red bricks of the new housing estate by the roundabout, where a few net curtains had now appeared at the windows. Circular washing lines and tubular climbing frames were planted on the squares of open ground at the backs of the houses, which might one day be gardens. In Corporation Street, round the corner from Lydia, the Electricity Board erected a pylon. It had one foot inside someone's front gate and the other foot inside someone else's. There was an outcry, and much talk of the consequences for people's health, and Dennis Rudgewick applied to the Department of Health for money to carry out a survey of consumer attitudes. The people inside whose front gate the pylon had appeared were quite old anyway, so the project fitted his general area of interest.

Lydia took to walking around Motley at night. It helped her with the metaphors of degeneration and decay she was working on for her book, and she also slept better afterwards. One night she set off as usual down Studfall Avenue, past Jilly's Dress Agency and the Frying Scotsman, where people queued to buy all sorts of things in batter. She'd seen Trent Lovett there once, his Candia Orange Max Alu bike outside strapped to itself with two U-locks, and a contingent of teenage boys trying to get their greasy hands on it. Trent had just smiled and waved, and Lydia had walked straight on. He clearly wanted her to believe he was a good thing, because shortly after this he'd sent her a copy of a report on children's attitudes to town centres. Only seven per cent loved them and seventy-six per cent thought them dirty. The word 'pretty' scored with only twenty-nine per cent. But, strangely, few children (only five per cent) thought city centres were actually *dangerous* places.

Lydia was idly looking in the window of the What Everyone Wants DIY Superstore at some multicoloured coffee machines when she saw a figure behind her in the glass. When she looked round, she could have sworn the legs she saw beating a retreat behind the bedding shop were Giles Tingey's. She followed them; but in the desert of the car park behind the shopping centre only a shopping trolley moved, drunkenly, in the wind, towards a dented and abandoned Vauxhall. There *was* a sense of menace in this urban wasteland, where in the daytime consumers came and consumed, and the thistles that stuck out of the gravelled surface were trampled by a clomping, urgent busyness, and tempers rustled even more than the plastic bags people crammed wildly into their car boots, defending themselves against the feeling of emptiness they had if they didn't buy, buy, buy.

Lydia walked on fast. Beyond the farcical Hawaiian Snack Shack, there was a row of lock-up garages to let and then a sign which said, CIVIC AMENITY TIP. She turned left onto the main road, where at least there would be cars passing, so she wouldn't be alone. After a bit, she felt foolish to have panicked back there in the car park. Dreadful things happened in the countryside and in London, but in the dingy metropolis of Motley the only things that moved after dark were the teenagers into nightclubs, and the lads who hungered after chips from places other than the Frying Scotsman. Lydia recalled, for some reason, that odd statement Giles Tingey had made when they'd met in that pub the day he'd woken her with his phone call: 'Some moments in history are more transitional than others.' Of course it was time to move on. Her reading of the *THES* job ads to Huneyball was comical, but the underlying motive was a perfectly serious one. But there was the chicken-and-the-egg problem. Should she resign before she got a new job, or should she land some superlative future first?

The low building on her right was Motley magistrates' court. It presented a squarely reassuring sense of law and order – that there should be such a building with such a function must surely say something important in itself. Beyond the roundabout was the city park and the boating lake. The water sparkled in the street light which penetrated the black lace of the trees. Something moved again. Don't be silly, said Lydia to herself. What my parents' generation used to call courting couples must have somewhere to go, even in October.

The water on the boating lake threw its satin coalface up at the autumn sky, which had begun to gather into itself the first sightings of winter. Lydia shivered. A low wind passed between the trees. Presence, and absence: and something in between. She buttoned her coat up, driven by a voice from childhood, those warnings that come back to all of us at odd and dangerous moments: keep warm; watch where you're going; cross the road if you think there's someone behind you; wash your hands before eating; smile, things could be worse. I did, and they were, thought Lydia. It was her mother's voice wrapping her in maternal reprimands and injunctions, all designed to protect. Repetition drives the point home; and who knows whether or not something said by a mother to her child will come back out of the void of the past like a comet whizzing its fiery point into the present, so that the words re-form and do their protective job again?

Lydia would have liked her mother to be alive now. She would have liked to have fallen back into that cocoon of familiarity that comes from being with the person who knew you even before you were born. Your early stirrings; all that tumbling and hiccuping in the womb; the sleeps and the purple-blue pulsations of the unborn child. The person who grasped you as you came tearing your way out, breathing pink and bloody for the first time, and held you, recognizing your smell, and saw in your infant grimaces and cries and silences this awesome continuity with the child before birth; time past and time present coalescing in the deep maternal knowledge of the moment. Yes, she would have liked to slip back into this comfortable and peaceful place – the very place, of course, that young people, such as Justin and Rosemary Leopard's Carey, try so hard to get out of.

Lydia's mother should still have been alive – she would have been only sixty-five now, and it would have been an active, demanding sixty-five, not an acquiescent, retiring one. But she'd died in the middle of Lydia's unpleasant fights with LSE about sex discrimination, of a suppurating breast cancer which raced its way through her body, and which left Lydia bereft of the opportunity to be a child ever again, and of the chance to measure herself against the necessary standard of what her mother was, and wanted for her.

The past is dreadfully powerful, but so is fear of the future. A clock chimed somewhere, and a car passed in an alcoholic frenzy, zigagging across the road. Motherhood was going to be Disa Loring's escape. Disa and Danny were having a baby in May. Disa was delighted, not only about the prospect of having a child, but because it seemed to solve the problem of her career at EMU. 'I'm going for the part-time post of European Officer,' Disa had told Lydia, when she'd confessed to the pregnancy. And all of this was under the careful tutelage of Fern Meredith, who instructed Disa and any other woman prepared to listen about the mythology of women's liberation. 'We can't do it all, and we shouldn't be expected to; we've been misled by our sisters,' she cried, sounding very like the general chorus of backlashers against feminism who occupied much space in the media these days. Men invented civilization and should be rewarded for it, so they said, whereas women invited rape and should stay home at night, and should certainly not do what Lydia was doing now.

Standing by the black boating lake, Lydia no longer had that sense of personal menace that had gripped her in the city centre. She felt almost like a tree; stationary, watching, inanimate. She was cold to the bone, and about to turn back and go home, when in the neon light between the trees loped something that had more legs than Giles Tingey. It was at least four feet long, and it had a wild arched tail, and it moved with such a speed that you would never have been able to countenance it unless you had the evidence right there in front of your eyes.

CHAPTER 14

Headlines

Justin, thoroughly back at work and feeling the strain, had been getting Jim Leonard's mail again. 'Test for RNase before it ruins your experiments,' shouted the green and white catalogue at him, 'The RNaseWatch Kit is a dipstick-based assay . . . if there is RNase contamination, a blue dot will appear on the membrane tab'.

How simple science is, thought Justin naively. It struck him that *social* scientists like him must be very clever people indeed to work with interviews and observations rather than dipsticks and experiments, and having to suss out many more forms of contamination using much more sophisticated means. But he did put his hand over his heart, feeling how grateful one ought nevertheless to be to medical science.

'Onwards, upwards and forwards,' was how Sir Stanley had put it at the presentation ceremony yesterday. Lots of students in gowns they would probably never wear again, the young men in their ill-fitting only suits, the young women tottering on and off the platform in unaccustomed high heels, and all with shining faces and Timotei-ed hair, and proud parents with hats and video cameras whirring.

Justin had sat on the platform with everyone else, biting his nails with hunger. He'd got his new diet sheet pinned up in his office, over the old one. The new one was more scientific, provided by the hospital dietician, so he had more faith in it than in Rosemary's witch-hunting manual. Muesli for breakfast, wholemeal bread and salad for lunch, grilled fish or chicken (without skin) and vegetables for supper. Nothing in between. Justin's abuse of his body had become a kind of eccentricity – the eating, smoking, drinking, non-exercising Justin Leopard. As cultural engagement with the mission of a healthy lifestyle increased, so Justin had turned the product of his unhealthy one, his unfit body, to his own advantage, becoming a sort of antitext for the biblical doctrines of the health-for-all movement. HFA: not even a decent acronym. Dennis Rudgewick and he had already had some verbal tussles about it. Justin was thankful he hadn't gone into health himself, because then he would have had to become healthy, just as medical students get all the diseases they read about. The next thing on the HFA agenda was jogging. Rosemary had bought him some of those ridiculous shiny shorts and a skimpy vest.

The good news was that Judy Sammons had decided to drop her case before Rosemary had had to find out about it. Lydia had said that Judy had felt sorry for him when he collapsed and went into the CCU. Justin wanted to believe this, but all of them found altruism a difficult concept these days, and he rather fancied there was more to it than that. The light of complicity had shone from Lydia's eyes when she'd told him the glad news. Justin had passed his supervisory role entirely over to Lydia now; whatever the truth of the matter, he could hardly meet Judy for an earnest behind-closed-doors discussion ever again. Justin was both disappointed and relieved; he was disappointed because for a while there Judy's *Claire's Knee* persona had rejuvenated his own energy and faith in the future; he was relieved because now he wouldn't have to read all that dense post-modernist stuff: Derrida, Irigaray, Cixous, someone called

Bell Hooks, who was apparently spelt bell hooks, which he'd kept correcting in Judy's quite promising but obscure Chapter One, and then this person called Cocks, which Justin had thought was another mistake, who wrote on political theory and the dialectics of opposition, and from whom Justin was especially glad to have been saved.

But Justin hadn't heard the end of Judy Sammons. The week after he returned to work, he got a call from the V-C's office asking him to come and see Sir Stanley immediately.

Justin had been told by his doctors always to take stairs rather than lifts, but this was easy at EMU, because there were very few lifts.

Sir Stanley was waving a newspaper around and looking unusually discomposed. Few of them had ever seen him looking anything other than his smooth, carefully put together, suave and suntanned self. It appeared that Judy had written a short piece for the *THES* about her research on the position of academic women. In it she'd cited the refusal of Sir Stanley to allow EMU to be used as a case-study, and suggested that the permission had been refused for malign reasons. There followed – Sir Stanley handed the piece over for Justin to see it with his own eyes – a statistical recitation which, Justin had to admit, looked on the surface quite convincing. Women as a percentage of professors at EMU, 2.7 per cent: of readers and senior lecturers, 5.8 per cent; of lecturers, 20 per cent; of miscellaneous others (including researchers – Beverley and Candida et al. would not be happy with this classification), 50.3 per cent. And all these figures were significantly different from the national picture. That is, worse.

'Well,' said Justin, standing on Sir Stanley's soft Wilton, and with Sir Stanley's relentlessly piercing eyes upon him, 'at least you're in good company. I mean you – we – weren't the only place to turn her down. See, it says here . . .'

'I know what it says there, Leopard, I've read it. Five other places said no. Well, no-one wants their dirty linen washed in public, do they? *You* didn't, after all.'

Justin didn't know quite where to look at this point, so he looked at Sir Stanley's pictures. Their poorly articulated limbs made him think of last night's news items about bits of bodies being found in black plastic sacs in Belgium. But why was Sir Stanley talking to him about all this? He wasn't even Judy's supervisor any more.

'Leopard,' said Sir Stanley, 'you're not concentrating. What I want to know is, where did the woman get these figures from? They're not published. So where did she get them?'

'Well, she didn't get them from me,' said Justin feebly.

There was a small photograph of Judy next to the headline, which said: 'THE SEXIST SECRETS OF EMU: STUDENT SPEAKS OUT.' At least, though he wouldn't have said so to Sir Stanley, he had reason to be grateful to Judy because she'd got him some publicity at last. She named him as one of her two supervisors, although the piece went on to say that, 'Professor Mallinder has been particularly supportive.'

'Get an apology,' barked Sir Stanley. 'I want an apology from this Miss Sammons. And I want them to publish it. Students have no business to be writing articles like this. If she doesn't apologize, I'll have to see what steps we should take.'

'Steps?'

'Something untoward is going on at this institution, Leopard.'

Justin thought everybody knew this, though there might well be various definitions of what 'untoward' meant.

'And I intend to find out what it is. I want you to do some detective work. Ask around. See what you can find out. Be careful with the Mallinder woman. She may be implicated. It seems we're high in the publicity stakes this week,' Sir Stanley went on, flicking a page from the *Motley Mercury* in Justin's direction. 'Miss Sammons's other supervisor has hit the headlines too.'

BIG CAT SIGHTED BY WOMAN PROFESSOR, shrieked this one. There was a picture of Lydia and one of a – not the – puma. The two creatures shared a certain long-limbed gracefulness. The article listed all the sightings there'd been of the puma recently (though omitting the Ford Fiesta episode), and described Lydia as a Professor of Women at the Study of Culture Department at the University (all in capital letters). '*Ms* Mallinder,' the paper went on to say with that habit the media have of disregarding the authority of women, 'had been out walking by the boating lake after midnight when she'd seen the animal.'

Justin wondered what Lydia had been doing out so late. 'Insomnia, probably,' he said out loud.

'Yes, probably,' echoed Sir Stanley. 'But I wish she'd keep her visions to herself. It doesn't look very good to have the university's name attached to gossipy stories like this.'

'You don't expect her to apologize as well, do you?' asked Justin nervously. 'I mean, I expect she did see it. The puma, I mean. I mean, she did think she saw it. Lydia's not a woman to lie.'

Justin wrote a firm letter to Judy Sammons, copied to Lydia and to Sir Stanley, making all the points Sir Stanley expected him to make. He got a note back the same day. It pointed out that the figures she'd quoted in the *THES* had dropped through her letterbox one day in a plain brown envelope. Her name and address had been printed in bold capitals on the front. There was no note inside. And that was that.

Justin asked Lydia about the puma.

'Of course I saw it.'

'That's what I said.'

'But people don't want to believe it, because it's matter out of place.'

'What?'

'Mary Douglas. *Purity and Danger*. Or Lévi-Strauss. The savage in the midst of the civilized. It's disturbing to think of wild animals in city centres. A bit like scholarship in universities. You never know what might happen.'

'I didn't think of that.'

'No,' agreed Lydia. 'But the point about the puma is that it does really exist. You tell that to Sir Stanley next time he asks.'

The other outcome of Lydia's peregrinations round the lake soon manifested itself when Sir Stanley got a letter from her. 'Dear Sir Stanley,' said the letter, 'It is with some regret that I write to inform you that I have decided to resign from my position as Professor of Gender Studies at EMU. Over the last year I have become increasingly unhappy about the way the university is being managed, and the impact this is having on my work and that of my colleagues. As I told you when we spoke confidentially last March, current university policy with respect to the resourcing of research poses a particular problem for me. I believe this policy is misguided. In short, I find my working conditions are no longer acceptable. I cannot do what I believe I am part of a university to do, and I regret this very much. I shall, of course, be taking my research grants with me when I leave. Yours sincerely, Lydia Mallinder.'

Lydia sent her letter and then took a week's sick leave. She *was* sick of it all. She shut herself up in her little house, put the answering machine on, and conversed only with

Huneyball, who'd excelled himself recently by jamming the f and the g on the computer keyboard with lumps of scabby fluff, falling off the television and dislocating something at the back (of the television), getting shut in her jersey cupboard for twenty-four hours and nearly dying of anoxia, and then throwing up all over a memo from Frank Flusfeder about missing wastepaper bins.

Lydia got on with her book. She was deep in a chapter on the implications of cyberculture for gendered subjectivities and experiences of space and time, and quite enjoying herself for a change, when she was shocked to hear a familiar voice on the answering machine. It was Giles Tingey. He said, 'Hallo Lydia, I'm going to read you a poem. It's called "The Scholar". It goes like this: "My days among the Dead are past./Around me I behold/Where'er these casual eyes are cast/The mighty minds of old./My never-failing friends are they/With whom I converse day by day." That's the first verse. The last one goes like this: "My hopes are with the Dead, anon/My place with them will be/And I with them shall travel on/Through all Futurity/Yet leaving here a name, I trust/That will not perish in the dust." I thought you'd like that word "Futurity". Goodbye.'

Lydia dialled 1471. 'You were called today at 16.07,' said the staccato, stuck-together voice. 'We do not have the caller's number to return the call.'

'What's going on, do you think, Huneyball?' The cat raised his head from his new position on the sloping front surface of her printer, which was currently disgorging the revised version of Chapter Twelve. Huneyball watched with sleepy curiosity the regular turns of the roller knob on the side. Lydia watched him watching it. Storm clouds jostled for space in the sky above the patio, and there was the far-off rumble of thunder, which at first Lydia mistook for

Huneyball's stomach. 'I ought to do something,' said Lydia. 'But what can I do? No-one knows where Giles is. He's obviously had a breakdown, but it's not my responsibility, is it?'

Outside, the metallic greyness deepened, and the sky's indigestion was amplified. Electricity leapt downwards in a startling orange blaze. Her eyes drawn away from the screen by the drama, Lydia wondered about the mammoth legs of the pylon round the corner. Were pylons transfigured by storms or unaffected by them? Might it just pick itself up and wander off, like Giles Tingey? After a few more rumbles of thunder, she started typing again. Chapter Thirteen was called 'Media Viruses'. She ought to get on with it. 'Popular mass media culture (these terms need to be carefully defined),' typed Lydia, 'cannot merely be dismissed as a coherent ideological apparatus, intellectually impoverished, politically subversive and, from the point of view of gender, powerfully hegemonic. For the cultural texts encoded in information technologies are not that simple.'

The thoughts and the words were coming fast and furious now. There was another bang of thunder, like an explosion just above the house; and another scarification of lightning across the sky. The screen went blank and sparks flew from the printer. Huneyball rose like a scorched phoenix and made for the odoriforous safety of the laundry basket. 'Shit!' said Lydia. She'd meant to set the computer to automatic save, but hadn't got round to it. 'Bloody hell!' She scraped her chair furiously back across the parquet floor, and looked out at the patio with loathing at nature, her enemy.

The doorbell rang. Outside, dripping, but not scorched, stood Disa Loring and Ola and Miriam and Veronica and Candida and Beverley. 'Sorry,' said Disa, 'we're sorry to intrude, but we are worried about you. Please send us away if you want to, but we'd rather come in. It's very wet out here.'

Lydia let them in. 'You've chosen a good moment. I've just lost the first half of Chapter Thirteen.'

'So you have locked yourself up to write your book?' asked Disa.

'Yes and no. I mean yes, I *am* trying to finish the book, but I've resigned from EMU and I've locked myself up to recover from making the decision.'

'But what are you going to *do*, Lydia?' asked all the women, when Lydia had made a pot of tea and Huneyball had come out and arranged himself round Disa's neck.

'I'm going freelance. I'm going to set up my own research consultancy centre. I've given in to the market, you see. If you can't beat 'em, join 'em. Winkett and Bacon would approve.'

'But what about your salary?' they chorused.

'The overheads will be quite enough. You see, what the university takes away from us is our lifeblood. What we make, we ought to keep. The first ethical principle of Marxism. I only want what belongs to me – my ideas, my texts, my overheads, my life!'

'Fine words,' said Disa admiringly.

'We admire your spirit,' said Ola, on behalf of the others.

'But what about us?' wailed Miriam, meaning her and the others whose jobs were funded by the research contracts, the overheads of which would now in Lydia's grand plan be used to pay her salary.

'You can come with me. Don't worry, mother will provide. I'll negotiate with the University of Peterborough for a formal link: we'll need to be part of an institution, at least initially, in order to be able to take the research money with us. And Peterborough's a proper town, which will be nice. Only forty-eight minutes from London. I don't see why UP won't let me keep my professorship and we'll probably come to some agreement whereby I do a bit of teaching, but I'd quite like to concentrate on research in the next phase of my life.'

There was no doubt that she *did* see it as the next phase of her life. It lay there, a sunlit plain of expectancy and experience, egging her on through what you didn't have to be a university professor or to be reviewed by a virginal management consultant to recognize as a moment of transition. Out of the morass of feeling and the moral confusion of the last months, as a result of the persecution of both Lydia and scholarship by the banshees of profit and market credibility, there had emerged a reasonably clear vision of what would or might happen next.

Disa shook her head with a worried look. 'But how can you be sure,' she asked, 'you won't get into exactly the same position at the University of Peterborough? They will want your overheads as well.'

'It'll be a different arrangement,' explained Lydia, 'they won't own me. I shall be in control.'

They could see she was so firmly persuaded of the wisdom of her plan that it'd be useless to argue. Huneyball jumped from Disa's neck onto her belly, which she was clutching maternally. The thunder and lightning had receded by now, but the rain went on, pounding the autumnal vegetation deep into the ground, and filling up all the potholes on the EMU campus.

After the women had gone out into the wet night again, Lydia searched her hard disk for remnants of Chapter Thirteen and found an earlier version. She put Huneyball on top of the printer and smacked him to teach him that he wasn't allowed to sleep there any more. He streaked off to the kitchen and went down a hole at the back of the cupboard below the sink to sulk.

She ate a bowl of the chocolate ice cream she kept in the

freezer for such occasions, and pulled the blinds down and curled up on the sofa and shut her eyes. She called Huneyball, but he was still sulking. In her head it was as dark as the wild night outside, but unlike the exterior world it admitted images, scenes, cameos, even snatches of conversation framed between double quote marks just as they would appear on a computer screen.

After a while, she got up and, without thinking much about it, got in her car and drove to Haddon House. The lights were on. Sidony – she knew it was Sidony – was playing the piano. It wasn't a classical melody, and at first Lydia didn't recognize it, and then she did – it was the theme from an Australian film called *My Brilliant Career*.

'Good God, child, I'm surprised anybody's out on a night like this.' Sidony sat her down in front of the Aga with a hot milk and whisky.

'Sidony,' said Lydia, 'do you happen to know where Giles Tingey went to?'

'No, dear, do you?'

'He phoned me this evening. There's something nobody knows, Sidony. You see, Giles and I were lovers.'

'Ah.'

'Don't be shocked, please.'

'I gave up being shocked by other people's exploits a long time ago. I'm not shocked, but I am *surprised*. I thought he was your enemy. Oh, I see,' she interrupted Lydia before she had a chance to respond to this, 'it's sleeping with the enemy, isn't it? Isn't that the title of another film? I understand the principle, though I would have thought it was rather uncomfortable.'

'He was a virgin. I think he's got an eating disorder. He's very obsessional as well. Tidy, I mean.'

'Oh dear. What a lot of complaints,' commented Sidony matter-of-factly. 'I don't think there's much wrong with tidiness. But do you think the virginity and the eating dis-order might be connected? I saw a television programme about that the other day. Was it good, dear? I hope it was. You deserve to have something nice happen to you. The sex, I mean.'

'Wonderful,' said Lydia dreamily.

'I'm so glad.'

Lydia started weeping. Sidony put her arms round her. Callum walked in and walked out again, nodding in an understanding way.

CHAPTER 15

The Discovery of Worrying

In the end it was Carey Leopard who found Giles Tingey. Just as the summer had been unusually hot, so the winter got off to a horribly cold start. The early frosts at the end of November cracked the plaster in the little red Tudor houses on the Willowbrook estate by the roundabout, and the handful of residents who'd been foolhardy enough to buy them got together and formed an action group to sue College Homes. In Motley proper, everyone rushed to their central heating timers, or in the poorer parts of the city to their rusty electric fires and those gas heaters with heavy blue canisters that run out when you need them the most.

Carey's shouting matches with her mother had died down somewhat since Justin's illness. This had given her mother something else to think about, and Carey herself had been shocked by the sight of Justin in hospital. Although she was of that age that considered anyone over forty old, she still hadn't equated age with infirmity. She chafed against her parents so much precisely because they were always there; the possibility that they might not be altered her disposition towards them. Not hugely, but enough to enable Justin and Rosemary to sigh and say, 'Perhaps it was just a phase.'

A leaflet had appeared through the letterbox: 'Surviving

Adolescence' it was called. It was by the Royal College of Psychiatrists. 'Refusal to go to school is commonly due to difficulties in separating from parents,' read Carey, cynically. 'Most young people do not break the law, and those that do are usually boys.'

'Well, that's a relief, you got that one right, didn't you?' she said to Rosemary.

On this particular late November night, Carey was in her favourite haunt, the Moon and Sixpence nightclub. It lay between the Snooker Club and the Autochoice Used Car Centre, not far, in fact, from the roundabout where the EMU campus sneaked off towards the Fens. Carey was with a gaggle of girls and boys from Motley Comprehensive where she'd persuaded her parents to let her transfer for her A-levels, on the grounds that she'd have fewer problems separating from them if she went there. Willow Girls' School had failed with Carey Leopard or she had failed it, it was hard to tell which. Her ambition now was to be an airline pilot.

She was practising separation in the Moon and Sixpence, with her third vodka and lemon, and sitting in the lap of Gilroy Broxham, whom she fancied like hell.

'Look at that really old bloke over there,' said Sarah Scutt. At first Carey had thought she was trying to distract Gilroy, but then she had looked and it was perfectly true. Through the smoke and the rainbow of flashing light she saw a man sitting alone with a line of empty beer bottles in front of him. He had longish hair, blond, and he wore a cheap shirt from the market which was so new you could see the creases in it from where it'd been folded in the packet. As everybody else in the Moon and Sixpence was under twenty, he did rather stand out. 'D'you think he's a policeman?' asked Sarah excitedly.

'No chance, look at the hair.'

'Go on, I dare you to go and chat him up and find out.'
The others joined in.

'Get me another drink first. What's the reward, anyway?'

The man looked with suspicion at the girl who slid onto the bench beside him with her long brown hair and untouched face. 'What do you want?' His speech was slurred. He was writing something in a large black notebook.

'Hallo,' she said. Her enchanting eyes had lashes like the tails of ponies. 'I just wondered what you were doing.'

He closed the black notebook. 'It's warm in here.'

'Yes.'

'It's warm, that's why I'm here.'

'You mean you've got no home to go to?' The space between the lashes widened.

'Oh yes I have,' he explained, 'but I choose not to go to it.'

Carey had found a point of conversation here: 'I know what you mean.'

He tipped the beer bottle down his throat. 'I doubt that you do.'

'Just because I'm young,' said Carey indignantly, 'doesn't mean I'm a person with no understanding.'

'Just because I'm not doesn't mean I have any.' He laughed.

Sarah Scutt called out to her from the other table. 'You alright, Carey? Need any help?'

'Nope. But you'd better bloody well leave Gilroy alone!' She turned her attention back to the man. 'I think you're rather a sad figure, aren't you?' she said, sounding like one of her own schoolteachers. 'It's not clever to sleep rough; anyone can do it. You're obviously a professional man like my father. You must have a problem. Or at least a deep dark secret. Why don't you tell me what it is?'

'Listen, love,' he flung an arm round her, and if she

hadn't been where she was in the middle of the Moon and Sixpence's smoke and noise, she might have been frightened by it, 'why don't you stop trying to find out about me, and I won't try to find out about you!' He held out his other hand, and she shook it.

'It's a deal.'

'What does your father do, then?' asked the man, immediately breaking the bargain.

'He's a professor at the university,' said Carey proudly.

'Ah,' said the man reflectively. 'I knew a few of those once.'

'What do you mean?'

'PHODs,' he said jeeringly. 'The university by the roundabout. I had an intimate connection there once.'

'And what happened?'

'Them and their PRICS and RIPS and ARQs and TRUs,' he expostulated. 'Who do they think they are?'

'You can't blind me with words,' pointed out Carey.

'No, but *they* are blind with words. Blind with their own words.'

'What happened to your intimate connection?' persisted Carey, still mindful of Sarah Scutt's proximity to Gilroy Broxham.

'She was too much for me,' he said. 'I wanted to die in her arms. She crucified me. Every day it's either her or me on the cross, dripping with blood and with letters, ARQ, TRU . . .'

Carey slipped quietly away from him and took her mobile phone out of her shiny black shoulder bag. Her parents never would have given it to her six months ago, but they trusted her now. Everyone had one, even Sarah Scutt.

'Dad!'

'What's the matter?' It was far too early for her to talk about absent taxis and give a picturesque account of the empty road and the wind howling round her midriff because she'd forgotten her jacket again.

'Listen to me, Dad! You remember that man who disappeared in the summer, the one you didn't like who came to find out whether all of you were up to any good?'

Justin's mind was a blank at first. 'Oh, Giles Tingey, you mean?'

'That's the one! Well, I've found him. He's here in the Moon and Sixpence.'

'That child's amazing,' said Justin to Rosemary. 'We should never underestimate her.'

They took Giles Tingey into Motley Regional Hospital. Justin told Callum, and Sidony phoned Lydia, who went to see him. Giles was lying in a bed with steel sides, and was even thinner and paler than she remembered him. But he didn't as much as open his eyes. The nurse, a young woman with an eating disorder the opposite of Giles' own, told Lydia he was heavily sedated.

Giles' mother arranged for him to go into a private mental hospital in Taunton. The psychiatric diagnosis was mild schizophrenia. Dr Gayle Rutherford, the grandmotherly psychiatrist who tried to probe his mind in thrice-weekly sessions, couldn't at first get any handle on what had provoked the breakdown. She talked to Boyde and to Roberta, but only got from them the impression of two ordinarily distant upper-class parents who'd probably never given Giles and his siblings the kind of devoted parental care John Bowlby and others recommended. But there wasn't anything unusual about this.

Giles would only quote reams of poetry at her. She recognized some lines, but not others – the ones which seemed to feature pricks and seeds and some sort of encounter with a wild animal. She thought this might represent a woman. 'We need to get him stabilized on drugs,' she determined.

'I can't get anywhere with this stuff.' And so they fed Giles pills, but kindly, and kept all visitors away from him, including, especially, his parents, and eventually he began to act and speak more normally. But this meant that, instead of living quite cheerfully in his own spider's web of musings and machinations, he fell out of it abruptly, and became depressed about how and why he'd ended up here, having made a mess of his life and a perfectly good career with Winkett and Bacon, and the absolutely promising beginning of a career relating to women which he ought to have started long ago.

He told Dr Rutherford this. And then he talked about his preoccupation with his body, and how unsavoury it must seem to others. She thought there might be a story of abuse in there somewhere, but Giles denied it, confessing only to normal longings for more of his mother's attention than she was willing to give, and for more paternal understanding, which, having met his father, Dr Rutherford could well understand. The abuse seemed to be Giles' own.

His uncle, who was a Sir of some sort, came to see her one day. Actually, he came to see Giles, not taking no for an answer, but still being refused, he had to make do with Dr Rutherford instead. She recognized the type as soon as he came in the room. Homosexual, probably the passive partner. Goes for younger men. Probably denied it for years. Doesn't flaunt it now, but has enough power for it not to matter.

'I think I might be able to help you,' Sir Stanley offered, much to her surprise.

'Giles had a twin, she died at birth. His mother won't have told you. Denies it absolutely. The only way to cope. She never stopped trying to turn him into something he wasn't. I intervened. Got them to send the boy off to prep school at seven. But in the school holidays Roberta went on worrying him, like a fox the dogs won't leave alone. Giles reacted by getting a thing about food. You see, Dr Rutherford,' Sir Stanley smiled from the back of his startling blue eyes, and a look of ineffably superior wisdom passed across his face, 'that's one of the main problems with gender.'

'I beg your pardon?'

'You don't need to. Or maybe you do. Both psychiatry and women have a lot to answer for. With all this talk about what a frightful time women have, most people forget how difficult things are for us lads as well. In fact,' he sat down and adjusted his new platinum cufflinks pretentiously, 'they're probably a good deal more difficult for men than women. We may have power, but we've got to get it in the first place. You don't get it handed to you on a plate. Despite what those wretched feminists say.

'Oh, I know what I'm saying is unfashionable, but I'm coming to the point, which will interest you professionally, with regard to Giles, I mean. You see, it only takes an unusually sensitive boy for the whole seamless architecture of masculinity to come crumbling down. As it did with me, in fact, although somewhat differently. I loved Giles like my own son, and I could see his suffering, but every man has to do it on his own. That, of course, is an essential part of the problem. Having a twin sister who died was what I understand you professionals call a provoking agent; that is, it was for his mother, and having a dotty mother who wants you to be the other gender doesn't help. He should have been gay like me. Maybe he is, really. But there's a lot that can't be explained, isn't there?'

There was a view from Giles' room; the restorative effect of a peaceful landscape with not too much moving in it was being recommended by slightly radical psychiatrists these days, although only those working in the private sector were in a position to secure it for their patients. Giles looked out on a formal garden with a lake and many evergreen hedges and borders. Ill people shouldn't look at dead wood. Some who'd been there a long time complained about the swathes of unchanging green. Beyond the garden were fields let to farmers for summer grazing. These now lay fallow, and the trees in them held out their branches like supplicants in old-fashioned lunatic asylums.

The lake which Giles saw whenever he looked out of his window reminded him of Motley. In those months when he'd felt he needed to escape detection, he'd spent hours by that lake, on which nothing much of any interest happened, and the children who did come with or without their parents and take boats out on it only induced in him a scourging self-pity; he believed that whole areas of experience were now closed off to him; and he was destined to be an outcast, a hanger-round the fringes of other people's lives, absolutely for ever.

There were times when he thought that in such a role he would merely be copying what he'd been asked to do at Winkett and Bacon. There he was a spectator, a voyeur; in his shadowy existence in Motley he'd been an onlooker, a bystander, an observer: what was the difference? The difference lay in his moral attitude towards what he watched. At the university he was charged with duties of interrogation and interpretation; it was up to him to draw some conclusions about what he saw. These conclusions would inevitably embody his own world-view, and /or that of Winkett and Bacon, and this world-view was likely to deviate in important respects from the meaning the people themselves attached to their activities. Indeed, that was the whole point of the exercise: to tell other people more about themselves than they themselves thought they knew. But it was knowledge in a narrow sense; presupposing a particular kind of moral judgement about the value of what human beings did, and assuming that what was important could be enumerated, and what couldn't be, wasn't. If you accepted this, then you could do a Winkett-and-Bacon job with a clear conscience. But if it troubled you, and Giles hadn't understood how much it had troubled him until he met Lydia Mallinder, then you couldn't do it without feeling very worried indeed.

Giles had a lot of time for reading and watching television in his room in the hospital. As might be expected, most of what he read and watched tapped into the deep personal obsessions which had led him to be in that room and which he discussed in his thrice-weekly sessions with Dr Ruther-ford. He found her attentive nature and friendly, open smile generally much more therapeutic than the technical insights she trotted out. They discussed many things. Giles had watched a television programme on weather fore-casting: now, that was an example of a profession that was neither art nor science. The meteorological tools available to weather forecasters gave their predictions a good deal of accuracy these days, but no-one knew how this compared with more traditional methods of anticipating the weather – a red sky at night, and so on. One believed that everything modern was better, but sometimes it might not be so. There were some characteristics of the weather that defied the science of the forecasters; humidity, for instance. No satis-factory way had yet been found of expressing humidity numerically. Some measures had been tried: wet-bulb tem-perature, wet-bulb potential temperature, dew-point humidity mixing ratio, specific humidity, vapour pressure. But all were defective. So forecasters fell back on the older, more qualitatively descriptive language of 'sultry', 'steamy', 'close' and so forth; only with such loosely defined and evocative adjectives could they give an impression of how much moisture was likely to be held in the air at any one time; these words served a dual purpose, for they also explained what it would *feel* like to be in the presence of so much moisture. This was what in the end most people were interested in. One lives in the world and it's through being in it that one knows it. Thus, all knowledge is an intensely personal thing. Therefore, knowledge doesn't exist apart from the knower.

These were the conclusions that Giles Tingey reached, and they enabled him to make sense of what had happened to him. He became interested in the history of knowledge and in different theories about what knowledge is, and fortunately there was a good library locally, and what he couldn't borrow his mother bought for him, although she had to apologize for the esoteric nature of her purchases to the man in Night Owl Books, who was more used to being asked for texts on restoring antique furniture or making pottery.

Giles read a book about chaos theory, and when he mentioned this to Dr Rutherford, she reminded him of the central role of chaos theory in the film *Jurassic Park*. Giles borrowed the video from the hospital library and watched it in the video room with another inmate who had to be taken away by the nurse because he hid under his seat with his hands over his ears when the dinosaurs rioted.

Chaos theory provided another helpful slant on his Winkett-and-Bacon experience. The model he had used was simple and appeared watertight: one assessed the value of a set of human activities in exclusively financial terms, and this then gave one a standard for judging whether a certain activity ought to be encouraged or not; but the lesson of chaos theory, as Giles understood it, was that such closed systems of thought were precisely the ones likely to give you the wrong answer. Because they were impermeable, they were also unresponsive to the necessary dialogue with, and feedback from, the real world. Their value as predictors was equivalent to the weather forecaster's measures of humidity. It was the *correspondence* between the thought system and the feeling of being in the world that mattered; without it, one was lost.

And so Giles Tingey worried in his own quiet, locked-up way about the great questions that have preoccupied scientists and thinkers of all kinds over the centuries. When we speak of animals 'worrying' their victims, this is the original meaning of the word: the violent pursuit of an object of desire. The cat that turns over the mangled sparrow with her thorny paw, and then again for the pleasure of it; the hunting dogs that frighten the fox; the baby lions left unattended for a hot and starving moment; the black vultures swooping and landing on the carcass of a zebra; all these worry their victims. Only in the nineteenth century is worrying something people do to themselves, and in the minds of the troubled, those who are called mentally ill, worrying is liable to become an entirely self-consuming passion. People learn how to prey on themselves, in the same way that bulimics and anorexics learn to starve themselves and suicides work out how to kill themselves, using the same means that are used for murder. The modern world is one in which the awful sins perpetrated on some people by others become at the same time sins they perpetrate on themselves.

Once Giles had understood this, he began to feel more charitable towards himself. He could see how what had happened to him wasn't his fault. As Justin Leopard had said with less understanding and in a different context, he was caught up in the great broad transforming sweep of culture; he was even an involuntary part of the said transformation. Without him and others like him, history wouldn't move on. Most people possess limited freedom of action because they must act in ways that are culturally sanctioned and approved. They *have* to be part of whatever great mistake is going on, otherwise the mistake will never happen.

One day in December, when they allowed him to have visitors again, Giles looked out of his window and saw Lydia walking up the path to the front door. He recognized her instantly, even though she wore a heavy red coat with a mock fur collar turned up against the weather forecasters' prediction of snow.

Lydia was nervous. Giles, wearing a pale blue V-neck cashmere sweater over a white shirt and a neatly knotted tie reminiscent of his Winkett-and-Bacon days, looked at her with a gentle expression on his soft-contoured face and a fall of golden hair across his troubled brow. He was exactly as she remembered him. She felt her body tremble with a sense of how it might have been between them; other nights, different skies, alternative confidences and consolations. But she and Giles were an invented oasis in the desert of both their lives which stretched on and on in different directions. He was not the answer to her problems, nor she to his. There were important resolutions to be sought elsewhere before any reunion between them could be anything more than a fictional device for generating a happy ending.

CHAPTER 16

A False Professor

The snow came in the first week of term, just as the students arrived back full of Christmas food and good intentions. Those doing the new combined honours in Freshwater Eco-toxicology had an opportunity to study at close quarters the effect of freezing on the soil and on fish and marine plants. Those with rooms in the oldest hall of residence had a bad time because short cuts had been taken in the summer during the installation of a new batch of washbasins, and the short cuts were now frozen. Refugees in search of water could be seen morning and evening crossing and recrossing the square of quickly grimy, trodden snow to another building which had water, though an overstrained central-heating system.

With the Christmas break, building had ceased on the new management consultancy centre, and although it was supposed to have restarted, the workmen said it was too cold to work. The MCC was Sir Stanley's pride and joy, and he would go and prowl round the site like a big cat, imagining all the benefits the MCC would bring to EMU, and plotting and scheming the way V-Cs do to bring about that state of affairs at the university that was his heart's desire and which he had got RIPS and PRIC to agree to without much difficulty.

Richard Winkett would be director of the MCC, and

under the new system for awarding honorary titles, Sir
Stanley had put a proposal to the Honorary Appointments
Committee which he'd made sure Callum Wormleighton
as its chair supported: Winkett would thus be given the title
of Professorial Fellow. This wasn't on the reduced list of
titles HAC had within its power to give out, but Sir Stanley
liked the title Professorial Fellow – it summed up nicely the
academic and gender status of the post. Besides which, he
doubted he could have got the title of Professor down the
throats of the HAC members; there were certain standards
that had to be upheld, he could hear them saying, and
making a chap with a third-class degree in Moral Sciences
a professor, even of the visiting sort, wasn't one of them.

It was a pity about young Giles; Sir Stanley had had high
hopes of his nephew, and would have wished him to have
been a feature of the EMU campus for some time to come.
His sister had good news about Giles, who was a lot better.
She thought he might be discharged soon, and he was talking about doing a degree in philosophy. This seemed a bit
of an indulgence to Sir Stanley. Philosophy was a very
unproductive topic. But everyone wanted the boy to get
well, and if this was what would do it, well who was he to
complain about it?

Sir Stanley had come to recognize that the safe sex in
St Nick's idea had been a mistake, even though the vicar,
who was himself gay, had welcomed it, provided the condom bins were located outside the boundaries of conse-
crated ground. The vicar's gayness wasn't widely known,
and of course none of them would have liked Sidony
Wormleighton or Phyllis from SAR or any other of the
Clean Up St Nick's brigade to have found out about it. The
money Sir Stanley had given to the END AIDS charity had
now been diverted to a health-education initiative for the
students of EMU, most of whom had already been over-

exposed to AIDS education at school. Unfortunately another row had now broken out about the new proposal. This was being masterminded by Dennis Rudgewick in Justin's department, who'd maintained that there was no evidence that health education worked, and how would they know whether this particular attempt did or not?

'We'll evaluate it,' Vincent Clover of the END AIDS charity had proclaimed. But Dennis had an answer to that as well: 'The students you interview will tell you they changed their behaviour because of the posters and the leaflets, but they'll probably be lying, and the worst offenders will be so busy offending they won't have time to be interviewed.'

Sir Stanley had to admit there was a certain logic to this. It did seem to be an overly political business. Both AIDS education and universities: for couldn't the question, Is Education Effective? equally well be applied to the whole university system? It was a frightening thought, so Sir Stanley dismissed it immediately. But he did decide he needed to do something about his own excessive workload. All these complications and negotiations and the huge rise there'd been in the number of grievance and harassment complaints from both students and staff meant that he was having to work much harder than he wanted to.

He needed a deputy V-C. Other universities had them, so why not EMU?

And then it came to him suddenly, quite out of the blue – Lydia Mallinder. He might have diverted the St Nick's money from END AIDS to EMU in the nick of time (as Elliot Blankthorn, with his fondness for clichés, would undoubtedly have phrased it), as Sidony Wormleighton's nosings around at Charities House had uncovered what she and others – and Sir Stanley had reason to believe that Lydia was one of them – had decided could be called a distinct bias against charitable work for *female* HIV and AIDS sufferers. A group of women-and-health educationalists, or whatever they were called, had got together and prepared a short document on END AIDS' work in relation to the true incidence of HIV infection. They sought legal advice. Might this fall under the terms of the Sex Discrimination Act, for instance? Was there no end to these inane charges of sexism, discrimination, harassment, bullying and patriarchy, Sir Stanley asked himself?

He rang up his granddaughter, Venetia, to ask her professional advice and to tell her his idea about Lydia. 'But have you asked her, Grandpa? Didn't you say she'd resigned? Wasn't it something to do with overheads?'

'Yes and yes,' said Sir Stanley. Lydia was due to leave at the end of the spring term. She was busy finding a house to rent from which she might conduct her freelance research enterprise. Her army of contract researchers had dug their heels in and said they weren't leaving Motley for the University of Peterborough. Motley was where they'd been hired to work, and Motley was where they were staying. The problem was that there were very few houses in Motley of the right kind. Lydia wanted something architecturally pleasing with at least ten rooms in a safe area with a good-sized parking place. The nearest she'd come to this was a couple of bay-windowed semis that could be knocked into one in Daffodil Close, a Neighbourhood Watch area. But the council had warned her she was unlikely to get planning permission for a change of use, and bay windows were not her ideal.

Lydia had hardened her heart against EMU, and was resolved to cut her losses. The future of scholarship, it was now clear to her, lay outside universities rather than inside them. She and Ola and Miriam and Veronica and the others and more (two new grant applications showed signs of bearing fruit) would ply their valuable trade from whatever building she would eventually find, and sod the rest of them. With the overheads she'd get back from Bill Budgen's tight-fisted hands, Lydia would be able to pay her own salary for two years, two months, plus rent and other expenses, and plus the salary of an administrator, for which purpose she hoped to lure the disaffected Phyllis away from the uncomfortable no-smoking spaces of the SAR room. In this plan, Lydia made no allowance for the fact that Phyllis fed off her disaffection like Huneyball his pilchards; without it she wouldn't know what to do. But this particular plan was for the moment safely locked away in Lydia's head.

Richard Winkett, from the nascent empire of his new MCC, had offered to help Lydia on her path to commercial autonomy. He knew, because of something Sir Stanley had said, that there'd been at least a frisson of a thing between Giles and Lydia. Richard felt he owed it to Giles to help her. She mightn't need a logo yet, or any promptings in the direction of a Mission statement, but women generally needed some help with money, and Lydia would definitely have to learn the same lesson as the universities had – how to make the overheads work for her.

But she wasn't stupid: two years, two months at the age of thirty-six wasn't very long. Going independent was a fine moral move, and would certainly make a valid point about undue appropriation by the new marketized higher education system of the human capital required to create knowledge. Judy Sammons was at this very moment composing a piece for the *THES* about it; she'd developed a nice sideline in journalistic stories about higher education, and had been asked to write a regular column for the paper, 'With a Student's Eye'.

Lydia had confronted Judy with the revelations of the W-A-S-H Internet group, and Judy had agreed that Justin hadn't actually attacked her, but, as Lydia knew Elliot Blankthorn had verbally sinned in this same direction, she decided the right and the wrong could be regarded as can-celling one another out. At least knowing the truth about Judy's allegations enabled Lydia to feel comfortable with Justin again. Justin and she were two of a kind, not only because they were the only two at EMU who'd managed to get, and hold onto, European research money, a feat much underestimated by everyone else, but because they were both, essentially, innocent victims. The only difference was her political awareness, which was much more developed than his, and she didn't have a wife to support her, she only had Huneyball.

Despite her resolve, Lydia knew that leaving the univer-sity system was hardly a career move. So she and Huneyball sat in the evenings with the snow either settled or falling outside composing and re-composing the curriculum of her vitae, in order to go for any jobs that were going. Huneyball had a morbid fear of the snow, and Lydia had to give him a litter tray inside which he would use only after she'd gone to bed and then with such a rattle that she'd wake up thinking someone had broken in.

She didn't feel safe in Motley any more, not since the puma. She tried not to walk at night alone, and as soon as she got home she'd pull the blinds down and light the lamps and turn the central heating up to make a little insulated world of safety out of which she could look at the whole white world from time to time. The wild animals which loped across the deserts of her soul could hardly be blamed for causing what people had.

One day when she had a meeting with Elliot about their joint MA (the harassment had stopped, and Elliot had totally refused to be drawn on the topic of his comments about Giles Tingey), he saw the pile of stiff brown envelopes lying in her out-tray. 'Ah,' exclaimed Elliot, 'I thought you would. I didn't think RCC would be enough for you.'

'RCC?'

'Like MCC: Research Consultancy Centre.'

'I hate the word consultancy,' said Lydia.

'You should have consulted me about this,' said Elliot. 'I've had vast experience of doing and redoing my CV because I've moved around the world so much. I'm still ready to help, if you'd like. Maybe you'd like a copy of mine, as a kinda model, you know?'

She wouldn't, but he gave it to her anyway. One evening, before Huneyball launched his humungous nightly attack on the litter tray, she picked it up and flipped idly through it. There were some publications on it that looked interesting. She dialled into the library system to see if EMU had them. 'Blankthorn, E, Ethics and Modernity' she typed, and then entered the search code. 'No such location.' Well, it was an American publisher, and quite recent, and there hadn't been any acquisitions in the library since the cuts. She tried another one: 'Developing a Conscience: How Children Think'. But that wasn't there, either. With a growing feeling of suspicion, she exited from the library system and went into the Library of Congress, but the Library of Congress had no record of Elliot Blankthorn's publications. By 2 AM she'd checked every single one of the eighty-six publications on Elliot's CV and found only three on record.

'You're a sham, Elliot,' she told him angrily the next day, waving his smartly printed CV in his face.

'Oh, that!'

'Has nobody ever suspected before?'

He had a remarkably casual attitude towards it. 'Nope. And it's got me a few good jobs in my time. Mind you, it *is* one reason why I didn't consider it wise to go for LSE or

Oxbridge or Harvard or Yale or Berkeley. The thing is, Lydia, few people realize how few books or articles are ever read by anybody. The average number of people who read an academic article is 4.6. Do you know how many books are published every year? About a quarter of a million in the UK and the States alone. Who needs them? I ask you! Most people write things just to put them on their CVs. So that's what I did, only I put them on my CV without writing them. It's been a kinda test of the moral status of the academy: a research project into ethics and everyday academic life, if you like. It's been fun.

'What we need, I often think,' he went on discursively, in a mode of which Giles Tingey, before his insanity, would have approved, 'is something like the set-aside mechanism of the Common Agricultural Policy. Farmers get paid for *not* growing crops, so we academics should get paid for *not* writing. As I have been, in effect. It'd make things a helluva lot easier. Just think: you wouldn't ever have to update student reading lists, all those journal editors would stop harassing you to review books, students'd have more money to spend on beer, libraries wouldn't have to keep expanding, and it'd be good for our eyesights as well,' he announced, blinking sagely through his Woody Allen glasses.

'The other thing, of course, let me tell you,' he persisted, 'is that I'm far more intelligent than most of the people who read my CV. It figures, doesn't it? Intelligence and publication are inversely related to one another: the cleverest people don't waste their time writing books, they get on with life.'

Suddenly Lydia understood. 'That warning you gave me wasn't about Giles Tingey at all, was it? It was about you.'

Elliot nodded, grinning. 'One man's much the same as another. Or so you feminists are always saying.'

'Why did you say it, Elliot?'

'I should have thought that was as plain as the nose on your face. I was jealous. Of you and you know who.'

'Well, I didn't suspect anything. Except about you and Judy.'

'You let Judy down,' said Elliot, surprisingly.

'I did not.'

'She thinks so. On the other hand, I don't mind being charitable here. Perhaps there aren't any goodies or baddies in this story, Lydia. Callum isn't John Wayne, and you aren't Annie Oakley, though there has been a good deal of sharp-shooting going on. I may have built a life on deceit, but I'm a reasonable human being apart from that. Others may have lives of transparent decency, but being boring is a kinda sin of its own, isn't it?'

'A man after my own heart,' thought Sir Stanley, when Lydia brought forward her appointment to see him in order to disclose her discovery about Elliot. She'd been difficult about giving Jevon a time she could make, when he'd requested an interview with her, because she couldn't imagine that he'd have anything useful to say to her.

'Is he a good teacher?' asked Sir Stanley, when Lydia had told him about Elliot's mythical CV.

'Yes, I think so. I haven't heard any complaints.'

'Neither have I. So he knows his stuff.'

'I suppose.'

'He landed a whacking great research grant last year,' observed Sir Stanley, looking at the file in front of him. 'Two hundred and ten k from the Brackenbury Trust. On ethics and child support. That's eighty k in overheads.'

'Grant-awarding bodies don't check on applicants' qualifications,' pointed out Lydia.

'No. That would increase their overheads, wouldn't it? I

was talking to Rodman about the ESRC yesterday, he said that the cost of grant administration is now running at about thirty per cent of the grants they give out. He said he's glad the *News of the World* haven't got hold of that yet. I've been wondering about the National Lottery as a source of research income. What do you think, Lydia?'

She noted, and wondered about, this use of her first name. 'As you know, Sir Stanley, I take the view that the whole system's much of a lottery anyway.'

'Yes, quite so.' The woman hadn't changed. She was still the same mixture of steel on the outside and something else on the inside.

'Well, leave Professor Blankthorn to me, will you? And don't tell the *News of the World*. What I wanted to see you about was this.' He pushed a piece of paper over the expansive desk towards her.

'East Midlands University Deputy Vice-Chancellor,' it said in, Lydia noticed, the same crisp font as Elliot Blankthorn's false CV. 'East Midlands University is an innovative HE institution located just south of Motley, an important business centre, in Northamptonshire. The University has significant links with local business and is also a nationally and internationally renowned centre for research on modern economic and social policy. The student body now numbers 10,500. The University has six Schools organized around an Interdepartmental Structure. The present Vice-Chancellor is Sir Stanley Oxborrow. The post of Deputy Vice-Chancellor will attract candidates with a high level of academic leadership and a proven track record in obtaining research funding. Candidates will be expected to support the University's commitment to close links with industry. An attractive remuneration package will be offered, and the appointment will be available for a term of five years, with further terms available subject to review. The appointment will be at Professorial level. A detailed job description and further information about EMU can be obtained by telephoning . . .'

'What do you think?' he asked.

'Where's the money coming from?' she asked.

'Ah, that's what I like to hear, a brain firmly rooted in bank accounts.' Lydia had an incongruous image of brains pickled in vinegar jars with pound signs plastered on the outside. 'It's coming from industry, of course. Local or otherwise. I won't tell you which, it might put you off.'

She stared at him blankly.

'You don't seem to have got there yet, my dear. I want *you* for this post. It'll be better for you than leaving us altogether. Oh, I'm not saying you wouldn't make it on your own, you undoubtedly would, but what a waste! Of everything you've learnt about universities and university committees, and students, bless their little cotton socks, and the writing and reading and efficient disposal of memos and filling in those wretched staff appraisal forms and sorting out those silly contracts Personnel will persist in providing, and so on and so forth. What a waste. And for us too. Now we've got to know you and your inestimable gifts, we'd be very stupid to lose you. I would have said all this when you sent me your resignation letter, but it's taken me a while to sew up the funding. So, what do you think?' he repeated.

Lydia looked sideways out of the picture window and saw snow gently falling again over the front of the Senate building, coating the tops of the letters 'East Midlands University' and the pseudo coat of arms with flaky white eyebrows. Traffic chuntered slowly across the A43, and round the roundabout, which had become a veritable skating rink. She was grateful for her little urban pad a mere ten minutes' snowy walk away.

Sir Stanley swung on his chair. His periwinkle eyes danced with amusement, so like Giles Tingey's, though it was really the other way around. He sat there in his crisp suit and no doubt silk thermal underwear and his posture and his expression were those of a man who knew fully what he was about. The imposing leather, brass-studded chair at a slight angle to the desk; the legs casually but neatly crossed, one arm lying loosely on the chair with its gold watch peeking out from under a starched cuff, the other propping up his light-brown cheek with all the tensile strength of an electricity pylon. She hated it, but she had to admire it.

The text of the job advertisement lay on the desk between them.

Lydia said, 'You only want my overheads.'

'I wouldn't say only.' He smiled, and the blue in his eyes deepened and her green eyes locked with his in a momentary connection of understanding, though the rest of her face gave nothing else away.

CHAPTER 17

Our Mission

Justin was sitting in the Strategic Objectives and Planning (SOP) meeting of the Committee on University Policy (CUP). It was an exercise that happened at about this time every year, although this one had been delayed because the Great Snow had been followed by the Great Thaw with resultant damage to a number of university buildings. The plumbing in the students' residence building had exploded, and the hole in the examination hall had expanded as though the roof itself were a patch of melting ice. Even the Senate Building had sprung some damp patches. Because Jeff, the Building Services Manager, had long since departed (he'd actually got another job so his rabbits had been spared), Phyllis had had to lean hard on the remaining members of Building Services and had been forced to augment their numbers by looking in the Yellow Pages.

Anyway, it was all mended now. 'At this point we need to turn to Appendix S/9591/3/A. The green one,' intoned Sir Stanley. 'This document presents our Strategic Objectives for the 1997–8 session. The top page summarizes it. In essence the plan highlights achievements since the previous plan and describes the success of the new organizational structure; details our research portfolio and achievements in professional development and continuing education; gives student planning figures for the three year period 1996–9;

reports on our recently instituted quality assurance procedures; describes our current staffing policies; provides details of our financial plans; and comments on our physical resources policy.'

Justin hadn't read it, but he skimmed through it now, like most of the others round the table. Jon Pitton was asleep already; it was the way Graham Piper stroked his goatee beard that did it. Even Justin found it mildly mesmerizing. John Mapstone sat next to him. He'd been let off the hook of the overseas PR work by his psychiatrist's report, and Roscoe Proudfoot had taken it on instead (for an appropriate addition to his salary). He was currently in Taiwan, making speeches about what a wonderful place EMU was and unloading large quantities of the glossy literature produced by EMU's new Press Office. This was staffed by a recruit from Instant Print who was quite good at desktop publishing, but a bit deficient as regards where to put apostrophes, the need for verbs in sentences and the desirability of not splitting infinitives. But most of the places Proudfoot would take the publicity material to probably wouldn't notice these technicalities.

'EMU's Mission, as we all know,' continued Sir Stanley, 'is to pursue research, scholarship and teaching of the highest quality. If we are not a leading centre in anything, then it's about time we became one. Freedom, specialization and accountability are keywords in the development of EMU's intellectual capital. It is important for all staff to feel a sense of ownership and responsibility for our collective mission.' He pronounced the words crisply, as though they meant something.

'Perhaps I could further summarize your summary, Sir Stanley,' ventured young Neal Burnell, Jeremy Krest's colleague who'd got the readership Disa hadn't. 'The new IDS has been a qualified success, but it depends who you ask.

We've got three more research grants than we had this time last year, but they're smaller ones. Professional development is a nice term, but we're still waiting to find out what it means. Ditto with quality assurance. We've got more students than we can cope with, so the need for Professor Proudfoot's PR exercises might be called into question. The budget deficit is down slightly, because twenty-seven staff have been made redundant, or are about to be, but there have been, well,' he coughed politely, 'other balancing forms of expenditure. As regards buildings, we've still got to get rid of the A43 and if standards in Catering don't improve, we may all get salmonella. That's about it, isn't it?'

There was a polite wave of laughter. Sir Stanley didn't disagree. In fact, he wondered what new jewel in its crown EMU might have got with Neal's promotion, and made a mental note to ask him to dinner at Keynes Hall soon.

'And Professor Leopard's three stone lighter,' said Justin to himself with the self-absorption of the true dieter. He could see his feet again. But he missed his food, and felt he understood a little better the strategies of bulimics, which seemed to him to be to do with eating your cake but not having it. He'd been rather miffed, as had a number of other people, when he'd learnt that Lydia Mallinder was going to be the new deputy V-C. Why her? Why not him? Or him? But he could see it was a stroke of genius on Sir Stanley's part, because Lydia represented all those creatively disruptive elements which so obstructed Sir Stanley in his desires and strategic objectives: equal opportunities; fairness; openness; the notion that the human capital of universities mattered more than any other sort. So by taking her in with him, he would contain all that criticism and turn it like nuclear power to the service of the system rather than to its destruction. Justin supposed that Lydia was getting a hefty salary increase as well. Well, if that was what she wanted. She wouldn't have time to write books any more, though.

The revelations of Elliot Blankthorn's non-existent ones had been a shock. Rosemary said she'd never liked him, and she was usually a good judge of character. But Rosie liked hardly anyone at EMU.

Elliot had to be thanked, now, though, because he'd reduced the deficit by giving up his chair and going back to the States, not to one of those wives whose names began with M (about whom, along with everything else in Elliot's life, one began to wonder), but surprise, surprise (they came in threes, Rosie said) with Judy Sammons. Judy was going to do her PhD in the States. She said it was a more accommodating climate. Moreover, and as Elliot had said, there really weren't any absolute goodies or downright baddies in this story. Almost alone among the men at EMU, Elliot had a deep respect for women. He'd harassed Lydia only because he thought she was eminently capable of taking it like a man.

The other news that had hit them at the same time as the Great Thaw was that Worms was moving on. It wasn't the fracas over sex and the M25, or the other one over sex and the churchyard, but the compulsory purchase order that had been slapped on Haddon House because a new motorway was being built (unfortunately it wouldn't relieve the A43 problem). So Worms and Mrs Worms were off to Rhodes University in South Africa.

Callum's job as Dean carried an extra £20k, and Justin was in line for it. It would mean that the Leopards could move out of the Thatch Palace and into something larger and more practical. At this point in his life, Justin felt he was definitely after quantity rather than quality – that probably had something to do with dieting as well.

'We come next to the reports on our computing and library services. Appendix S/9542/B41. The salmon pink one,' said Sir Stanley. Perhaps the point about salmonella had hit home. 'EMU is committed to increasing the provision of computing equipment to staff and students. Equipment will be replaced where necessary when financial resources permit. The system has recently been enhanced with the installation of a Sun Spaceserver 1000. This is working well most of the time.'

'Except on Monday mornings and Friday afternoons,' complained Dennis Rudgewick, digging horse manure out from underneath his fingernails. He loved the transition of the spring, when there was all that ploughing of the earth to do, with much chopping up of juicy worms and other rejuvenating activities. 'And why do they have to shut down whenever I'm in the middle of my data?'

Sir Stanley merely nodded. 'As I said, *most of the time*. And as you will see from Appendix S/9542/B41, a major projected initiative for this coming academic year will be the introduction of computerized Management Administration Data Systems – MADS for short – which will provide invaluable support for the not-so-new IDS.'

'Isn't it time for coffee?' asked someone.

'Next, the library. Here EMU's role as a centre of excellence – what? – will be maintained. Collection development policies are being reviewed in the light of our recently agreed Mission statement. This means that we'll try to have ten copies of all books used for teaching instead of eight. Selective charging for services will be introduced, with particular emphasis on external users. A new independent computer system in the library will be installed whenever external users have been charged enough to cover the cost of it. The system will, in the full ripeness of time, be fully integrated with other networked electronic data sources.'

Sir Stanley looked round the table with what he hoped was a satisfied air. It was important to rehearse in front of these people the rhetoric of progress in terms they would understand.

The coffee trolley was wheeled in, and Justin, as usual, leapt up to be Mum. If he didn't, then a woman would, and this would hardly be consistent with EMU's equal opportunities policy. 'Do you realize, Leopard,' muttered Alan Livingstone, helping Justin with the little tubs of non-milk, 'there's a direct relationship between the rise in student numbers and the fall in the number of biscuits provided for university meetings? We just don't get enough of them these days.'

'Now,' said Sir Stanley, when they were all settled with their cups of coffee. (Was it time for a move to polystyrene, he asked himself, looking at the china cups and the way they were all slopping coffee into their saucers.) 'Now, are there any issues anyone would like to raise about the report on Strategic Objectives?'

'Well,' said Marcia from Personnel, a striking and vociferous woman who wasn't bad at her job when she was there, 'I may have missed it, I wasn't at the last meeting because of all that trouble I had with my mouth, but I wonder if you could just remind us, Sir Stanley, what the Mission Working Party finally decided about the Mission?'

Sir Stanley turned to Jevon, who was rifling through the back pages of his shorthand notebook.

'You won't find it there,' said Phyllis, matter-of-factly. 'You won't find it anywhere. They didn't.'

'Didn't what?'

'Didn't decide.'

'I thought you put it quite well earlier, Sir Stanley,' suggested Stephanie Kershaw. Not for nothing had they given her a personal chair.

'What did I say?'

'Something about specialization and being accountable. I think the concept of freedom was also mentioned.'

'Good, that'll do then, won't it,' said Sir Stanley, brightly and much relieved. 'Justin, pass me another of the pink biscuits, will you?'

In the second part of the meeting, Sir Stanley ran through what he regarded as the attractive new feathers in EMU's cap: the MCC, of course (due to open shortly); the European Office (run happily for the time being by Disa, though what would happen when she had her baby no-one had quite grappled with yet); and the Press Office, which was making a valiant job not only of manufacturing glossy literature, but of trying to publicize the academic output of the university. The new policy was that every publication by a member of staff was handled by the Press Office, which issued a press release and had a launch party, usually well after the book was published. Occasionally people did prove to be interested in something someone at EMU had written. This was true for much of what Jeremy Krest wrote. Trent Lovett's work on risk and intimacy also went down surprisingly well. Of course, Sir Stanley knew it would; that's why he'd slipped Trent in. He had a nose for these things. He also knew the fuss they'd all make would settle down in time, that is, as soon as they had something else to complain about.

He wasn't displeased with his achievements at EMU. He'd got them out of the red and knocked a bit of sense into them, even if his scheme for doing this by means of the new technology of management consultancy hadn't quite come off. It was the human element; one could never control that. This was a lesson he'd brought with him from all his experiences in industry and with the British Council, here and abroad. EMU had proved to be exactly the same as everywhere else. Well, perhaps not exactly, because the degree of idiosyncrasy that had been allowed to flourish on this unattractive campus had got rather out of hand. In order to get it under control, one had to lay on one side the masturbatory tangles of wordy memos and agendas and minutes and promissory notes that delivered little more than the cheap coloured paper they were inscribed on. One had to see all this both as a diversion from, and a response to, the real issues, most of which were tied up with the profit motive.

Sir Stanley thought of it as a kind of symphony, a clashing, atonal symphony of marketization. It seemed to him to be distinctly in tune with EMU's dishevelled rural location. The cocks that crowed at all the wrong times; the broods of mis-laying hens; the dampening mists that rolled in from the fens; the foxes and more human forms that haunted profane and sacred cesspits – all these signified a demand for order to be imposed. The quantifiable order of the market was as good as any other and better than some. Indeed, hadn't Giles, his beloved but unfortunate nephew, ranted on, before Roberta had had him consigned to That Place, about farming overheads and the transferability of rural lessons to the meanderings of people like those seated now round this table, whom he had the misfortune to be steering through yet another meeting, strategic or otherwise?

CHAPTER 18

Appendix S/1036/A9

At the beginning of summer, just as the students began to fill the examination hall once again, the renovations to the catering block were finished, and the MCC embarked on its first profitable consultancy-development course (for university managers and others who might feather Winkett and Bacon's – and thus also EMU's – nest), and the hedge-rows in the countryside round Motley were filled with creamy cow parsley and pale red saxifrage and yellow cat-sear and violet bellflowers again, Giles Tingey came out of hospital, passed briefly through his parents' house, and took the train to Motley. (The distinguished green Volvo had been sold.)

It was pleasant to be able to look at the passing rural and urban scenes and watch, with the revitalized vision of one who's been away from it all, the way figures located themselves and moved in and through these landscapes, being at the same time part of them and not part of them. Giles wondered about happiness. He wondered about it the way young people do, when it first strikes them that happiness is no longer something provided by parents, but that one has some responsibility for it oneself. Were most of those people he could see through the windows of the 3.58 to Motley happy? The man sitting with his legs splayed and stomach bared to the sun on a garish canvas chair in his small back garden, can of lager in hand? The woman pegging trousers on the washing line, with a small fat child lumping across the patch of dandelioned grass? The workers in their allotments sloping down to the railway line, banging their bean poles in and anticipating the staircases of redorange flowers, up which Jack in the Beanstalk would be able to climb, all the way to heaven? What about the gaggle of boys who boarded the train, sweating in their gabardine school uniforms, ties adrift, sports bags dumped anywhere on the seat, early shadows on their chins, shouting and full of bravado, going home for their tea?

Giles' head was still filling up with poetry. He'd banished it for too long, and now it was having its revenge. '"Out of the night that covers me/Black as the pit from pole to pole/I thank whatever gods may be/For my unconquerable soul"', he muttered *sotto voce*, but the boys were too self-occupied to notice. '"It matters not how strait the gate/ How charged with punishments the scroll/I am the master of my fate/I am the captain of my soul"'.'

Giles did feel victorious. He was doing what he had earlier threatened, and was enrolling in a taught-MA in the Philosophy of the Natural and Social Sciences. He could have gone to many other universities, where he would have got better value for his money and had an easier and more productive time. But there was something about EMU, and about Motley, that drew him back. Its position between town and country, eponymic of the urbanized gangrene of the rural idyll; a vacuously supposed bridge between the domain of ideas, in which Giles now travelled, and the territory of money, from which he had come. Perhaps he was the only one of them who truly realized that it wasn't all disaffection and decline. The endless conversations and interlocutions at EMU, most of its afflictions – budget cuts, failing building stock, illiterate students, demoralized and/

or lazy staff, a superfluity of acronyms, a campus rent by gender and ethnic divisions – were common to most universities these days, after all. The people at EMU were confident creatures really; they had a place and most of them knew what it was. The plodding, complaining spirit that kept them all going was heroic in its own way. It was in the nature of the best aspirations, thought Giles, that they had no chance of becoming anything else.

Sometimes the people at EMU appeared to him as characters in a dream: *Alice in Wonderland*, and *Through the Looking Glass*, both. They inhabited a crazy land which gave them a quite spurious grandeur; but they knew this really, and weren't at all taken in by it. Only the truly brilliant or the mad have the talent to see the skeleton of what really hangs there: a series of questions about who knows what and why, and what kind of human happiness can be chiselled from the pursuit of understanding. You don't have to keep the kind of black notebook Giles had done, or the red one of a small-minded academic bureaucrat (Giles remembered Frank Flusfeder's jottings about Lydia with particular distaste) to understand that there *are* objects of desire: ideas, people, places, things, concepts of identity; but our understanding of the logic of the chase is much less than our aspiration to be part of it. Knowledge is an awesomely wonderful thing, whether we mean by this science or art; and the aesthetic imperative owes its strength to the lack of true division between the two.

Academics have a bad press. This is, after all, why Sir Stanley had set up a Press Office, and had sent the nauseating Professor Proudfoot off on more of his global escapades. But these sorts of gesture wouldn't do much for the public regard of academics; it was as true as Proudfoot's TRUs that we as a culture have yet to find a way of democratizing knowledge. If knowledge belongs to the people, it's more likely to aid understanding as the paramount object of desire. If spawned and controlled by an elite, it may have the longevity that one finds in the closeted colleges of Oxbridge, but it'll lack the strength and ingenuity of a virus capable of contaminating the world. So places like EMU are in the vanguard of the democratization of knowledge, and have a historical significance after all.

Thus Giles ruminated on the train, which ploughed its way through a countryside covered in thunderflies yet again. The sudden warm weather had caused them to rise from their normal habitat of the cornfields and carry out displaced mating rituals in towns, houses and on people's skins. On the walk from the station he had to pick them out of his hair, his nostrils and his ears, and when he got to The Country Pie, he noticed with amazement how clouds of them had managed to wend their way past nailed mahogany frames to insert themselves cunningly and uselessly between the glass and the quite awful representations of gladioli on the wall of his room – still the same one, they hadn't kept it for him, but they gave it back to him, because they remembered him as a kind, quiet, cultured and well-dressed man whose presence gave a facelift to the place.

Presumably the thunderflies had behaved like this last year, but Giles hadn't been in a mood to notice them then. Without his Volvo he was transportless, and buses to the EMU campus were few and far between, so he asked the hotel to rent a bicycle for him. At 5.30 he put rubber bands round the bottoms of his trousers and got on it and set off for the famous roundabout and the churning, divisive A43. He was going both back to EMU and to see Lydia Mallinder, but he was also tying his reappearance into the reception that would mark the launch of operations at the MCC.

Giles tied his bicycle to the railings at the back of the Library in the company of a number of others, some with seats or wheels missing, or both. A new bicycle park had been built, Trent Lovett had seen to that, but unfortunately the firm hired to do it had underestimated the width of most bicycle tyres, so only the slimmest could successfully be inserted between the steel bars. Huge new wheelie rubbish bins had appeared on campus since Giles was last here; great green monsters with the word SULO plastered on their fronts in large orange letters. Plaintains grew in the asphalt cracks; one ground-floor office had a festive display of trailing scented red geraniums, but Dennis Rudgewick's motion to have the campus landscape-gardened hadn't yet got far enough up the PRIC agenda to be debated.

They were all there. Sir Stanley, in a new beige shantung suit with a red rose in his neatly pressed lapel; Richard Winkett, darkly dressed and weathering well the competitive experience of the consultancy market, with only a slight onset of silver appearing at the sides of his gleaming dark hair; the deans of five of the six Schools, including Worms in the last weeks of his Deanship; Stephanie Kershaw, flushed with the triumph of having finally weaned Jeremy Krest away from his wife; Jeremy Krest himself, flushed from Stephanie Kershaw, and also from the success of marketing the hormones Biological Sciences manufactured from Motley Regional Hospital's never-ending supply of placentas (it was this that caused the nasty effluent from the chimney); Roscoe Proudfoot, brimming with a herd of new-old ideas infused by an exceptionally long train journey from Perth to Alice Springs (a conference on Transport Economics); Disa Loring, wrapped in milk and maternity with her pink infant son; Alan Livingstone; Trent Lovett; Elliot Blankthorn; Gaynor Scudamore; John Mapstone; and so on and so forth. Even Phyllis. When Giles Tingey popped up at the back, his height immediately gave the game away. Sir Stanley, preparing to make one of his polished speeches, nudged Professorial Fellow Richard Winkett, who looked around for the new Deputy V-C Lydia Mallinder, and saw her in a sparkling pale blue Agnès B summer suit conversing with Richard Winkett's partner, Conway Bacon, and not seeing Giles Tingey's head above the crowd.

'Well, I never,' they all said.

'It was so sad, what happened to him,' said Richard Winkett in a whisper. 'He had a very promising career with us.'

'He's got a very promising career with us, now,' promised Sir Stanley, his eyes twinkling with the old bright blue light. 'Haven't you, dear boy?' He took Giles by the hand and led him to the centre of things. There was proper champagne and stuffed olives and caviar and tiny falafel and pockets of salmon and crème fraîche – no Twiglets for this lot.

'I can't drink, Uncle, it's the drugs.'

'Of course, of course. There's some gassy grape juice around somewhere, I think.' Sir Stanley went off to find it, and into the space he vacated drifted the Agnès B suit.

'Lydia. You look great.'

'Thank you. You don't look too bad, yourself.' She could almost have been looking at a different person. Gone were the suit and the meticulously polished shoes; Giles wore an open-necked shirt and a cardigan, and suede loafers. The whole appearance was softer, as though he no longer wanted to make an impression on anyone, but just hoped to sidle in and out of the picture-frame of their lives as a slightly blurred and therefore unmemorable image. He was fatter, too; she could see that from his face.

He couldn't take his eyes off her; they rested on her like a butterfly with still white wings. She looked quite wonderful. Very composed, and in control; with her hair, still pinned in a coil at the back of her head, much neater than he recalled it, and a couple of little diamond pendants in her ears, and a tracery of a silver chain about that delicate neck, and she looked up at him with such a sweet, painful look. All his suffering, and hers as well, was encapsulated in it.

'It goes with the promotion, I expect. One up, one down,' he said.

'Meaning?'

'You've gone up and I've gone down. I'm to be a mere student again. I expect you've heard. When we first met, I was the one with power and status. Now it's you.' Giles smiled at her gently; there was absolutely no bitterness in his voice or his face.

Instinctively, Lydia reached out to touch him. 'I'm glad you're better,' she said. She was, yes, she certainly was; but she also felt a nostalgia for the person Giles had been before, when she'd both hated and loved him for it. That night when they'd conjugated under the stars and Huneyball had wailed for his dinner, she'd really thought, like Giles, that it was the beginning of something momentous. Perhaps it had been. But this was the end.

'It'll be strange being a student again.'

'I should think it will be.'

'And you, look at you! Why did you do it, Lydia?'

'Well, I suppose it's rather like the question I asked you,' she reflected. 'Why did you change your mind about me? I was an experiment, you know. I was *your* experiment, and then Judy Sammons, the student to whom you sent those figures . . .' He raised his eyebrows, slightly. 'I was an experiment to her, as well.'

'All academic women are an experiment, Lydia,' suggested Giles. 'The philosophy of science, of knowledge . . .'

'Is a gendered thing in itself,' finished Lydia, 'yes I know. You *will* make a good student, Giles. I didn't answer your question, did I? Well, I don't think you actually answered mine, at the time. I've just put the results of the two experi-

ments together, that's all. You found that I and my department were a success at EMU – in your terms, that is. We
were cheap; we brought in a lot of money. But the system
was designed to prevent us knowing that; to make us feel
lowly and demeaned, to force me always to fight for things
which should have been ours by right. Judy Sammons was
disappointed in me. She wanted to find radical women at
the top, but what she found was that the system gets rid
of radicalism. Power is gendered. It's male. When you get
power, however paltry the power you get, you become
male with it. It contaminates.' She gazed at him, and saw
again the person he had been before. 'Oh it excites, but it
corrupts. So I thought I might as well sell my soul to the
devil.'

   She laughed, and he saw the old Lydia. The one whose
quirky optimism burst like a melting sun through the clouds
of whatever problems assailed him. 'I didn't really want to
go freelance. It was a gesture. They can keep their overheads.' She laughed again. 'I'm stuck with the system, Giles,
and it's stuck with me. At least now I might be able to
change a few things about it. The only hope of changing a
system is to become part of it. I thought of my mother, as
well. Dying of a female disease. I really don't want to do
that.'

   'Would you like it to have been different, Lydia?' Giles
meant both the university and their relationship. His reflec-
tions over the past few months had led him to see the whole
grand edifice of the higher education system as poised on
the edge of a cliff, waiting either to be propped up, or to
fall into a sea quite as deep and as blue as his dear uncle,
Sir Stanley Oxborrow's, eyes. The problem was that demo-
cratized knowledge requires a fundamental alteration in the
way knowledge is produced. And that's the nut EMU hadn't
cracked. It tried to keep bright assertive students like Judy

Sammons down; it attempted to exclude from hierarchies of power difficult women like Lydia Mallinder. And if it couldn't, it put them in places where they wouldn't ever have a chance of doing anything creative again.

But Lydia heard Giles' question only as an interrogation about them. She smoothed the pale blue linen over her hips and altered her position slightly, as though this would divert the directness of his question. 'Wouldn't you?'

It all came flooding back to him. *His* desire and hers; and her release of his. Their joint pursuit of something other than knowledge, although perhaps it was the same thing in the end. He'd been thinking about that fairly intensively as well over the last few months. 'Can I ask you something else?'

'People who ask that always will anyway,' she observed, smiling.

'Marry me. Marry me!'

Lydia shook her head. 'I'm sorry, I'm really sorry.'

'No? You won't even think about it? It's not the Student and the Deputy Vice-Chancellor thing, it can't be that!' he puzzled.

'No, of course it isn't that.'

'Well, what is it, then? I'm a reformed character. I'm a much nicer person now. I won't be on these drugs forever. You liked me before, I know you did, so why can't you like me again?'

He pleaded; she felt bad about resisting him, and there was still something about him that had to be resisted. For an instant, which would be fixed in Lydia's mind forever, the whole context in which they were standing melted away – all the conversations, all the people, the air in the champagne and the grape drink Sir Stanley was bringing for his nephew, everything obvious and everything that wasn't – it all went, and there in the thin summer air she stood alone with Giles Tingey in the presence of these questions about their past and their future, about him and what had happened to him, and about her and what had happened to her, thoroughly enmeshed in a tightly woven fabric of What if? and Why not? hardly able to breathe, and not at all conscious of anything else that might be more important. Despite all these circumlocutions and interrogations, it was as though for this moment Giles and Lydia were creatures utterly without culture. They just existed: they were naked in the world and before each other. Faced with the living solidity of the body, the rest of material reality receded. And in this purely corporeal attitude Lydia could feel, but not imagine, that future Giles would lead her into; and she knew (but wouldn't have been able to articulate) both how good and how bad this might be. The goodness seduced, like Giles himself, but the odours of badness rose up with a familiar strangling motion.

Eventually, the moment passed. Lydia relaxed, released from its grip. In this place where there were far too many of them, words didn't come easily to her; and then the context itself came flooding back – the people, EMU, the birds beyond the campus chattering their bedtime song, Huneyball, Disa's baby, and Lydia's own forthcoming book – a totally different future; and Sir Stanley came over and pushed the glass of grape juice for Giles between them, and Giles looked at her sadly, and Lydia said 'Sorry' again, and moved away from him, thinking how people's lives are lived in time, and that time changes things, and that things, once changed, move on and people with them, whatever alternative futures may, from time to time, be held out to them.